IN THE HANDS OF A MASTER

Sarah thought she was quite able to counter the moves of men in the game of love, but too late she realized that she was no match for Lord Wexford.

How else could she explain why her lips willingly opened under his when he kissed her?

When at last she broke free, she could only say, "So that is what it is like to be held in a man's arms and kissed. What a very good thing it is that girls do not learn how marvelous it is until they are betrothed."

Then she realized what she had said, and hastily added, "I hope you do not think that I kissed you to entrap you, m'lord."

"Entrap me?" he said with a smile, following her as she backed away, his eyes as intent as a tiger stalking his prey. . . .

Lady
at Risk

Barbara Hazard

A SIGNET BOOK

SIGNET
Published by the Penguin Group
Penguin Books USA Inc., 375 Hudson Street,
New York, New York 10014, U.S.A.
Penguin Books Ltd, 27 Wrights Lane,
London W8 5TZ, England
Penguin Books Australia Ltd, Ringwood,
Victoria, Australia
Penguin Books Canada Ltd, 10 Alcorn Avenue,
Toronto, Ontario, Canada M4V 3B2
Penguin Books (N.Z.) Ltd, 182–190 Wairau Road,
Auckland 10, New Zealand

Penguin Books Ltd, Registered Offices:
Harmondsworth, Middlesex, England

First published by Signet, an imprint of Dutton Signet,
a division of Penguin Books USA Inc.

First Printing, February, 1997
10 9 8 7 6 5 4 3 2 1

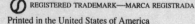 REGISTERED TRADEMARK—MARCA REGISTRADA

Printed in the United States of America

Prologue

The Marquis of Wexford's manservant had removed the covers and placed the decanter of port near his master's right hand before he bowed himself away. As the door closed softly behind him, the lady who remained at the table, against all established manners, rested her chin on both fists. Then she said thoughtfully, "Do you know, I find it astonishing that this is the first time I've ever been here."

"How so?" her host asked lazily.

"Well, we are cousins, are we not? And I've visited your estate in Kent many times. But never have you invited me to this little hidey-hole you keep. Indeed, I recall asking you once if I might come, and you refused me. Curtly, too."

"I should hope so," the other gentleman at the table remarked, his gray eyes glinting as he raised his glass to the lady in a silent toast.

"Why do you say that, Drake?" she demanded.

"Because, dear bride, it would not have been at all proper for Miles to entertain you here without a suitable chaperon."

"What fustian!" she exclaimed, tossing her head. "Have you forgotten that you entertained me, completely alone, during that snowstorm this past winter in Yorkshire? I didn't even have my maid with me."

"Ah, but no one knew of that, and as you know only too well, Eliza, I'm not in the least bit proper."

The lady blushed a little before she continued, "Still, Miles and I are related, and at the time I begged the invitation, I was a widow as well. And widows, if you remember, my darling Drake, may do just as they please. I certainly did."

"No they may not," her cousin interrupted. "Not if they want to remain in the ton's good graces, that is. No wonder your father insisted I keep an eye on you after James Chalmers died. I can't tell you how relieved I was to turn the post of watchdog over to your new husband."

He raised his glass and added, "To your good health, sir. To your *very* good health."

As the Earl of Darrin chuckled, he went on, "No doubt it is Eliza's propensity for doing outrageous things that prompts your removal to Darrin Castle? Most understandable."

"As usual, you are being provocative, Miles, but I shall not regard it," the new Countess of Darrin said, at her most forbearing. "Surely you can see that the reason we are going to Yorkshire is because I am no longer fit to be seen."

The two gentlemen wisely held their tongues. It was true Eliza Darrin had lost her slim figure now she was six months with child, but the high-waisted gowns currently in fashion hid her condition very well.

"And you are not to change the subject, Miles, as you are so wont to do when you do not care to discuss something. I insist on knowing what you use this little house for. It is too small for entertaining, and it cannot be considering a hunting box, for I know this is indifferent hunting country. But stay!"

She sat up straight and regarded her cousin with eyes full of mischief. A small smile hovered on her lips. "I have it," she crowed, bouncing a little on her seat. "It is too far from town for you to install a mistress here, but can it be you've brought a *lady*? I was vastly amused to hear some gossip just recently about your possible involvement with the Duchess of . . ."

"No," her host said so loudly and firmly she fell silent at once. "You will not mention the lady's name, not even among ourselves, Eliza. What a terrible trial you are. I don't envy your bridegroom in the slightest."

"You might well do so, sir," she said quickly, color rising in her cheeks. "I assure you, he is more than content. Aren't you, Drake? Well, aren't you?"

"If you say so, my love," the earl said so meekly, she forgot to be angry and dissolved in laughter.

"The things I am forced to put up with," she said when she could speak again. "You are both of you very bad.

"But seriously, Miles, surely it was unusual for you to leave town when the Season is only just coming to a close. Why, even Prinny has not left for Brighton yet, and most of your cronies are still in London."

"Perhaps I was tired of the Season. Perhaps I felt the need for solitude."

"Then, we must apologize for coming and disturbing it on our way north," the Earl of Darrin said, holding out his glass as the marquis gestured with the decanter.

"There is no need. I am delighted you came, for it is sure to be some time before I see my madcap cousin again. And no doubt due to some ghastly bad judgment on my part, I admit a fondness for her."

"Well, I like that!"

"Do you make a long stay?" the earl persisted. "Eliza and I would be happy to have you visit Darrin Castle. It is lovely in Yorkshire at this time of year."

"It is indeed, cuz. It only gets horrid in the winter. Honestly."

"I may take you up on your offer. But, except for the occasional trip back to town, I rather think I'll remain in East Anglia for some time yet. The neighborhood is all atwitter awaiting the latest heiress's arrival."

His mobile mouth quirked in a tight smile. "Can it be hope springs eternal? Even though I know, as surely as I am sitting here, the lady will be the most unattractive creature alive?"

"But haven't I heard it said all heiresses are beautiful, sir?" Eliza asked pertly.

"Of course they are," he agreed. "Strange, is it not, how their beauty increases in proportion to the weight of their purses?"

"Well, why would you care?" Eliza asked carelessly.

"You're all of thirty-five, and you've told me over and over you've no taste for marriage. And everyone in the family gave up hope long ago you might succumb to *anyone,* never mind someone rich and ravishing."

"Eliza," the earl said, his tone of voice a warning. She stared at him defiantly for a moment, but something she saw in his keen gray eyes made her look down first.

"You are too forward, ma'am," he went on. "Surely Miles's bachelorhood is his own concern."

The gentleman under discussion waved a careless hand. "No need to defend me, old friend. I've held my own with that saucy wench of yours since she was in leading strings."

"Who is this heiress?" Eliza demanded.

"A Miss Eaton. Her grandfather, Jonah Eaton, was one of the biggest landowners for miles around. He died some months ago, and Miss Eaton was named in his will to inherit all. She'll have a tidy sum, too. Besides the rents on the estate, her grandfather was a canny investor in various manufacturing schemes; canal building as well."

"There were no male heirs?" the earl inquired, sounding surprised. "Surely it is almost unheard of for a young woman to inherit a fortune."

"Yes, and there's a mystery there that intrigues me. The girl's father, Samuel Eaton, is old Jonah's only child. They must have had a falling out some time ago, so serious it prompted the old gentleman to pass over his son in favor of his granddaughter. Of course the estate was not entailed, and there's no title involved, so he was free to leave his wealth where he chose."

"But what a terrible blow for Mr. Samuel Eaton," Eliza said, looking thoughtful. "How difficult it must have been to watch everything go to his child."

"A female one, at that," her cousin reminded her. "That would make it doubly galling, which of course was no doubt what the old man had intended."

"I don't think I care for him at all. He sounds horrid," Eliza remarked, frowning now. Over her head the two gentlemen exchanged bemused glances. It was most unlike the countess to let a man deride her sex without a heated argument.

Suddenly the earl saw her cover her mouth to hide a yawn, and he rose at once.

"Time you were in bed, Eliza," he said as he came to hold the chair for her.

She smiled at him over her shoulder as she rose obediently. He bent and put his arms around her before he kissed the deep dimple in her cheek. Their host suddenly became intent on the wine left in his glass.

"Ordinarily I might argue that, sir, but I confess I am tired tonight. I'll leave you then. Mind you don't stay up till all hours drinking port, you two."

Miles Griffin rose to hug her briefly before he raised her hand to his lips. "I don't think I've ever seen you look so handsome, Eliza," he complimented her, his dark eyes admiring. "Marriage and approaching motherhood agree with you."

She curtsied to them both. "Thank you, sir. You really should try it, Miles. It is such a shame you are missing all the joy and happiness it can bring."

His dark brows rose, and for a moment his sleepy eyes widened. "I, Eliza? Dear me, I don't think I should care for it, even if it turned me into another Byron. I confess, I prefer to remain my ugly self. And as for motherhood, I could not possibly consider it. Too, too confining."

He listened to her gay laughter as she went up the stairs before he took his seat again, and refilled both the earl's glass and his own.

Chapter 1

A long time later, Sarah Eaton would marvel that she had not had some premonition—some faint quiver of unease—about what would happen to her on her return to England. Instead she had felt nothing but eagerness for the adventure, and more than a little impatience that it should all be taking so long.

The unbearably steamy conditions on board the ship that carried her back from India had to be endured, and her mother had to be nursed throughout the journey. Mrs. Marion Eaton was often ill. She could not abide the motion of the ship in any kind of rough weather; indeed, even long swells were enough to send her to her bunk with a basin handy beside her.

Sarah reveled in the storms they met, however, for then the ship gathered speed, digging her forefoot into the waves and tossing them aside as she sped toward home.

Sarah had traveled to India with her mother and father when she was eighteen. The Reverend Mr. Eaton went to take up the post of missionary to the natives there, the first Methodist preacher to do so. That had been seven long years ago, and remembering, Sarah's mouth tightened. She had not thought the natives at all receptive to her father's teaching, for they appeared more than content with their own religions. Sometimes only a handful attended Sunday services. But her father had not been discouraged. He believed fervently in his faith, and he was never so happy as when he was preaching God's word. He didn't seem to notice the poverty his family was forced to endure, the run-down quarters, the poorest food, and the old, patched

clothes—even the impossibility of sending his wife and
daughter to the hills during the worst of the brutal monsoon
season. Sarah thought it too bad she didn't have her father's
vocation, for she did mind such things—dreadfully.

But now her father was dead of a fever, and although she
mourned him sincerely, his death had freed her to go home
at last. Strange, she mused as she clung to the ship's rail
and stared far out to sea. Her only other relative, her Grandfather Eaton, had also died, three months prior to her father.
The letter that had arrived in India telling of his demise had
come right after the funeral when Marion Eaton was still in
deep mourning and trying desperately to think whom she
might call on to assist her and her daughter, left as they
were almost penniless.

Sarah smiled a little, remembering how her mother had
exclaimed as she read the letter from Jonah Eaton's solicitors; how she had called it the answer to her prayers. It had
not only asked Sarah to return; there had been a large draft
on the East India Company's bank enclosed to ease her way.

Sarah had worried that her mother might not want to
leave her husband to his lonely grave, but Mrs. Eaton was
much more practical than that. She knew there was no future for them in India, and she longed for home as fervently
as her daughter.

The ship reached London at last very early one July
morning, to tie up at the company's new enclosed docks.
Fast asleep in her cabin below, Sarah missed that excitement, but she was dressed and on deck as soon as it was
light. There was a cool damp breeze blowing off the
Thames, and she wrapped her shawl tighter around her
shoulders, reveling in the fresh, briny air. Her eyes were
wide as she watched the unloading and inspected the closed
warehouses nearby, admiring the hustle and bustle before
her. And the voices she heard made her smile broadly; they
were so *English*. It had been far too long since she had
heard such fluent conversations in her own language spoken by so many people. And most of it at the top of their
lungs, too.

She caught the sweet smell of saffron from a small basket nearby and the piercing tang of cloves in a barrel next to that. For a moment she was back in India in the blanketing, claustrophobic heat, surrounded by the usual throngs of dark-skinned people in their loosely draped saris and robes. And over all would be the thick odors of cattle and people and dung, spices and hot food, permeating the air and seeming able to enter one's very pores. Sometimes her eyes had teared, it had been so powerful. She was recalled to the London docks as an officer near her bellowed to the lascars to look lively there! Sarah told herself India was a three-month journey away, and she would never have to see it again. She was *home*. To stay.

Two hours later, the Eaton ladies left the ship. Sarah then sent a note to her grandfather's solicitor, informing him of their arrival. Shortly thereafter a large carriage came to transfer them and their baggage to Grillon's Hotel, where they were to stay while in town. The solicitor had professed himself all eagerness to attend to their every wish, and a time had been set for Sarah to call on him the following morning when they would be more rested from the journey.

Marion Eaton sighed gustily as the carriage lurched into motion, and her daughter looked at her, a question in her eyes.

"I am having the greatest difficulty believing we are really here at last, Sarah, and off that dreadful vessel," she explained. "Especially when I can still feel the motion. I tell you, my dear, I shall never set foot in so much as a punt again."

Then she looked down at her black gown and frowned. "But I am afraid we are both of us dreadfully out of fashion. We must purchase new clothes at once, for we cannot appear in public looking as dowdy as this."

Sarah inspected her own black gown. It was faded and much the worse for wear after three months at sea. "No, we can't," she agreed. "Why don't we go shopping as soon as we're settled in the hotel? We can always unpack what we will need for our stay there later this evening."

Mrs. Eaton smiled and nodded, her eyes twinkling. Sarah looked at her fondly. She knew her mother had been a great beauty as a girl, and traces of that beauty were still apparent, although she was careworn and fragile now. For a moment Sarah felt a surge of anger at her father for making her mother's life so difficult. If she had married someone else, she might have been pampered and cared for, and able to keep her beauty. And was any of it worth it? Sarah asked herself. How many souls did my father save when all was said and done? If she were to be honest, she would have had to admit he had even lost one, for she no longer found her religion a comfort or an inspiration. It was something she had kept very much to herself, and she had no intention of ever revealing her falling away to her mother, lest it distress her.

"Dear, do look there!" that lady was saying, pointing out the side window to where a middle-aged woman dressed in a narrow silk gown and large elaborate turban was waiting to cross the street. She was attended by both a maid and a footman, and she had a pale blue silk parasol to guard her face from the sun.

"How grand," Marion Eaton breathed as their carriage swept past. "Did you see the blue kid gloves she wore, daughter?"

She sighed again as she smoothed her own black cotton ones. Sarah saw the darned fingertips, knowing without looking her own gloves were just as disreputable.

"Tell me, Sarah, is it *wrong* of me to be looking forward to our home? To new clothes and comfort and ease? Is it disloyal to your father's memory, do you suppose? Somehow I feel guilty."

"Nonsense," Sarah said briskly. "After the life we have lived in India we deserve it, Mother. And I don't want to hear a single word about how wrong it is to be worldly and how wealth is a danger to our immortal souls. Surely God would not be at all pleased if we scorned this bounty He has bestowed on us."

"Do you really think so?" Marion Eaton asked eagerly. "Well, in that case I shall not repine. I most assuredly have no desire to appear ungrateful for any of *His* blessings, far from it."

Sarah was delighted to see they had arrived at the hotel before her mother remembered it had been old Jonah Eaton who had provided their newfound wealth, and not the Lord.

Grillon's seemed very elegant to the Eaton ladies, and quite a bit daunting. Sarah ignored the stares and whispers of some ladies who had inspected their appearance and seemed incredulous that anyone so clothed could expect to be housed there. But the clerk who welcomed them at the desk and had them sign the register had no such misgivings. Horton, Horton, and Gavin was a very well-respected firm; if the Eaton ladies were clients of theirs, they would be well able to pay their bill, no matter how dreary and provincial they looked.

For a moment of weakness, Sarah wished they might remain in the large, pleasant rooms they had been shown to, but after the baggage had been delivered, she put up her chin and escorted her mother back through the gauntlet in the lobby. She asked the doorman to summon a hackney cab, and inquired of him the best place to shop.

As the cab conveyed them to Bond Street, she stared out at the passing scene. She had been to London but once before in her life, and then only to travel through it to the docks and the ship that was to take them to India. But now, she realized, she could stay as long as she wished, see all the sights she had only been able to read about before, buy beautiful clothes, eat marvelous food. *English* food. Roast beef and fat sausages, prawns and creamed soups, puddings and cakes . . . She laughed a little to herself. If she did not take care, she would gain so much weight she would not be able to fit into the handsome clothes she intended to buy.

The shop they entered a short time later was fortunately empty of other customers, and although the tiny Frenchwoman who came to serve them seemed startled by their garb, she was soon all smiles. As it happened, she had several black gowns already made up, for mourning clothes were always in great demand and must be ready to don as soon as any member of a family died. Measurements were taken and other fabrics and patterns chosen, some for simple day gowns, others for evening. Sarah also ordered a few white gowns of silk and muslin. It was summer and warm, and in India white was often worn for mourning.

By the time the Eatons returned to Grillon's, they looked vastly different. Both clad in new black gowns and sandals, and sporting elegant bonnets, they had their hands full of parcels. The doorman hastened to call some boys to help, and Sarah took a great deal of pleasure in sweeping through the lobby, the equal of anyone there.

The new clothes also gave her courage when she and her mother arrived at the solicitor's late the following morning.

"Mrs. Eaton, Miss Eaton," the elder Mr. Horton said, rising and bowing as they were ushered into his office. "May I suggest a cup of tea before we turn to business?"

Sarah nodded, and he gestured to his clerk before he seated the ladies in comfortable chairs before his desk. "You had a pleasant journey from India, ma'am?" he asked Mrs. Eaton. "Ah, how clumsy of me! My condolences on the loss of your husband, ma'am. Most unfortunate. Most."

Marion Eaton was nowhere near as composed as her daughter, and she was barely able to stammer a response. Kindly ignoring her discomfort, the solicitor turned to Sarah.

"I hope you are content to be home, Miss Eaton," he said. His bushy eyebrows rose and fell in such a comical way as he spoke, Sarah had to swallow the laughter she could feel bubbling up and threatening to disgrace her.

"More than content, I am glad, sir," she said with her warm smile. "I did not care for India."

"Sarah," her mother scolded. "We were there so your father could do the Lord's work."

"I know Mother, but that does not alter the fact that it was a most unpleasant place."

The appearance of a tea tray cut short any more detrimental comments about India. As they drank their tea and ate the little biscuits provided, Mr. Horton spoke at length about what had been happening in England during their long absence. He concluded by telling them that on no account should they miss the fireworks planned for the first of August in St. James's Park to commemorate the final victory over Napoleon. "Sir William Congreve has agreed to serve as rocket master, so we may be sure they will be outstanding," he said.

Mrs. Eaton spoke up then. "Excuse me, sir, but I fear that would never do. The hotel where we are staying is much too grand, and, I am sure, very expensive. And the first of August is not for two weeks yet."

"My dear ma'am, I assure you, you have nothing to worry about as far as money is concerned. Not a bit of it. On my honor, your daughter could buy Grillon's if she had a mind to." Turning to Sarah, he added, "And now, shall we get down to business, Miss Eaton?"

Sarah nodded, still a little stunned at the wealth he implied was now hers. She was even more stunned half an hour later, and her mother so white, Sarah was afraid she might faint. All that land, hundreds and hundreds of acres of it, the bounteous rents, the shrewd investments that brought in so much money month after month—it was hard to take it all in at once. It seemed her grandfather had not only had the knack of making money, he had not spent much of it. But twenty thousand pounds a year, my word! Her father had only had three hundred. Remembering then how she had lived in poverty all her life, she was furious with her grandfather. How easy it would have been for him to ease their way. How little it would have taken to make their lives more comfortable. Mr. Horton's voice recalled her to the present.

"No doubt you will wish to make many changes at Woodingham Hall. It is old-fashioned. Send all the bills to me to deal with. I'll also place a sum for you to draw on at a bank here in London. Just let me know when you need more.

"The Hall is fully staffed, although you may wish to add more servants, or at least change some of them. The butler is elderly. He should be pensioned off, as I took the liberty of doing with your grandfather's valet. No doubt, you intend to hire ladies' maids? May I suggest the Free Registry for Faithful Servants? I'll write down the address for you. And it would not be amiss for you to inspect some warehouses and open accounts in them. You'll need to order new carpets and material for draperies and bed hangings. My late wife preferred Brown's, but the Prince Regent favors Sanford and Sons. When you have seen the Hall and decided what must be done, you can send to them for samples. They're both reputable firms."

He paused for a moment, looking uncomfortable. "There is something else I must say, Miss Eaton," he began, not looking at her now.

"Yes?" Sarah prompted, suddenly uneasy.

"You have the look of a sensible young woman, so I hope you will not be offended."

He moved some papers restlessly on his desk for a moment, then coughed behind his hand before he went on. "As you have discovered this morning, you have become a considerable heiress. There are very few women in England who have as much. But even though wealth brings comfort, it also brings responsibilities, even danger. I shall do all I can to guide you, but there is one area where I cannot help you. You see, Miss Eaton, you are about to become one of the most sought-after women in the realm. And I do most earnestly beg you to be on your guard against fortune hunters and Captain Sharps."

He looked doubtfully at Mrs. Eaton before he smiled gently. "I know your good mother will be on her guard as well. But, may I suggest, before you make any decisions about a possible husband, you send me his credentials so I can check them?"

Sarah nodded thoughtfully, and he held up his hand. "Yes, that is easy enough to agree to now, but later you may not find it so. It will seem as if you do not trust the man you have chosen. However, I can tell you with the greatest confidence that no man could possibly object to such a procedure unless he had something to hide."

He rose then, terminating the interview. As Sarah followed his example, she grasped her reticule tighter and took a deep breath. "Thank you, sir," she said. "You've been most helpful. I think we will remain in town for at least a few days, even though I am anxious to inspect the

Hall. Should I see about purchasing a carriage and pair to take us there?"

"There's no need to do that," Mr. Horton said as he walked both ladies to the door. "Let me knew when you plan to leave town, and I'll send a message to the Hall, ordering a carriage be sent for you and your maids."

Sarah managed to get her mother from the premises before she could inform the solicitor she had never had a personal maid and had no intention of hiring one now, fortune or no. They hailed another hackney cab, one Sarah dismissed at the Stanhope Gate.

Hyde Park was not crowded at this hour. There were only a few walkers like themselves, some children with their nannies, and the occasional rider trotting down Rotten Row.

"Well, I never in all my born days ever expected to hear such things as I did this morning," Mrs. Eaton confided as she took her daughter's arm. "In fact, I'm still having trouble believing I even did hear it. All that money! It is—it is *obscene* for anyone to have so much."

"No doubt, you're right, Mother, but there is nothing we can do about it now. And do consider the good we will accomplish, using some of it to help others."

Marion Eaton's troubled face brightened a little.

"Of course I'm sure there are many unscrupulous persons about who would be delighted to relieve us of it, all in a good cause, naturally," Sarah pointed out as they moved aside to let a little boy rolling a hoop run by them. "I suggest we ask Mr. Horton to investigate them as well as the hoards of suitors he imagines will beat a path to my door. Now, that *I* find hard to believe."

"Why, my dear? You're a most personable young lady, and thanks to your upbringing, well-educated and mannerly. You will make any man an excellent, frugal wife—oh, how silly of me. You don't have to be frugal anymore, do you?"

"When did madame say our gowns would be ready?" Sarah thought to ask.

"Sometime next week, although she did request we come

in for a fitting before that. I don't know, Sarah. Why is that necessary? We've been making our own gowns for years. I'm sure we can alter these if they need it. Do let's leave for Essex as soon as we can. Madame can send the gowns on to us."

Sarah stopped and turned her mother to face her. Looking down into that dear, worried face, she said, "I know you don't like any of this, Mother. But we can't run away from it. We must learn to live differently, learn to be easy in our new circumstances. Don't you see? We can't keep on being the widow and daughter of an impoverished Methodist preacher anymore. That life is gone—behind us now."

To her dismay, her mother began to cry a little. Sarah rummaged in her reticule for a clean handkerchief, and handed it to her to wipe her eyes.

"I know. I'm silly," Mrs. Eaton said at last. "I'll try, Sarah. I do promise to try. But I'm missing your father, and I think I'm still weary from the voyage. In time, I'm sure I'll be better.

"Now then, what would you like to do this afternoon?" she asked brightly, making a great effort to hide her still very real misgivings. "Shall we go to those cloth warehouses? I do hope you'll choose Brown's. It would quite undo me to even step inside the one the Prince Regent fancies."

"But there's no reason it should, Mother. Do turn around and see who is riding down the Row right now."

Obediently, Mrs. Eaton turned to see a corpulent figure in beautiful riding dress with a handsome, florid face, riding a large gray gelding toward them. She knew who it was immediately, for he was attended by several gentlemen. As he drew abreast, both the Eaton ladies dropped him deep curtsies. To Sarah's surprise and her mother's overwhelming delight, the man who would someday be George the Fourth not only nodded genially to them both, he also raised his hand in salute and smiled.

Chapter 2

At the end of July, the Eatons found themselves still residing at Grillon's Hotel. There had been a great many things to do besides the shopping, not the least of which had been to see the sights. Marion Eaton stopped fretting about the time it was all taking, and the expense, when she saw the Palace of Westminster and the Abbey, Whitehall and St. James's Palace. And when Sarah went off to hire a ladies' maid, she tripped off herself to visit a few of her late husband's friends in the ministry, to try and discover where some of her daughter's vast wealth could be put to best advantage. She assured Sarah she had no intention of revealing that wealth, but would only listen to these good people as they discussed the Methodists' most pressing needs.

Sarah was glad her mother was more comfortable now, although she knew it might be a long time before she was able to accept their new circumstances and was truly at home with them. Sometimes Sarah wondered if she ever would be. Still, she had enjoyed the Royal Menagerie, and she so cherished their encounter with the Prince Regent, she mentioned it often. Sarah was sure she would still be telling people of it when she was a very old lady. And she had enjoyed the concert of sacred music they had attended one evening.

Sarah would have liked to have gone to a play or an opera, but she knew her mother would have nothing to do with something so frivolous and worldly. Wisely, Sarah did not insist on it. She knew she was standing on fragile ground. By all rights, as the heiress, she was in charge of things, and her mother her dependent. Dear to be sure, but

still only a dependent. But Sarah could never bring herself
to consider Marion Eaton that way. For one thing, she had
bowed to her judgment all her life. Of course, sometimes in
the past she had chafed at the restrictions her mother had
laid down for her, and longed to rebel, but for the most
part, she had held her tongue. How much more important it
was now that she continue to do so. Otherwise she would
appear proud and overbearing, and her mother made to feel
secondary and unimportant. That would never do.

The maid Sarah finally engaged was even younger than
she was, but Sarah felt comfortable with her, something she
had not done with the older, very superior abigail the pro-
prietress of the registry had suggested first. Sarah told herself she had no need for such a smart maid, for soon she
would be going to the country. She was in mourning, too.
She was sure young Betsy Borden would do very well for
her.

On August first, Sarah persuaded her mother it would do
no harm to go to St. James's Park to see the wondrous fireworks everyone was talking about. They themselves had
watched the workmen putting up the wooden frames of the
display with a great deal of interest. Since Betsy was to accompany them, Mrs. Eaton agreed.

An older, wiser maid would have been quick to point out
that ladies did not stroll about London at night by themselves, and certainly not on an evening that was sure to at-
tract not only the nobility and gentry, but crowds of others
as well—pickpockets and prostitutes, beggars and bel-
dames—all sorts of rogues and rascals. Unfortunately,
however, Betsy was too anxious to see the fireworks herself
to consider the propriety of it.

After they had dinner as usual in the hotel dining room,
Sarah and her mother, followed discreetly by Betsy, set out
on foot about nine o'clock. Sarah had not realized they
would need tickets, and when they reached the park she
was disappointed they could not join the others already
within the gates.

"There now, missus, not ter fret," the ticket taker said
with a wink. "Jest ye go 'round by the 'orse Guards, then

along the Parade ter the Mall, an' ye'll see it all grand, that ye will."

Sarah thanked him gravely and shepherded her mother and Betsy in the direction he had indicated. As they walked, she pondered the kindness of strangers, and wondered if it occurred because she and her mother were so obviously mourning.

The route they were taking was becoming uncomfortably crowded, and people, intent on getting a good vantage place, pushed past them rudely. Marion Eaton reminded Sarah to keep a tight hold of her reticule. She frowned as she said it, for she could not like the company they found themselves in, nor the conversations that came to her ears as they went on their way. She had heard doxies propositioning men quite blatantly, and other men taking the name of the Lord in vain. That they were probably drunk was no excuse. And she could not like the way these people smelled, of liquor and sweat and dirt. It was as bad as the swarming, odorous streets of Bombay. But she knew how Sarah was looking forward to seeing the fireworks, how eagerly she had waited for this particular night, so she said nothing. After all, she told herself, we've lived abroad. We're not country folks anymore, ripe for the picking. And at twenty-five, Sarah was no longer a girl who needed protection. It was something she was trying very hard to remember, now that her daughter was home and an heiress.

At last they found themselves opposite a large architectural piece designed by John Nash. Sarah heard a man passing by telling his companions it was called the Temple of Concord. Betsy pushed forward, clearing a space for them toward the front of the crowd, near the high iron fence that separated the general public from the more elegant ticket holders inside the park.

The three women prepared themselves for a long wait. Sarah amused herself by eavesdropping on conversations nearby, and smiling at a little boy who was perched on his father's shoulders, the better to see. Betsy squealed suddenly, and whirled to confront a pair of costermongers, from the smell of them, who had dared to pinch her. They faded away as Marion Eaton glared at them.

The fireworks began promptly at ten. The piece they were facing was lit up first as the Temple of Discord showing all the fire and devastation that symbolized war and its horror. Sarah thought she had never seen anything so stunning, or so shocking. Betsy clutched her arm tightly in her astonishment, but Sarah did not reprimand her. A glance at her mother's face showed her Mrs. Eaton was also affected. As they stared up at some rockets filling the night sky with bright streamers of colored flame, the scene within the temple changed. Now it became a beautiful structure lit by many lamps and featuring transparent paintings. Sarah had no idea how such an effect had been obtained, but although her eyes were beginning to sting from the smoke, she did not blink lest she miss something important. She knew others were similarly affected, for she could hear the gasps and excited cries, and a quick glance showed her the little boy's eyes were round with awe.

She only wished the ever-growing crowd would stop pressing forward. She felt quite helpless, hemmed in as she was, and she took a tighter grip on her reticule, winding its strings around her fingers as a further precaution.

Suddenly there was a huge blast. For a moment Sarah was sure it must be part of the show. But only moments later, as Nash's great pagoda burst into flame and people began to scream, she realized all was not well. The fire spread rapidly, and some rockets meant to be set off later exploded with a thunderous roar. Now the crowd panicked, pushing and shoving others in their desperation to escape before any of the flaming pieces of wood and canvas could shower down on them.

Gasping, Sarah put her arms around her frailer mother to protect her, spreading her feet as far as she could in the narrow-skirted gown she wore in order to keep her balance. She called out to a burly fellow to watch where he was going. He did not reply as he shoved the Eatons out of his way. Sarah felt her mother stagger, and she was sure it was only a matter of time before they fell and were trampled underfoot. She could no longer feel Betsy's hand on her arm, and she had no idea what had become of the maid. She hoped she was all right, yes, and that the little boy she had seen was still perched on his father's shoulders, high above the crowd.

She felt a strong arm grasp her around the waist, and heard a deep voice say, "Hold on to me! All this will be over soon!" As she obeyed, she looked up to see the man who had taken both she and her mother into a strong embrace, even turned them slightly to protect them. Sarah felt enormously grateful to him, whoever he was, putting himself in jeopardy to save strangers.

For some moments more they continued to be buffeted, and once Sarah heard her mother cry out in pain. But eventually the worst was over, and the man who had come to their rescue let her go, although he continued to support Mrs. Eaton. Sarah could only see part of his face, the side that was lit by the flames behind them. The rest of it was in shadow. But she could tell he was a gentleman by his educated speech and his air of calm authority.

"You are all right, ma'am?" he asked Marion Eaton.

Sarah could see the lines of pain on her face, and she took her hands and said, "Mother! Have you been hurt?"

"It was so stupid of me," Mrs. Eaton murmured, and the two taller people on either side of her bent closer. "Someone stepped on me in what feels like must have been hobnailed boots."

She tried a tentative step, and her face grew ashen. Sarah gasped. To her relief, the gentleman with them lifted her mother in his arms. "No, you must not put any weight on it, ma'am," he said, his deep voice gentle. "We do not know if it is broken, and you might only make it worse." He turned to Sarah then and said curtly, "Follow me. I've a carriage nearby."

Not waiting to see if she obeyed, he set off, Sarah close behind. Two blocks away from the park and the fire and the confusion, the gentleman called a brisk order, and a servant in livery hastened to open the door of a large, fashionable carriage.

Suddenly reminded of the impropriety of allowing a stranger to assist them, and all too well aware she did not even know their savior's name, nor his real purpose for what appeared on the surface to be an act of kindness, Sarah said, "Oh, please, sir, do not trouble yourself further. I believe we can manage from here. If you would be so good as to fetch us a hansom, I'm sure . . ."

"It's important a doctor see to your mother as soon as possible, miss," he interrupted her impatiently as he deposited Mrs. Eaton on the leather seat. "Can you put your injured foot up on the opposite seat, ma'am?" he asked, his tone gentle again. "I think it best if you keep it elevated."

"I—I think so," Marion Eaton told him, but she bit her lip in pain as she tried to obey. Carefully he reached down and helped.

Admitting defeat, Sarah hurried forward, and he assisted her into the carriage.

"Your address?" he asked.

"We are staying at Grillon's Hotel," she confessed after a brief moment of silence. Half of her warned her to tell him nothing, while the other, more practical half said she must if she wanted to make her mother easy.

He turned away to give directions to his coachman before he joined them, taking the seat facing back, carefully avoiding Marion Eaton's injured foot.

"It was most unwise of you to visit the display without a man to assure your safety," he began, looking straight at Sarah. She stiffened at the criticism, and he went on, "I must say I was astonished to see ladies like you in such a lowly crowd."

"How came you to be there, then, sir?" Sarah asked before she blushed hotly and hoped the dim sidelights did not reveal it. Beside her, Marion Eaton gasped at her boldness.

"The ticket I held was only good for the area around Storey's Gate. I left the enclosure to get a better view, of course. But I am a man, used to London, and armed as well."

"It is true it was not wise, perhaps, but we were so anxious to see the fireworks," Marion Eaton contributed. "And we have not been in London for some years. Indeed, we have only recently returned from . . ."

Sarah interrupted lest her mother reveal their circumstances. She did not want this gentleman to know their name, or anything about them. She wondered why she felt so strongly about this. Now they were facing each other in the close confines of the carriage, she could see he was surely a gentleman, well dressed, and if not precisely handsome, pleasant enough looking with his long, intelligent face, those sleepy eyelids that so successfully hid his expressions, the firm jaw and high cheekbones.

"We must thank you for all your help, sir," she said quickly.

"Yes, indeed," Mrs. Eaton contributed. "You have been so kind, so good, sir."

He waved away their thanks. "But why didn't you bring a maid with you, or better still, a footman?" he persisted.

"Betsy!" Sarah exclaimed, her hand coming up to cover her mouth. "Oh, dear, I wonder where she is? She was torn away from us by the crowd."

Their companion shrugged. "If she escaped the initial panicking surge of humanity, no doubt she will find her way back to you," he said, not sounding very interested in the maid's fate.

For a moment the three rode in silence. The carriage was of necessity traveling slowly for the streets were still crowded. Sarah felt the silence stretching into awkwardness, and she said, "It was a marvelous exhibit all the same. I am so glad we saw it."

"I'll be very surprised if someone wasn't killed," he said, his voice frosty. "These fireworks displays are extremely dangerous."

There seemed to be nothing further to say, and Sarah was delighted when the carriage halted before Grillon's a few minutes later. As soon as the groom helped her alight, she went to speak to the doorman. Mindful of Mr. Horton's advice, she had no intention of allowing this stranger to carry her mother up the stairs to their rooms. The doorman summoned two sturdy footmen to support Mrs. Eaton between them.

The tall gentleman stood beside his carriage, watching Sarah organize all this activity. He had the suggestion of a smile on his face. It was as if he divined her reasons all too clearly, and worse, found them amusing. Sarah frowned a little, but still she put out her hand to him. He bowed slightly, but he did not take it, not did he reply to her stammered thanks.

"Oh, yes, thank you, sir, and may God bless you," Mrs. Eaton said, smiling valiantly through her tears as the servants lifted her.

He did smile then before he turned back to Sarah. "Be sure you have a physician come and see to that foot, miss," he said.

Not waiting for a reply, he climbed back into the carriage, the groom slammed the door behind him, and the coachman set the team in motion.

As Sarah followed her mother through the lobby and up the stairs, she told herself it didn't matter that she didn't know the gentleman's name or address. He had not seemed the type who would stand much on ceremony. No doubt he would consider any written thanks of hers not only excessive, but a crashing bore.

Besides, she was an heiress now. She must take care. As she hurried forward to open the door to their rooms to admit the men carrying her mother, she told herself it was just as well she had been so cautious and ended all this right now. For even though he had appeared the gentleman, who knows who he might have been, or what he might have been up to?

Chapter 3

The physician the hotel recommended came promptly, and after a thorough examination, which Mrs. Eaton bore with a great deal of fortitude, proclaimed himself satisfied that no bones had been broken. As he measured out some drops to dull the pain, he said to Sarah, "Although I'm sure she doesn't think so right now, your mother was very lucky to have escaped with only a severe sprain. However, she must rest her foot for several days, and put no weight on it."

When Sarah inquired if she would be able to travel soon, he gave it as his opinion that it would do no harm in three or four days' time. "Before that, the motion of the carriage would cause severe discomfort," he said, adding that he would stop in again the next day to see how the patient went on.

Betsy Borden returned a few minutes later. She had a dirty face and a bruised cheekbone, and her gown was ripped near the hem, but she had escaped serious danger. Horrified at the injury to Mrs. Eaton's foot, she hurried to wash before she went to try and make the lady more comfortable. Sarah reminded herself she must hire someone to help her mother, whether she wanted a maid or not. The doctor had said she would be incapacitated for some time, and it was not fair to ask Betsy to maid them both.

She discussed this with her mother the next morning after breakfast. Mrs. Eaton could not like it still, but she saw the wisdom of it, and she agreed, looking resigned.

Sarah kissed her lightly before she went to write a note to Mr. Horton telling him what had happened, and asking him to arrange for the carriage to take them to Essex in four days' time. She also asked if she might see him again. She had been going over everything he had told her, and she had come to realize it would be wise if she knew more about her grandfather's investments.

Half an hour later, a huge bouquet of flowers arrived for Marion Eaton. It was delivered by Mr. Horton's nephew Daniel, another partner in the firm. As Sarah admitted him to their rooms, she thanked him gravely for the flowers. When he smiled at her, she blushed a little, then scolded herself for such a girlish display.

Daniel Horton was a man of only medium height, with blond hair cut in a fashionable crop and bright blue eyes. She judged him to be in his early thirties.

"My uncle tells me you've expressed a desire to become familiar with your grandfather's business matters. Most commendable, Miss Eaton, most commendable indeed," he said. "Of course, you are welcome to visit the firm anytime, but wouldn't it be easier for you if I came here? I do assure you I'm as cognizant as my uncle about these matters. In fact, I thought we could make a start today, unless you are busy now. I'll certainly understand if you are, for it was forward of me to assume you might be able to see me."

"Not at all. I should be delighted," Sarah told him, indicating a table and chairs near the window. "Shall we sit there, sir?"

Mr. Horton opened a leather case he had brought with him and took out some papers. In a short time Sarah was deep in a discussion of shares, assets and debits, interest rates, and markets. Daniel Horton was as good as his word, and before he left an hour later, he had done a great deal to initiate her into the intricate world of finance.

"Not, of course, that this is anything but the barest outline, Miss Eaton," he said, his blue eyes twinkling as he gathered up his things. "May I say how impressed I am at your quick understanding? You do your grandfather proud."

As she walked with him to the door, he added, "If it is convenient, I'll come tomorrow at the same time."

"You are too kind. Thank you. And thank you for bearing with my ignorance."

He stepped a little closer to take her hands in his. "It was my pleasure," he told her. "Finances, investments, are not matters women generally understand. However, I do assure you, you may leave the day-to-day matters of the estate in our hands, ma'am."

Sarah was a little disconcerted. He seemed very near, and she wondered he had taken her hands in such an intimate clasp. But she also noted he was not even as tall as she was herself, and somehow this reassured her. Still, when her mother called for her a moment later, she was glad to free her hands and step away.

"Tomorrow at ten, Miss Eaton," Daniel Horton said, so businesslike now Sarah was sure she had misinterpreted his gesture. "Do give your mother my regards and my best wishes for a quick recovery."

This, however, Sarah forgot to do, for when she went into her mother's room, she discovered a very young, very thin little maid standing beside the bed looking pathetic. It was obvious the girl had been crying, for her eyes were all red, and so was the tip of her long, narrow nose. Sarah was not a bit surprised to find her mother patting her hand to comfort her.

"Sarah, dear, this is Mathilda Dents. I've just engaged her to be my maid. Wasn't it the most fortuitous thing? She came to clean the rooms, and I heard her crying and coughing. It seems she is not happy in London, and the work at the hotel is too hard for her. But surely she will do famously as my maid, and she will have the chance to live in the country, eat nourishing food, and breathe fresh, healthy air."

As the maid coughed, Sarah sighed. Her mother was much too trusting. After all, what did they know about this girl? She herself could not like the way her eyes darted from her face to her mother's, the pale freckled skin and watery eyes, the droop of her mouth and her limp ash-blond hair.

"I don't know," she said at last. "Besides, I've already

written to Mr. Horton asking him to engage a maid for you."

Marion Eaton's face fell, and the little maid darted a venomous glance at Sarah, so quickly gone Sarah was sure she must have imagined it.

"But couldn't you write again and tell him not to bother?" her mother said. "I'm sure I'll be happy with Mathilda's services, and we'll deal extremely well together. And she needs me, Sarah, she does."

Sarah was not proof against the pleading she saw in her eyes. "Of course I can, if that is what you wish, Mother," she said.

The doctor's arrival forestalled any more discussion, but as he examined her mother's foot, then rebound it carefully, Sarah told herself it would be easy enough to dismiss the girl later if she did not suit.

True to his word, Daniel Horton came at ten the following morning. They worked till twelve. Although grateful, Sarah was surprised he remained so long, and she felt a little guilty she was taking up so much of his valuable time. But she was even more surprised when he invited her to join him for a repast in the hotel dining room.

"I'm sure we've earned a respite, aren't you, Miss Eaton?" he asked, bowing a little as he rose from the table.

"It is very kind of you, sir, but . . ."

"Now, now, please don't say no," he implored, his blue eyes laughing at her.

"I would enjoy it very much, but I'm not sure it is the correct thing to do," she admitted.

He threw out his hands. "I do beg you to believe I would never have extended the invitation if it were not. A meal in a hotel dining room cannot be criticized by even the highest stickler."

Sarah felt like a provincial know-nothing. Of course he wouldn't put her in an awkward position. What had she been thinking? She excused herself for a moment and went into her mother's room to tell her where she was going. The little maid her mother had hired was nowhere in sight.

"Where is Mathilda?" Sarah asked as she settled her bonnet on her hair before the glass. She thought it was a shame she had to wear it. She would tower over Mr. Horton, and she did not like to repay his kindness by embarrassing him.

"I sent her down to get us a bite to eat, dear. You run along. I'll be fine alone, truly, and if I need anything, I can always ring for Betsy."

Reassured, Sarah rejoined Mr. Horton. He took her arm to help her down the stairs, talking lightly of London all the while. After they were seated in the dining room, he asked Sarah how she was enjoying her stay in town.

"Very much. If only my mother had not injured herself, I would have said wonderfully. Still, she is mending well, and that is all that's important."

He asked for details of the accident, and Sarah found herself telling him of the stranger who had come to their aid. "I do wonder who he was," she said as the waiter put bowls of soup before them. "He gave me a tongue-lashing for being so rash as to go to the exhibit without a man along for protection."

"How forward of him," Daniel Horton remarked with a frown. "After all, it was none of his concern.

"Still," he added as he stirred his soup, "I suppose I would have been tempted to do the same thing. But I shall not scold you, ma'am. Instead, please tell me something about yourself. Where you grew up, what you like to do— your time in India."

Sarah told him a little and before long she saw his eyes were twinkling. She found it impossible not to smile back when he looked so engaging. She even wondered if he were married.

"I sense you did not care for India, though, did you?" he said. "Perhaps because it was so different? But you need not consider that anymore. You're home now."

"Yes, thanks to my grandfather, and I've no intention of leaving England again," Sarah agreed.

By the time they had finished their meal, Sarah was a great deal easier with Daniel Horton. He had been a perfect host, easy to talk to and pleasant to be with, and he did not seem to mind in the slightest that she was taller than he.

She agreed readily when he asked if he might come again the following day, in the afternoon.

"Some tiresome bit of business I must take care of in the morning, ma'am," he told her as they stood together in the lobby. "But perhaps after we have finished tomorrow, you would permit me to take you for a drive in the park? Five is the fashionable hour to be seen there, and you must not go to the country before you have witnessed the ton parading. It is not as inflammatory a sight as the fireworks, but it is every bit as colorful. What a shame your mother cannot join us."

When they left two days later, Sarah was sorry to have to say good-bye to Daniel Horton. He had come to the hotel early that morning to assist them. She felt she had made a good friend, and a most knowledgeable one at that, and she was delighted when he said he would come to Essex in a week or so to see how she was getting on. He also begged her to write to him if she had any questions or problems he could help her with. She did not object when he took her hand in farewell, and before he released her, she returned the pressure of his fingers.

It was early evening when they clattered through the village of Woodingham and turned into the gates that separated it from the grounds of the Hall. Sarah was glad of the concealing dusk, for it meant her mother had not been able to see the small cottage that stood alone on the edge of the village, where she had spent almost all her married life before traveling to India. Sarah knew she would have to deal with that situation before much longer, and she only hoped it did not bring back too many sad memories and make her mother cry. Now, however, she was too tired to worry about it; tired and anxious to see the Hall itself, even though part of her dreaded it. She almost wished she could bang on the roof, order the coach to halt, then turn back to London. She scolded herself mentally for her cowardice.

As they traveled up the drive, she recalled the one and only time she had been here before. Her father had brought her along on one of his rare visits to his father. Only five at the time, she had wondered since if he had hoped her little girl's ingenuous ways would soften her grandfather's attitude toward his only son and his family. She could not remember clearly, although she knew that for a long time after the visit, she had had trouble sleeping in a darkened room. Because the Hall seemed full of dark rooms, vast and cold? Or was it because her grandfather had glared at her, and shouted at her father, until he frightened her? She did not know.

The bulk of Woodingham Hall rose before them, ghostly in the pale light of a half-moon. Sarah was surprised no torches had been lit at the door for them.

Beside her, her mother coughed a little and lowered her head to rummage through her reticule. Sarah wondered if she had done so so she would not have to look at a place where she had never been welcome but must now call home. As the coach halted, the groom leapt from his perch and hurried up the steps to sound a large brass knocker. It seemed quite some time before the door opened and an elderly butler stood surveying them, a lamp in his hand held high. Really, Sarah thought, this becomes ludicrous. All we need is a baying hound! If I had read of it in a book, I would have laughed aloud at the melodrama. Somehow this thought gave her courage, and without waiting for the groom's assistance, she stepped down to climb the shallow steps, her chin high.

"Assist my mother, then see to the unloading of the baggage," she ordered the groom as she passed him.

"Good evening," she said to the old butler as she entered the Hall. "I am Sarah Eaton, your new mistress. Kindly summon some footmen to help us. My mother has had an accident and cannot walk easily."

The butler bowed and shuffled away, and Sarah realized she had forgotten to ask his name. She shrugged as she removed her bonnet and looked about her.

The foyer where she stood was not especially large, but it was crowded with all manner of tables and chairs, dim paintings, and even a suit of armor. In the light of the flickering candles she could make out that it seemed clean but neglected. Of course, she reminded herself as she heard footsteps approaching, it had been over three months since her grandfather's death, and no one had been living here except the servants.

She thought she recognized both the footmen as they bowed to her. Surely they had grown up in the village, hadn't they? Still, she gave no sign she knew them as they went to fetch her mother.

"Forgive me, I forgot to ask your name," she said to the elderly butler. She remembered to smile.

"Ferris, ma'am," he said in a quavering voice.

"Well, Ferris, please fetch the housekeeper for me, and see about a light supper. We did not stop to eat on the road. Oh, and someone must show our maids where we are to sleep. But perhaps I should take that up with the house-keeper."

Sarah made herself stop and take a deep breath. She knew she was babbling, and she was sure the butler must know she had never run a household, never mind one the size of Woodingham Hall and despised her for her igno-rance.

"Yes, ma'am. At once, ma'am," he said in his faint old voice as he bowed and left her.

No sooner had he disappeared than the tallest footman was at the door, Marion Eaton in his arms. Wildly, Sarah was reminded of a bride being carried over the threshold. And what a macabre thought that was when her mother had not only been denied here, but loathed from the day she had married the son of the house.

Quickly Sarah picked up a branch of candles and led the way into a drawing room nearby. The furniture was cov-ered with dustcovers, and she whisked one off a sofa so the footman could put her mother there.

After ordering the footman to light more candles and start a small fire in the fireplace to take away the chill of an unused room, she went to sit beside her mother and take her hands.

"Yes, it is a bit overwhelming, isn't it?" she asked in a soft voice, trying to ignore the busy footman.

"I wish we had not had to come here," Marion Eaton confessed, her face troubled. "I can't forget how your grandfather felt about me, and . . ."

"But he is dead now, Mother, and everything has changed," Sarah interrupted. "Now *I'm* the owner of the Hall. I only wish I knew how to behave as that owner. Mind you help me."

It was perhaps just as well Mrs. Eaton did not inquire how she was to do that when, as the daughter of a cabinet-maker in a small shop in Ipswich, she had no idea, either. Fortunately, the housekeeper entered the room then. Sarah immediately disliked the woman. Her curtsy was so shallow it bordered on insolence, and the gaze that carefully inspected the two women was sullen.

"You are?" Sarah prompted, her chin up again and her voice challenging.

"Mrs. Quigley. Ma'am."

"Well, Mrs. Quigley, please inform our maids where we are to sleep."

"There's no rooms ready. Ma'am."

"And why is that? Surely, you expected us."

There was only a cold silence, and in it, Sarah rose. She was glad of her height now, for she towered over the shorter, older woman.

"I mean, I thought you'd want to choose your rooms yourself. Ma'am," came the grudging reply.

"It is much too late to inspect the Hall tonight. I shall do so in the morning. For tonight, just have any two rooms prepared. And I've instructed the butler to serve us a light supper."

The housekeeper nodded and turned away. Sarah's voice stopped her in mid-stride. "Have you forgotten something, Mrs. Quigley? Your curtsy, if you please."

For a moment Sarah was sure the woman would not obey, but just as she was wondering what on earth she was to do about such insolence, the housekeeper turned and dropped another shallow bob.

As she turned to go, Sarah said, "This is my mother,

Mrs. Marion Eaton. You will obey her orders as you would
mine."

Mrs. Quigley had only turned her head slightly, and now
her nod was barely perceptible. Sarah did not push the
issue. She intended to replace the housekeeper as soon as
possible. She would write to Daniel Horton tomorrow and
ask him to send her someone else immediately.

Chapter 4

There began a period then in Sarah Eaton's life that she would eventually look back on and wonder that she had ever lived through it. Although busy from morning to night, giving orders and making sure those orders were carried out took only a bit of time every day. But she had also to interview her grandfather's agent and the outdoor staff of gardeners and stable men. She was an immediate success with these gentlemen, since, knowing nothing of such matters, she only told them to carry on as they were wont to do. The elderly head gardener immediately dug up some bushes Mr. Eaton had insisted he plant, and the agent went off to plan extensive changes in crops the following year.

Sarah had also written to Daniel Horton about the housekeeper and had had an almost immediate reply. In it, he had begged her to endure Mrs. Quigley until such time as he was able to interview replacements. A press of business at the current time prohibited him from giving the matter the attention it deserved. Sarah did her best, but the woman continued to be insolent and cold.

Since the Hall needed a great deal of attention, she herself set the maids to scrubbing and polishing, and oversaw the results rather than depend on Mrs. Quigley. That the housekeeper probably resented her interference did not concern her.

She did have a gentle talk with the butler about retirement. He had agreed readily he was beyond the work now, although his eyes grew damp as he told her how he had come here to be boot boy sixty years before. To Sarah's surprise, he was not at all interested in a cottage in the vil-

lage. Instead he said he intended to move to Devon, where
he had a widowed sister. Relieved that this problem had
been solved so easily, Sarah turned her attention to the two
footmen to try and discover if either were worthy of promo-
tion. She could not like the idea, however. She had grown
up with the taller one, and as a small child he had frightened her, he had been such a bully. Now his sly knowing
looks, the odd little quirk of his mouth when she gave him
an order, told her he had not forgotten her humble begin-
nings, and never would. The other footman was younger
and the weaker of the two. It was obvious Dennis Carten
had bullied him unceasingly. Sarah doubted he would ever
get over it. She decided to put this particular problem aside
until she could discuss it with Mr. Horton.

To her surprise, her mother seemed to have accepted her
new home with more ease than her daughter had thought
possible. Of course, because of her injured foot, she spent
most of her time in her room, attended by the depressing
Mathilda Dents, and so had little contact with the other servants. Sometimes Sarah envied her her isolation. She herself was so very much aware of every glance, every
whisper. And aware as well of her complete ignorance of
elegant wealthy households, and how they should be run.
She could feel herself growing tense, and she often went to
bed with a blazing headache after a day of tiptoeing around,
trying to appear at ease and in charge.

One pleasant afternoon when she had had as much as she
could stand, Sarah ordered the landau and had her mother
carried downstairs so they could both enjoy the sunlight
and fresh air, and she could have the respite she felt she
more than deserved.

They both smiled to everyone they saw as they went
through the village. Sarah noted very few people smiled
back, and she frowned a little. It would not be pleasant living here if she was to be treated like a pariah. She had not
considered that possibility. Was it because she was a
woman, and women did not inherit wealth? Or was it because she had grown up here as poor as they were, and they
resented her good fortune?

The carriage bowled along the country roads, the village lost to sight behind them, and Sarah put those concerns from her mind for now. It was such a lovely sunny day. She was amused to see her mother pull her shawl closer, and she knew she was feeling chilled after all those years in India. For herself, she could hardly wait for winter.

It was on their return an hour later that the groom inadvertently drove them past their old cottage. Marion Eaton saw it first and begged to stop.

Resigned to something she had known must be faced sooner or later, Sarah gave the necessary orders. Helping her mother alight, she asked the groom to return in half an hour as Marion Eaton limped eagerly to the gate, leaning heavily on her cane. As Sarah had feared, her eyes filled with tears as she did so, and she sobbed a little in her distress.

"Oh, dear, how it does bring back the memories," she said softly as she wiped her eyes on her handkerchief. "Your father brought me here right after our wedding when your grandfather refused to admit us to the Hall. But how happy we were, here in our dear wee house."

Sarah stared at the tiny cottage. There was nothing dear about it as far as she was concerned. She remembered only too well the windowless loft where she had slept as a child, the cold scullery, the smoking fireplace that never drew well, even the crude furniture and chipped dishes. But it had been all Samuel Eaton could afford, for the writing he turned to after his father withdrew his support had never been a success.

"Do you think the people who own it now would mind if we looked inside?" Marion Eaton asked, recalling her daughter to the present.

"It looks empty to me—deserted," Sarah replied as she pushed the gate open. It creaked on its hinges just as it always had, and she shivered a little. The garden was overgrown and weedy, although the pink tea rose near the door her mother had tended so faithfully was full of flowers and as fragrant as ever. Mrs. Eaton pulled off a few faded blooms, then plucked a freshly opened bud and held it to her nose, her eyes closed.

"How often I dreamt of doing this in India," she said softly.

Sarah did not reply. She was not at all sure her mother had even been speaking to her.

Mrs. Eaton opened her eyes and looked around. Her face brightened when she saw that although the rustic bench under the beech tree was covered with moss, it was still there. Before it, the little brook that fronted the cottage went its familiar way until it disappeared in the woods beyond.

"What a lovely place this is," she mused to herself.

Sarah tried to see the cottage as her mother did, but she was not successful. To her it was poor and humble; so badly built it had been cold in winter and stifling in summer. Even when the garden had been carefully tended, it had not been able to hide the necessary, the broken-down stable, or the hen coop. Thinking back to how her mother had toiled here day after day, her lips tightened. Marion Eaton would never do so again. She would see to that.

Her mother wiped away another tear before she reached up over the door and felt the top of the jamb. Surprisingly the key was still where she had left it seven years before. Looking a little nervous, she unlocked the door and pushed it open.

Dust motes lay heavy in the air, clearly visible in the golden light that came through one of the dirty windows.

For no reason she could understand, Sarah was suddenly alarmed.

"Don't go in there, Mother!" she said, grasping her arm more tightly.

Startled, Marion Eaton stared up at her. "Why ever not, dear?" she asked. "There now, you can stay out here if you cannot bear it. I understand. Just wait for me. I won't be long."

She pulled gently away to step over the threshold. Sarah hung back, stunned her mother had thought her affected by grief or nostalgia. Turning away, she walked back to the gate, wanting to put as much space as possible between herself and the cottage.

As she reached the gate, the familiar figure of the curate, Mr. Forrest Blake, mounted on a chestnut mare, came around the bend in the road.

"Why, if it isn't Miss Eaton!" the gentleman exclaimed, his face lit with a warm smile. "I heard you had returned to Woodingham, but I was loathe to call until you were more settled. How delightful this chance encounter is."

To Sarah's surprise, he dismounted and tied his horse to the gate before he came to stand before her. His gray eyes were intent on her face. They seemed to be searching for something. She wondered if he had found it—whatever it was.

"Yes, you have changed, haven't you?" he said, nodding a little. "India did affect you. May I say I hope it did not alter your character?"

Sarah curtsied. She felt flustered. Even as a young girl she had secretly thought the curate the handsomest man she had ever seen. He was about ten years her senior, and she had sat rapt throughout his lengthy Sunday sermons, admiring his black curly hair, those flashing gray eyes as well as his expressive hands, firm jawline, and tempting mouth. If the truth were known, she had barely heard a word of what he said. No, for she had sat dreaming of him holding her close to him, and wondering what it would be like to kiss him and feel his caresses. What a good thing he did not suspect how wayward a character she had possessed.

Still, she remembered that after her father had become a Methodist, she had spent no more time in the village church. Samuel Eaton had conducted his own services in a nearby barn for his family and those few others he had persuaded to his new beliefs. She remembered that although Mr. Blake had not ridiculed her father, the vicar had; yes, held him up to censure and scorn as well, and she stiffened.

"Have you remembered something unpleasant, Miss Eaton? About me?" he asked seriously, leaving her to wonder if he could read minds. Pray not! "Let me assure you I've since regretted my silent condemnation of your father's beliefs. No matter how misguided I still must consider him, it was—it was not Christian of me. And now he is dead. My sincere condolences to you, and to your mother."

"Thank you," Sarah managed to say.

He bent a little closer, as if to search her face again. "I know it is much too soon, but I must say how gratified I would be if you would return to the fold, come to church again, and allow me to serve humbly as your spiritual adviser. Everyone would be so pleased to see you take your place in the Eaton pew. After all, you are Jonah Eaton's granddaughter. But I shall not press you at this time. As I've said, it is too soon. But you may believe, Miss Eaton, I do most sincerely have your best interests at heart."

"You are too kind, sir," Sarah said, and was delighted to hear her mother shutting the cottage door behind her.

Before she could excuse herself, Mr. Blake exclaimed as he brushed by her to hurry up the flagstone path to help her mother.

"Why, Mrs. Eaton, you are injured," he said, all but lifting her off her feet and carrying her down the walk.

"It is only a sprained foot," Marion Eaton said, her color heightened as he set her down beside her daughter. "But I—I do thank you, er, sir."

The curate removed his hat and bowed. "Mr. Forrest Blake, ma'am. Curate of St. John's, St. Agnes's, and St. Matthew in the Meadow."

"Indeed?" Mrs. Eaton replied, her voice suddenly frosty.

Suddenly Sarah was startled to see her face light up in a welcoming smile, her vigorous wave, and she turned to see a smart black phaeton approaching. To her continued amazement, the gentleman who had come to their aid in London was driving the rig. He halted his team before them, gave a short order to the groom clinging to the perch behind, and climbed down to the dusty road.

"Well met, ma'am," he said, smiling at her. "You are almost recovered now?"

"Indeed I am, and I am so glad to see you again, sir," Marion Eaton said as she curtsied. "I never did have the opportunity to thank you properly after you came to our assistance at the fireworks. And here you are in the country. How extraordinary."

"Believe me, no more thanks are necessary, ma'am," he said brusquely. His glance inspected both Sarah and the curate. "As for being in the neighborhood, I have a house here."

Sarah sensed Mr. Blake was becoming impatient now this stranger had invaded their little group and he was being ignored.

"I do not believe we have met, sir," he said as he stepped forward and bowed. "I am Forrest Blake, curate of several local churches."

"Are you," the stranger said, his lazy voice showing how much this fascinating information bored him. "Well, sir, since we are introducing ourselves, I am Miles Griffin. Er, the Marquis of Wexford."

"I do not believe I have seen you in any of my churches, sir," Blake persisted. Sarah spared him a passing pang of sympathy. She did not think he would fare well in any contest of wits with Lord Wexford. Then she wondered how she could be so sure of that.

"How could you? I've never attended," Wexford told him. "Nor, sir, to spare your breath, is there any likelihood I shall."

He turned to Sarah then. "You are visiting in East Anglia, miss?" he asked, giving the poor cottage beyond the gate a dubious glance.

Sarah was sure he only inquired to be spared any more conversation with the curate, so she was not flattered by this attention.

"No, we are come to live, sir," she said. Then she wondered if somehow he had found out she was an heiress and followed her here. It seemed highly unlikely. She told herself she must stop being suspicious of everyone she met. Almost she wished Mr. Horton had not put such ideas into her head. Lord Wexford's being here was probably just a coincidence. He had said he had a house in the neighborhood. She supposed many gentlemen possessed country homes to retreat to when the noise and ceaseless activity of London became irksome.

For himself, Miles Griffin was confused. There was no nearby carriage, and surely the ladies had not walked from their home, not with the elder one still leaning on a cane. And he refused to believe they occupied the run-down cottage. Where, then, did they live?

As if in answer to his question, a handsome landau, driven by a proper groom, drove up.

"Here is the carriage now, Mother," the younger lady said.

Did he detect a note of relief in her voice, he wondered. Relief that she could now escape the prosy parson? Or was it he himself?

"Allow me to assist you, ma'am," he said, offering the elder lady his arm. He noted with some amusement, the curate hastening to help her daughter.

As they took their seats in the carriage, Mr. Blake said, "I shall do myself the honor of calling on you in the near future, Miss Eaton. Mrs. Eaton, ma'am, your very good health."

He stepped back, and startled, Miles Griffin followed suit.

"Give you good day, sir," the elder lady he knew now for the heiress's mother said. Then she turned to him and smiled.

"And to you as well, sir. We would be pleased if you would call, too."

The leave-taking of the two men left standing in the road was curt. As the marquis drove away, he considered what he had learned. So, that was the new heiress, was it? Why had he never suspected it when he came upon them here in Essex today?

He smiled a little. No matter what his cousin Eliza had said about heiresses, no one could call this one ravishing. Miss Eaton was far too tall for one thing and in no way outstanding. True, she had a pleasant face—when she remembered to smile—and attractive hazel eyes flecked with gold. But her nut-brown hair was much too long and thick for the current fashions, and she wore it in a prim chignon low on her nape. He applauded her lovely complexion and her excellent figure, but in a ballroom crowded with the elite, she would go unnoticed.

Not that it mattered, of course, what she looked like. Eliza had been right about that. The beaux and fortune hunters would be after her as soon as they discovered her whereabouts. And if he were not mistaken, that country parson was the first to enter the lists. He had disliked the man on sight, and not because he had the handsome good looks of an Adonis. The marquis had come to terms with his own lack of masculine beauty long ago. No, it had been the man's manner. He had been polite yet somehow *oily*. Concerned, yet self-seeking. Obsequious but, he suspected, under that humble facade, conceited.

He smiled again as he halted the team to let a flock of sheep cross the road. Mrs. Eaton had asked him to call. Perhaps he would do so. It might be amusing to see how the ladies went on, and he found he was interested in them both. The elder because he sensed the very real gentility she had had been hard earned, and the younger because her wariness of this new situation she found herself in, and a gallant resolve to do well in it that he did not think he was imagining, was intriguing.

Besides, he had yet to discover why old Jonah Eaton had passed over his only son and bestowed his land and his wealth on his granddaughter. And the marquis would be the first to admit he had more than his share of vulgar curiosity.

Chapter 5

Daniel Horton arrived in Essex early the following week. Sarah was delighted he had come at last, and practically ran down the stairs to greet him. He laughed at her fulsome welcome before he introduced the woman who had accompanied him.

"Here is Eudalia Bonnet, Miss Eaton," he said. "She is a distant relation of mine, and although she has never been employed as a housekeeper, she has a great deal of experience running a large establishment. Her husband had a sizable holding in Devon. He is gone from us now, and she was replaced by the new heirs, so she is delighted to be able to assist you at this time."

"How kind of you, ma'am," Sarah said with a smile. Mrs. Bonnet returned it, and Sarah, observing her ample curves, that round friendly face, felt herself relaxing. She would send Mrs. Quigley on her way tomorrow.

She rang for a maid and asked the girl to show Mrs. Bonnet to her room and give her any assistance she might need.

As the door closed behind the two, Daniel Horton said, "I pray you do not think me too forward, to be bringing my dear old Dalia here, Miss Eaton. But really, I could find no one else suitable. And employing her would be an act of kindness, for deprived of both her husband and her household, she was quite bewildered."

"The poor thing," Sarah sympathized. "I hope she'll be happy here. But what a bad hostess I am! Please be seated, sir."

Mr. Horton took the chair across from the one she chose. As he did so, Sarah said, "I fear I have another problem for you, sir. Dear, dear, how tiresome I'm becoming. I'm sure you must be rueing the day my grandfather took his business to your firm."

"Hardly," Daniel Horton told her so dryly she had to laugh.

"It's the butler. As you suspected, he wants to retire, but I cannot like either of the footmen as his replacement. I hope you can find another man for me. It will not matter if he is not well versed in social matters, for we intend to live very simply here."

"Of course, for the time being. But eventually you will wish to give entertainments, dinners, or parties. You'll need someone knowledgeable, then. Leave all to me. I'll endeavor to find someone suitable."

As they continued to converse, Sarah learned he had taken a room at the Woodingham Arms, and she insisted on sending a groom to fetch his baggage.

"No, no, you must not stay at the inn, sir! You will be much more comfortable here, and besides, it will give us the chance to discuss all these problems more easily. Er, I do hope your uncle is well?"

She wondered at the small frown that darkened his face for a moment. "Yes, he is well," he said briefly. "He sends you and your mother his regards."

Tea was brought in then, and Sarah waited until the servants had bowed themselves away before she went on, "I hope you will have time to advise me about the farms and the estate, sir. I've told my grandfather's agent just to carry on, for I haven't the slightest idea what on earth I could have told him else. I am so—so helplessly incompetent."

Daniel Horton put down his cup and leaned forward, holding her gaze with his own. "Yes, I can see why you might feel that way, Miss Eaton," he said easily. "And why not? All this is very new to you. But you must remember it would be the same for anyone else, man or woman. You'll learn as you go along. Just don't be afraid to ask questions if you don't understand something. And if there is something you cannot like, by all means change it! I shall always be available to help you, you know."

She smiled at him warmly. "I know. You are too good. I must take care I don't impose on your good nature and valuable time. I rely on you to inform me if I become tiresome."

Before he could reply, she offered to refill his cup, and as she did so, she changed the subject.

After tea, Sarah suggested a stroll through the grounds. They were admiring a sunken rose garden when a footman came to tell Sarah Mr. Forrest Blake had called and begged a few minutes of her time.

Sarah frowned, but finally she nodded, and asked him to tell Mr. Blake she would be with him shortly.

"Ah, I see the gentlemen are already beginning to assemble in pursuit," Mr. Horton said as he helped her up a shallow flight of stairs. "I did not think it would take them long."

"No such thing," Sarah protested. "Mr. Blake is the local curate. He is merely determined to save my soul by convincing me my place is in the Eaton pew in the village church."

Daniel Horton only smiled at her, but he appeared deep in thought when he caught a glimpse of the handsome curate a little later.

Another gentleman called the following afternoon. Miles Griffin asked for Mrs. Eaton, and the lady was delighted to receive him, although he thought she seemed uncomfortable in the ornate, formal drawing room. When he asked her if there wasn't another room she preferred, she confessed she had grown fond of a small morning room that faced the garden. The marquis suggested she receive her visitors there.

"No need for all this pomp, ma'am," he said with a smile as he stared around at the dark brown velvet draperies, the beige brocaded chairs and sofas, and the walls covered with murky oils of long-deceased relatives and depressing landscapes. "I find it, er, more than a little dreary myself. I wonder what Mr. Eaton was thinking of, to select these colors?"

"The butler told me his wife chose the decorations, and he never cared to alter them," Mrs. Eaton explained.

"A typical male excuse," the marquis murmured. "I suppose he hoped people would imagine it was because he revered her memory so, he could not bear to, when in reality, he was only lazy."

His hostess's delighted laughter brought a smile to his long, stern face.

"Sarah does intend to change things, after we have lived here for a while," she confided. "But she hesitated to rush into alterations too soon."

"Tell her there is not a moment to lose," Miles urged. "Assure you, must make haste lest you both expire from constant contact with gloom and somberness.

"Now, a pale blue drapery with gold accents would do nicely in here. And a striped paper, don't you think? It would brighten the room up considerably."

"Are you interested in decorating, m'lord? How unusual for a man."

"Not at all. I'm interested in any number of things. But perhaps it's because I've never married that I began to study the art of decoration."

Mrs. Eaton asked him if he would be kind enough to go through the ground-floor rooms with her and give her the benefit of his expertise. They were deep in a discussion of whether scarlet or royal blue would be better in the dining room, when Sarah and Mr. Horton, fresh from a drive around the estate, came in and found them.

Informed of the marquis's assistance, Sarah stiffened a little. She could not have said why exactly, for surely it was kind of him to bother. But perhaps it was because she considered it impertinent? Although he had come to their aid in London, they did not know him very well after all. And had he offered because, knowing her background, he considered her incapable? Incompetent, even? No, she told herself, she must not make too much of what might be merely a kindness. After all, he probably had more than his share of male arrogance, and considered his taste superior to any woman's. And she didn't have to follow his advice if she didn't care to. Still, she had to admit the peach and soft green he suggested would look lovely in the room her mother so admired.

When he took his leave at last, and Mrs. Eaton went up to rest, Daniel Horton said in a teasing manner, "But surely the marquis has no interest in your religious beliefs, Miss Eaton. I beg you not to pretend that is why *he* calls."

"Of course not, sir," Sarah was quick to say. "For some reason he seems intrigued by my mother. We met when he came to our aid at the fireworks."

"Did he? Well, there are worse ways to become an intimate of the family," he persisted as he held the library door for her. "I know my uncle cautioned you to beware of fortune hunters, so I shall say no more. But would it upset you if I looked into the Marquis of Wexford's financial affairs? Sometimes noblemen, feeling as they do superior to the rest of us ordinary human begins, are careless about money. They gamble incessantly, and many have been brought low by losing all their wealth to the table or the Fancy. Er, that is horse racing, Miss Eaton. There have been a number of nobles who sought to recoup their fortunes by an advantageous marriage to an innocent heiress. Some even stoop to marrying Cits."

Sarah gave her permission, but much later when she was getting ready for bed, she wondered about Daniel Horton. Surely he was seeing fortune hunters at every turn; why, he was even worse than she. Still, she told herself as she climbed into bed, she was grateful for his concern and his care. And for his expertise as well. He had suggested a number of things she might set in train to keep the estate profitable, and he had mentioned several investment schemes for her to consider as well. She hoped he could stay for a long time.

The next morning she asked the housekeeper to come to her in the library, to tell her her employment at Woodingham Hall was at an end.

"You and I were obviously not going to deal well together, Mrs. Quigley," she said. "Your dislike of me and my mother has been most marked. However, I'm prepared to write you a reference, and you may remain until the end of the week."

"Ah, don't put yourself to the bother, you poor excuse for a lady," Mrs. Quigley said quickly. She leaned over the desk, and Sarah was hard put not to recoil. The house-keeper's round face was scarlet, and in her anger a thin line of spittle had escaped the corner of her mouth. "I'm not going to work for anyone ever again. I've enough put by, aye, I made sure Mr. Eaton saw to that, long before he died. And there's things I know about the Hall. Things I could tell if I wanted to. So I'm going to a cottage I own in the village, and I'll be keeping an eye on things here. You can count on it."

"But surely it would be more pleasant to live somewhere else?" Sarah suggested. The very thought of this virago crouched outside the gates, possibly making trouble for her, was horrible to contemplate. And what did she mean, she knew things about the Hall?

The woman laughed. "You'd like that, wouldn't you? Out of sight, out of mind. But this here is England. I guess I can live where I want. And you don't *own* the village."

She turned then and went to the door. Once there, she sneered at Sarah and said, "Think you're something, don't you? Think just because you came into a lot of money, you're better than everyone else. But you're not. Everyone here remembers you growing up, and poorer than the poor-est church mouse you were. Almost dressed in rags, too. Aye, your fine feathers now can't change that, Miss-High-and-Mighty-Eaton. And money can't make you noble, or even landed gentry. You were born common, and common is what you'll always be. I wouldn't work for *you* if I was starving, I wouldn't!"

Sarah sat frozen as she stormed out and slammed the door behind her. Mrs. Quigley had not bothered to lower her voice. She was sure everyone within earshot had heard her shouted condemnation—those terrible insults.

She swallowed hard. I won't cry, she told herself fiercely, I won't. She is wrong. I'm not common. My father was an Eaton, and until his father cast him off, a member of the landed gentry. I am his daughter. I'll not pay any attention to what she said, but I'll see she leaves this house today. She has lost the right to any consideration I might have shown her.

After instructing the butler to relay her order, she left the Hall. She wanted to put as much space between her and the ugly scene just past as she could.

She walked quickly through the gardens, not even seeing the profusion of colorful blooms there, nor the old gardener's stiff salute. She did not slow her pace until she reached the woods, where she knew she could not be seen from the Hall. She paused then to catch her breath, leaning against a huge oak that was marked with the king's broad arrow to show it had been chosen for some future ship of the Royal Navy.

As the wind ruffled her hair, she realized she had come out without a bonnet or gloves. No lady would ever be so remiss, and for a minute the housekeeper's hateful words came back to taunt her. She put up her chin. No more, she told herself. I'll just ignore her.

But even though she tried to think of a million things else as she went deeper into the woods, she only completely forgot when she came to a small pond and sat down to watch the dragonflies hovering over it, and the ripples a small fish made as it jumped to escape some larger predator. The sun was warm on her face, but there was a cool breeze. When she dipped her fingers into the water, it was cool, too. This would be a good place to bathe, she thought. It was certainly private.

Eventually, when the position of the sun told her it was getting late and her mother would be wondering where she was, she stood up and smoothed her muslin skirts. She was wearing a white gown today, and it was very wrinkled. She would have to change before tea. Daniel Horton was going to join her for that. He had been with her agent all day, going over future plans. What a good man he was, Sarah thought as she headed for home, to spend so much time with me. Why, surely he exceeds his duties as one of my solicitors. She wondered if his uncle approved.

At the edge of the woods again, she paused to stare at the Hall she could see a little distance away. As she did so, Mrs. Quigley's face, her words, even what amounted to her threats, returned to her mind, and she frowned.

The Marquis of Wexford, who had been about to make a call on her mother, saw her there, and leaving the graveled drive, rode over to meet her. He wondered as he did so at her frown, and at her casual attire. It seemed unlike her somehow, for he suspected she wanted to appear the perfect chatelaine of Woodingham Hall. Still, he admired her figure when the wind pressed the gown against her, and acknowledged she was much better looking now that the self-same breeze had loosened some of her hair from its tight arrangement. He was reminded of the Herrick poem about a slight disorder in a woman's dress being more bewitching than a perfect turnout, and found himself more than agreeing.

"Miss Eaton, well met," he called out as he neared her. He saw her look around as if for some way to escape, and he smiled to himself. Between her and the Hall were only the gardens. There was no place she could hide. She brushed back the little curls at her forehead before she hid her gloveless hands in the folds of her gown. The marquis dismounted and, taking his horse's bridle, began to walk at her side.

"I hope you don't mind that I join you without an invitation," he said, smiling down at her.

Sarah had the incongruous thought that it was very pleasant to stroll along beside a much taller gentleman. Why, the top of her head barely reached his chin. Remembering to be polite, she said as she stared straight ahead, "Have you come to call on my mother, m'lord?"

"Perhaps I came to call on you," he replied. His horse snorted then, almost as if in disbelief, and Sarah forgot to frown.

"Ah, I'm glad to see a smile replacing that serious face you've been sporting," he went on smoothly. "Is anything the matter?"

Sarah looked at him and was surprised to see his dark

eyes boring down into hers, as if he were trying to read her mind. She shrugged. "Just an annoying bit of household trouble," she said as lightly as she could.

"But there is no such thing. Everything that affects the household is of the utmost importance, for if it isn't run smoothly, without wrangling and upsets, it is a miserable place.

"Just consider if you will, Miss Eaton. The butler gives one of the footmen a set-down. The footman then snarls at the upstairs maid, who had fond dreams of the two of them marrying someday. She suffers a fit of crying and quarrels with the boot boy. In the kitchen, the boot boy pushes the scullery maid out of his way, causing her to drop the cook's favorite mixing bowl. That breakage and the cook's resulting foul temper result in a dinner sent up, that, although perfectly adequate, somehow does not satisfy. Could it be the slightly burned taste of the soup? Or could it be the dryness of the roast? The limp vegetables? The tartness of the berry pies? And all this because a footman's livery had lost a button. No, no, Miss Eaton, you must never say household business is of little consequence!"

Sarah had begun to smile during his explanation, and now she said, "And you would hate that, wouldn't you, m'lord? I am sure your home is a paragon of order and felicity."

"Yes, it is. But please don't try to turn the subject. You may confide in me. I'm a good listener, and I keep what I hear to myself. Perhaps I can help—advise you. I'd like to try."

Sarah considered. He had sounded sincere, and there wasn't anyone else she could confide in. Telling her mother would only upset her, and she knew she shouldn't bring every little problem to Daniel Horton's attention.

Resigned, she said, "I just had a most distressing interview with my housekeeper. I am letting her go, for she has been insolent, indeed unsatisfactory ever since our arrival. Mr. Horton, my solicitor, brought another housekeeper from London. But Mrs. Quigley insulted me, and she says she is going to live in the village and keep her eye on me. I suppose it is silly of me, but it upset me."

"Yes, I'm sure it was unpleasant. But there is nothing she can do but talk behind your back. The villagers might believe her, or they might not. And after they get to know you, I'm sure they'll put her backbiting down to sour grapes. It is strange that she's not looking for another post, however. Most servants have little money saved."

"She told me she had seen to it long ago that she had enough money from my grandfather."

"Ah, I understand now. It is entirely possible this Mrs. Quigley served your grandfather in quite another capacity than just his housekeeper. He had been a widower for some time? She is an attractive woman?"

"I wouldn't say so. She's in her late forties with black hair and a high complexion, and she is, mm, robustly built. But what do you mean, another capacity? I don't understand."

She saw his astonishment and wondered at it.

"Why, I meant the woman must have been his mistress, of course," he drawled. "There is nothing else she could have been to have enough money to live independently now. Perhaps she is disgruntled because she expected him to leave her more in his will. Perhaps she even thought she'd get the Hall, since he had quarreled so finally with your father. It's a good thing you got rid of her when you did, for when a servant begins to get ideas above her station, it usually means . . . why, Miss Eaton! What is the matter?"

The marquis's sideways glance had shown him how pale his companion had become, how she had turned a little away from him and covered her mouth with one hand.

"Are you feeling ill?" he demanded. "Tell me."

"How dare you speak of such things to me, sir?" she managed to say. "I have never been so insulted."

He seemed dumbstruck for a moment before he recovered to say, "Of course, I must beg your pardon for offending you, ma'am, but because you are older and more widely traveled than the usual young thing, I assumed such a conversation would not offend you."

Sarah closed her eyes. "I may not be an innocent sixteen, m'lord, but I am hardly the sophisticate you believe. Indeed, I have lived a most sheltered life. But that is neither here nor there. I do not care to talk to you any longer. I wish you would go away. Now! At once!"

Chapter 6

But the Marquis of Wexford did not go away. Instead he looked around calmly and raised his hand to summon a gardener working in a perennial bed nearby.

"Take my horse to the stable," he ordered as the boy came running up.

Sarah stood there quietly seething. So, he was going to ignore her order, was he? Well, she had no intention of talking to him further. She picked up her skirt and was prepared to walk away with her head held high when he took her arm in his.

"There, this is much better," he said easily. "Besides, I did not care to trail a horse through your gardens.

"Now, Miss Eaton, I've apologized, and you may be sure I'll watch my tongue from now on. However, what I said was nothing but the truth, and if you want to hide from that truth behind a veil of simpering modesty, you are not the young woman I believed."

He paused, but when Sarah had nothing to say, he went on smoothly, "I like that blue and white bed of larkspur and phlox. It is a handsome conceit. I'll have to try the scheme at Wexford. That is my estate in Kent, you understand. Perhaps I should introduce some scarlet as well? Or do you think that too obvious?"

There was another silence, and he stopped and turned her toward him. His dark eyes under their sleepy lids burned down into hers, and she lowered her eyes immediately.

"You don't feel your behavior at the moment is slightly, oh, just the *merest* bit childish, Miss Eaton?" he asked. "I am your guest. You must say something to me eventually."

"I was rather hoping that might be good-bye," Sarah retorted, stung now.

He grinned at her in genuine amusement. "Excellent, excellent. I am delighted to see you have a sharp wit, ma'am. But come, shall we sit on that bench over there and admire the flowers?"

Sarah wished she might excuse herself and run into the Hall to change for tea, but he was so urbane, she hardly knew how to manage that without appearing even more gauche than she was sure she had already seemed. She nodded, feeling in turn both hot and cold, and furious with herself for being tricked into behaving as she had.

"Tell me something of India, if you would be so kind," he said as they seated themselves."

"I wonder why everyone asks me that first?" she mused, determined to control herself from now on. No matter what. "It is a vast, crowded country with extreme heat and a prolonged rainy season. I'm delighted to be home."

"Your father was a missionary there, I believe?"

"Yes, we went out when I was just turned eighteen."

"With the risk of upsetting you again, I must say I am surprised you returned unwed. I understood that there are few English girls in India, and between the Company and the army, far too many men."

"Yes, that's true. But you must remember I was not your ordinary English miss. I was the undowered daughter of a poor Methodist missionary, and therefore an unsuitable choice. No matter how they might long for the comforts a wife could bring them, men are practical beings."

"You must find it amusing to contemplate how they would flock to your side all smiles and compliments, now you are an heiress."

She smiled herself. "Oh, I do. Even those shorter than I. And there were several of those. I've heard myself called a Long Meg many times."

"How fortunate there are also taller men. But tell me, Miss Eaton, where did you grow up?"

"Why, here."

"Here at the Hall? But I understood there had been an estrangement . . ."

"There was indeed. We lived in that cottage where you met us the other day. My mother told me she and my father went there right after their marriage when my grandfather refused them admittance at the Hall."

"So you never saw him?"

"Yes, once. My father brought me with him on a visit here when I was five. All I remember is how my grandfather glowered at us, and the way he shouted. He frightened me."

"It must have been sad for your father, and upsetting for your mother as well, to live so close yet be so estranged."

Sarah's face darkened. "I think my father felt it the most. He was a wonderful man, so caring and full of love for all. To be cast off by his father was hard for him. Of course, since he insisted on marrying my mother in spite of the dire consequences his father had threatened, he knew what was going to happen. But it wasn't until he turned to Methodism, after hearing John Wesley preach, that the final breach came. My grandfather hated the Methodists. He thought them troublemakers, bent on overturning the Church of England. They were not like that. For years Wesley hoped to bring reform to the Church. He never meant his followers to leave it."

She sighed. "Well, it's true we've had a hard life. My father, with the best will in the world, was not practical. He had no idea how to care for himself, never mind a wife and child. I remember when we were packing for India, my mother said the move was most fortunate, for now we would not have to worry about warm winter garments. Sometimes it seems so different now, I have to pinch myself to make sure it's real."

She turned to him then and added with a rueful smile, "But I have been speaking entirely too much of myself. Tell me of your life, m'lord."

"So you can compare it?" Miles asked lightly. "It was vastly different and nowhere near as fascinating as yours. A life of ease, and wealth, and status. So predictable and measured, it was often boring."

"I would have settled for more than a little boredom if it had made life easier. But that is all behind me now. For some strange reason, my grandfather left me the Hall and all his wealth. I intend to be a good steward, and to see my mother lives a luxurious life from now on."

She rose and shook out her skirts. "Shall we go up to the Hall now? I must change for tea."

As they strolled beside a brick wall lined with espaliered fruit trees, she added, "That may be difficult, however. My mother is so used to poverty, she considers anything else frivolous. I do believe she would give all our money to the poor if she could."

"Yes, she is a unique woman," he agreed. "A real lady in the best sense of the word."

Sarah stopped and looked at him. "Oh, may I tell her you said so? She will be so pleased by such a lovely compliment."

"Of course you may, but there is no need. Your mother knows who she is very well."

After leaving the marquis in the drawing room to await Mrs. Eaton, Sarah went upstairs to change her gown. She wondered she had been so open with the Marquis of Wexford, and right after he had been so free with his speech, too. For a moment she blushed, remembering. Was it possible an old man like her grandfather had really . . . and with Mrs. Quigley, too. She could hardly credit such a thing.

Below in the depressing brown drawing room, Miles Griffin stared out the window and pondered the conversation he had just had with Sarah Eaton. What a funny contradiction she was, first indignant and ruffled to be told the facts of life, then so calm and open discussing her past. And what a past she had had. She had not dwelt on the hardship and want, but he could imagine it. And now to be thrown into all this wealth and privilege. No wonder she was wary, a little shy and stiff under the circumstances. And when all was said and done, he imagined she had heard herself called more than just a Long Meg. Jonah

Eaton had not been the only Englishman who hated Methodism. He was also sure that the former housekeeper had added to her pain today with her harsh insults and scoffing remarks. It was too bad.

Mrs. Eaton came in then and curtsied. She had confided to Sarah that knowing their savior was a nobleman had almost made her dislike him. But when he continued kind and attentive, she had changed her mind.

"He may not be a churchgoing man, but I believe he is a good one," she had said. "And he may yet see the error of his ways."

Sarah had held her tongue. Remembering the occasionally wicked look in Miles Griffin's sleepy eyes, his acerbic wit and sophistication, she was not at all as sure as her mother that he had any intention of being saved.

Daniel Horton left the next day. He had received a special billet from London calling him back, and he told Sarah he did not dare delay.

"My uncle rarely interferes with my comings and goings," he said at the breakfast table, where the two were sitting. "Something dire must have happened to make him so anxious. But never fear, Miss Eaton, I'll be back."

Sarah promised to study the proposals for new investments he had given her, and make a decision before his return. She walked with him to the door later, and gave him her hand in farewell. She stayed to watch the carriage go down the drive until it disappeared. Only then did she return to the Hall, wondering why she felt so bereft. It was true she was growing fond of Daniel Horton. He was a very nice man. But surely she had only imagined that his gaze had lingered on her mouth—his air of regret as he bid her good-bye.

"He is such a nice man, Daniel, isn't he?" Mrs. Bonnet remarked as she came to the front door. "Although of course, I shouldn't say so since we are distantly related. But there, you've no time for such maundering thoughts as mine, I'm sure, ma'am.

"I've brought the menus for next week. Should you care to go over them and see if they please you?"

The two women went into the library, the tiny, round Mrs. Bonnet almost skipping as she attempted to keep up with her taller, long-legged mistress.

When the housekeeper bustled away later, Sarah sat back at the desk and considered. She was delighted that Mrs. Bonnet was working out so well. The household ran smoothly now, and everything was done as she ordered. But there was something about the woman. She seemed overfamiliar somehow, and there was a sharp look about her at times that Sarah found unnerving. Then she scoffed at herself. It was not necessary for her to take Mrs. Bonnet to her heart. It was enough the woman did her job and did it well. Still, she reminded herself to ask her mother what she thought of the housekeeper.

She picked up the package of samples that had come from the cloth warehouse in London and went to the drawing room to try and decide which fabrics and colors she would like. As she did so, she thought of the marquis and almost wished he were here to help. He was so sure of himself and his taste. No doubt that was because of his upbringing, whereas she was a quivering mass of doubt. As she spread a sample over the back of one of the sofas and stepped back to scrutinize it, she told herself she would have to muddle through somehow. And if she made a bad choice, well, there was plenty of money to do it over.

Still, as she looked round the drawing room, she wondered if she would ever be able to make the Hall a gracious, pleasant home. It seemed depressing even on a bright sunny day. And there was a heavy atmosphere to it, almost as if it were brooding about some long past misfortune that had happened here.

But of all the rooms in the Hall, she found her grandfather's bedroom, which she had appropriated as her own, the most daunting. She had almost decided she would choose another, for she was not sleeping well there. Not at all.

Later that morning when she went up to see how her

mother was doing, she discovered her watching Mathilda
Dents eat a large custard. The maid jumped to her feet
when Sarah came in, and hung her head.

"No, no, sit down do, Mathilda child," Mrs. Eaton urged.
"You need not stand on ceremony with Sarah."

The maid obeyed, her eyes lowered, although Sarah
could have sworn she wore a triumphant little smile, carefully hidden. She drew her mother into the adjacent dressing room and closed the door firmly behind them.

"What is this all about, Mother?" she asked, careful to
keep her voice low. "Mathilda is supposed to be taking care
of you, not indulging herself with treats."

"Oh, but she is, and very nicely, too, but she is still so
thin and pale. I've taken to ordering a large custard for her
every morning. Don't be angry with me, Sarah. She is to be
pitied, indeed, her life has been one horror after another,
starting with the foundling home, where she grew up until
they sent her out to make her way in the world. And at
twelve, too! Such wickedness!"

Her eyes were flashing, and Sarah hugged her. "You
shall do exactly as you please, my dear," she said softly.
"Oh, by the way, didn't you say you wanted to learn how to
drive the dogcart? I've spoken to the head groom. He'll
have it ready for you this afternoon with a gentle pony to
pull it, and he'll give you instructions himself."

"Oh, that will be wonderful, dear."

"I suppose you want to learn so you can tool Mathilda
around the countryside in the fresh air," Sarah remarked,
and she laughed when she saw how self-conscious her
mother was looking.

She had intended to go down to the stable yard to watch
the first lesson, but she was prevented from doing so by the
arrival of Forrest Blake. Although she was well aware most
clergymen never dressed in any particular religious fashion,
she could not help but think his coat a very bright blue for a
pious gentleman. And his cravat as well was so elaborate,
his black curls so handsomely arranged, a dandy would not
have scoffed to own them. Still, she smiled and offered him

a glass of wine when they were seated together in the drawing room.

"Thank you, my dear Miss Eaton," he said, bending that magical smile of his on her. "Your grandfather kept an excellent cellar. I have enjoyed a glass of Madeira here many and many a time."

When the wine came, he admired its amber color before he raised the glass to her in a silent toast.

"My compliments that you do not join me, Miss Eaton. I've never considered wine suitable for the weaker sex."

"And why is that, sir?" Sarah asked.

"Because, dear lady, women are inclined to be giddy creatures, quick to act foolishly if they are not guided by a strong, sensible man. When they drink spirits, they lose all sense of right and wrong. They laugh immoderately and loudly, utter fatuous remarks, and disgrace themselves in general. But since you are an abstainer, there is no danger of that happening to you."

Sarah swallowed her comment that she had often seen men in much worse condition, and said instead, "Then, perhaps there is some good in Methodism?"

He frowned. "I would wish all women of good taste to abstain, whatever their beliefs. But I am glad you mentioned your father's theology, for I wish to speak to you about your own."

"I thought you said it was too soon to do so."

"I have reconsidered. Indeed, after careful prayer I've come to realize that not a moment must be lost restoring you to the true flock. Every day you continue on this errant path, your soul is in danger. Watch, Miss Eaton! Watch, for the night is coming!"

Sarah realized she much preferred to listen to Mr. Blake when he was occupying a pulpit. Being alone with him, his only audience, was most uncomfortable. Furthermore, she wished he had not hitched his chair closer to hers. Their knees were almost touching. It was unnerving.

He smiled at her then, the expression in his gray eyes softening. "But no more now. I'll bring you some tracts to read and consider. You must believe I am only concerned with your welfare, Miss Eaton," he said.

"But we must not be so serious. You've changed a great deal since you went out to India. Naturally you are more mature. Was it a difficult time for you?"

"I suppose you might say so," she admitted, although she was determined not to portray her father in a bad light. Not to Forrest Blake.

"And you are glad to be home?" he persisted.

"Certainly."

"As we are all glad to have you with us again," he said, putting his hand briefly over hers before he leaned back in his chair. He smiled at her, and not proof against his virile good looks, Sarah returned that smile. He certainly was a handsome man, she thought, feeling a little tide of warmth begin somewhere deep inside. She hoped it would not reach her face and betray her. But could it be possible she was still attracted to the curate? Even now that she was, as he had told her, so mature? Surely not!

Chapter 7

Marion Eaton spent most of dinnertime describing her first driving lesson. Sarah listened, glad she had found an interest. Since her mother had never had the luxury of being idle, Sarah had worried she might be bored here. It was why she had suggested the two of them begin a new set of chair covers for the dining room, knowing full well her mother would complete most of the twelve herself. Marion Eaton enjoyed fine needlework and excelled at it, while Sarah considered it a tiresome chore.

After dinner they went to one of the smaller drawing rooms. It was cool for August, and a fire burned in the grate to take away the evening chill. Sarah decided to order some for the bedrooms later. Perhaps a fire might even make her grandfather's bedroom more appealing. She again thought about choosing another room. Heaven knew the Hall boasted a number of them. Still, she did like being on the front of the house, overlooking the drive, and the room had handsome proportions and a huge dressing room.

The two women worked on their needlepoint until the tea tray was brought in. Sarah ordered those bedroom fires, and the footman, Dennis Carten, nodded. She thought his bow almost mocking as he backed away and closed the door, but she said nothing. Until Mr. Horton found a new butler and footmen for her, she would have to put up with his barely concealed insolence. And she knew, after the scene she had had with Mrs. Quigley, she was not at all anxious for another confrontation.

When she went up to her room later, the fire she had asked for was well alight. She stood before it for a moment, enjoying its warmth. She heard Betsy in the dressing room getting her night things ready, and she went to join her. Just before she climbed into bed, she opened the window for some fresh air. As she pulled the covers up and closed her eyes, Sarah wondered if she had wanted the fire more for cheer and to banish her grandfather's ghost, than from any real need. Unlike her mother, she did not shiver in the Essex breeze, nor did she reach for a shawl in the early mornings.

She never did know what woke her from a sound sleep much later. She was still half asleep, but she knew something was wrong. Very wrong. As her eyes strained to pierce the blackness, she smelled the smoke that was already filling the room.

Her first thought was to escape. Every sense alert now, she threw back the covers and struggled into her robe before she began to make her way to the door. She made herself move slowly as she tried to remember the layout of the room and the furniture; exactly where the door was located. Her eyes were tearing now from irritation, and she had to cough almost continually. She pulled her robe up over her mouth and concentrated on taking shallow breaths. It didn't seem to help much.

The room was still completely dark, but although she knew she should be relieved by the absence of flames, somehow the blackness made the situation even more awful than it was. And after she stumbled into a large wing chair and upset the table beside it, she wished she had taken a moment to light a candle.

Sarah was brought up short when she walked right into the wall. She felt around desperately, but there was no door and no doorknob anywhere in reach. She was almost frantic for fresh air now, and she had to force herself to remain calm. The door was here somewhere. She must have lost her direction when she stubbed her toe on the wing chair. Moving slowly, her arms extended, she edged along the wall, praying she was going in the right direction. She touched the frame of a large oil painting, but that didn't help her. The walls were covered with them. Beyond the

painting, however, was a big chest of drawers. She gasped
in relief, then had to cough even harder. The smoke was so
heavy now, it felt as if the ceiling was pressing down on
her. But that didn't bother her. She knew the door was only
a few feet beyond that chest.

She was about to turn the knob when she wondered if the
fire was contained here in her room, or if it were even now
engulfing the hall. When she opened the door would she be
met by a wall of flame? Praying as hard as she could, she
opened the door and stepped into the hall.

It was pitch-black, but the air was fresher, and she took a
deep steadying breath. At least she had been spared an in-
ferno devouring everything in its reach, and her mother—
all the household—were sleeping peacefully in their beds.

"Fire!" she screamed as she hurried down the hall, using
the banister to guide her. "Everyone, get up! The Hall is on
fire!"

She went first to her mother's room. Marion Eaton rose
quickly and put on her robe and slippers. In the hall again,
Sarah saw the two footmen come clattering down from the
attics, followed more slowly by the elderly butler. They
were carrying candles and in various stages of undress, but
she was not tempted to smile. She explained the situation in
a few terse words as the rest of the staff tumbled down
behind them.

"We'll have to form a chain to pass the water up," Dennis Carten said crisply. "See to that, Ned, and fetch the stable men to help while I find out how bad the fire is."

He disappeared in the dark smoke that was now beginning to fill the hallway. Sarah wondered if she had left her
door open. She couldn't remember. Still, she was glad for
Carten's quick understanding; the way he had taken charge
so competently. Poor old Ferris was no use. He was as
white as a ghost, and his hands were shaking. She looked
around until she saw Betsy and indicated the butler with a
nod of her head. To her relief, the maid went to him to lead
him down the stairs.

"Just you come along with me, Mr. Ferris," she said
kindly. "We've work to do."

Reminded of his duties, the elderly butler nodded, and with a visible effort, straightened his shoulders.

When Carten came back, he told them the fire was contained for the moment in Sarah's dressing room. "If we hurry, it won't do too much damage," he said over his shoulder as he ran halfway down the stairs to fetch the first of the buckets and pans the maids were filling in the kitchen and passing up. The servants seemed a very thin line of defense even with Sarah and her mother taking their place beside them, and she despaired until the men from the stables arrived with larger buckets, and the situation eased a little.

Sarah could hear the crackling of the fire now, and she could see some flames licking at the hall rug. Don't let me lose the Hall, she prayed as she took another pail from the scullery maid and passed it up to Ned, the second footman. Not when I've just been given it for my own!

Her arms were beginning to ache from the weight of the heavy buckets; she could feel them trembling when she raised them. How her mother was faring she could only imagine until she took a moment to look around and saw Marion Eaton and her little maid lifting a large stock pan between them.

No one spoke but Dennis Carten, and he only to urge the others to make haste. He had positioned himself nearest the fire, right outside Sarah's dressing room door, and he was lost from sight in the smoke that swirled around it. Sarah could only hear his voice and the hiss of the fire as water was poured over it. It sounded like a particularly angry snake. The stench from the burning made her gag.

"We're gaining on it," Carten yelled. "More water! Come on, all of you! Work faster!"

It seemed an endless time, although later Sarah would realize it had probably only been a matter of some minutes, before he announced the fire was out. One of the maids sobbed a little in relief as she put the empty bucket she was sending back for more water on the step and sank down beside it, her head in her arms. Sarah slumped against the railing herself for a moment to catch her breath before she went to her mother's side. Vaguely she was aware Carten was still giving orders, this time about the removal of the burned furniture and rugs, the mopping up to follow.

"But what could have happened, dear?" Marion Eaton asked, her eyes wide. "How did it get started?"

Sarah shook her head. She supposed it had to have been the fire she had ordered. But if a stray coal had rolled out of the grate, how could the blaze have begun in her dressing room? True, that room backed up to the fireplace wall, but how could fire get through bricks and mortar?

She patted her mother's shoulder and went down the hall toward her room. The rug was ruined, half-burned and thoroughly soaked. The door to the dressing room was gone. So was the large armoire where she had stored her clothes. So much for all her new finery, she thought wryly, wondering what she was to wear until she could acquire more. Then she forgot such mundane problems when she saw Dennis Carten. He stood before her, breathing hard. His hair was full of ashes from the fire, and the whites of his eyes were startling in his blackened face.

"Thank you," Sarah said, and meant it sincerely. "You were wonderful, Dennis. I am sure we would have lost the Hall if you had not been here to take charge."

He shrugged. "Maybe not. It was only a small fire after all, and we got to it in time."

"Have you any idea how it might have started?" Sarah asked, peering into the dressing room beyond his shoulder.

"Did you or your maid leave a candle burning here, by mistake-like?" he asked. "It's the only thing I can think of."

"I'll ask her. I know I didn't," Sarah told him.

Mrs. Bonnet arrived then to survey the damage, her round little body tightly belted in a blue wool robe. "I've set the maids to preparing another room for you, ma'am," she said. "What a terrible thing to happen! Now, you just come downstairs with your mother and have a glass of brandy while the men clean up this mess. And I do think everyone should have a tot of it as well, especially Mr. Ferris. Poor old dear! He's quite undone by this. He told me that never in over sixty years has such a thing happened at the Hall."

She had wrapped an arm around Sarah and led her away, talking all the while. Sarah told herself she would have to do something special for Dennis Carten, to reward him.

The brandy made her choke. She was reminded of the curate's dislike of women who drank spirits. But it warmed her all the way down to her stomach, and it brought the color back to her mother's face, so she swallowed it all. When Betsy came to tell her her new room was ready, she asked her about the candle.

The maid looked indignant. "I never," she said at once. "Why, I never would do such a thing, Miss Sarah, not on your life. Took the candle away with me to light me upstairs, I did, and there's none can say other!"

"It's all right, Betsy, I believe you," Sarah assured her. "But it was the only thing Carten could think of that could have started the fire. Best you get to bed now, too. You'll have to go into Ipswich tomorrow and buy me some clothes. I'll have to be sequestered in my room until I have something to wear."

But later the following morning, Sarah was able to come down, for one of her mother's gowns had been altered to fit her by adding two additional flounces to the hem, and letting out the waist. Sarah was sure she looked a perfect fright in this concoction and her bedroom slippers, but she was glad to leave her isolation even so.

The Marquis of Wexford arrived right after the ladies had finished a light luncheon.

"I understand you had some excitement here last night," he said as he bowed to Mrs. Eaton and nodded to Sarah. "You are quite all right?"

"How on earth did you hear so fast?" she asked, very conscious of her unfashionable attire.

"Word travels quickly in the country; sometimes I think it is borne by the wind," he said as he took a seat beside Marion Eaton. "A fire, I believe? What was the cause?"

"We've no idea," Mrs. Eaton told him, looking concerned. "We did have bedroom fires last night, but Sarah

says there was no way a fire in her bedroom could have ig-
nited her dressing room."

"That is where the fire started? In your dressing room,
Miss Eaton?"

"Yes, and as my mother says, it's a real mystery. One I
am sure we'd be happy to do without."

The marquis was frowning now. "Would it be possible
for me to see this dressing room?" he asked. "Perhaps I can
shed some light on the subject."

"Why—why, of course, if you would care to," Sarah
said.

She led the way upstairs and down the hall. Marion
Eaton remained below.

The servants had cleared away all the charred wood, the
burned rug, and the maids had mopped up the dirty water,
but the dressing room was still a depressing sight. Miles
Griffin stepped inside, his eyes keen as he looked around.
He spent a long time studying one particular spot. Sarah
saw it was the most heavily burned.

"Was there some piece of furniture here?" he asied, and
when she told him about the armoire, he nodded.

He moved away then and pushed the half-burned door to
her bedroom open. The maids had left the windows up to
air it out, but following him, Sarah noticed the smoke smell
still lingered.

"How did you stand it in here?" the marquis murmured
as he inspected the dreary colors, the heavy old furniture,
and the depressing pictures that lined the walls. Sarah saw
the room through his eyes, and for some reason was very
conscious of the huge four-poster bed.

"I was only in here to sleep," she said, wondering why
she was so quick to tell him anything he asked when surely
what she did, or where, was none of his business.

"Well, at least the fire gives you an excellent reason to
redecorate," he said as he went to one of the windows that
overlooked the drive.

"How do you think the fire started?" Sarah asked.

"It had to have been set, of course," he told her. She
gasped.

"Oh, yes, fires don't start by themselves. The fact that it began among your clothes is very telling, don't you think? Someone meant to harm you, or at least destroy your belongings. Perhaps as a warning?"

"Don't tell my mother these things," Sarah said quickly. "It would frighten her so."

"Of course I won't. Credit me, if you please, with a little common sense. But I think you suspected my same conclusions, long before I voiced them, did you not?"

She nodded, her face serious. "Yes, I did. But—but *who*?"

"I do not mean to imply you are not unique, Miss Eaton, when I say everyone has enemies, or at least people who dislike them enough to wish them harm. In your case there is that disgruntled housekeeper . . ."

"Mrs. Quigley," Sarah supplied when he paused. "But she left the Hall two days ago, right after I dismissed her."

"And only went as far as the village, I believe you told me? As the former housekeeper, and, forgive me, an intimate of the Hall for so many years, surely it would have been easy for her to return, say, late at night? She might even have retained a key. Simplicity itself, if she were bent on mischief."

Sarah went over to the wall to straighten the oil painting she had disarranged when she was trying to escape the smoke. She also did so to give herself time to think. "I would hate to imagine that what you say might be so, m'lord," she said at last, and when she turned, Miles Griffin saw the very real worry in her eyes.

"Even if she had nothing to do with the fire, to suspect she might come and go here as she pleased is very distressing. It makes me feel . . . violated somehow."

He dropped the curtain he had pulled aside and came toward her. "Yes, if she is indeed making free here, she must be stopped. I'll have a word with her, if you like. Perhaps a threat of possible legal action might make her pause."

"But what if it *isn't* Mrs. Quigley? It would be terrible to accuse her, if she is not guilty."

"I've no intention of accusing her," he said, his voice

haughty. Sarah wondered if he expected her to beg his pardon, something she had no intention of doing. "Do you mean to say you have another enemy or two? You *have* been busy haven't you?"

For a moment Dennis Carten's timely actions the previous night came to mind, and Sarah almost shook her head. But she also remembered his scornful attitude, and she said reluctantly, "Well, there is one of the footmen. He's been almost insolent since our arrival. I think it's because we were children together in the village, and now he dislikes me being mistress here. But last night, he was the one who organized the servants to fight the fire—he was closest to it and he did the most to put it out."

"I see. Well, it is the mystery you claimed," he said more softly, almost as if he suspected someone was listening outside the door. "And I do not mean to cry wolf, Miss Eaton, but I believe you may still be in danger. You see, having tried once to harm you, and failed in the attempt, the arsonist may well try again."

"But people don't attempt murder just because you discharged them, or grew up with them," Sarah protested. Her heart was beating faster now just considering the possibilities of what he had said.

"Not normal people," he agreed.

It was quiet then in the dark, somber bedroom. Sarah moved away from the marquis to go and stand before the fireplace. Only cold ashes remained in the grate.

"You're frightening me," she said finally over her shoulder.

"Good."

As she turned to him, a question in her eyes, he explained, "I want you to be on guard. Do you have a pistol?"

"Of course not. I've never fired one. And I doubt I could, even to save my life."

The marquis strolled up to stand beside her again, his long face dark with thought. "You will probably dislike my next suggestion just as vehemently, but I don't see any other way.

"Miss Eaton, I suggest I come and stay with you and

your mother, here at the Hall. I would be right on the scene, and perhaps I might find out who set that fire. We could let people think I was just here to help you and your mother with your decorating schemes. Unexceptional, I assure you. And perhaps having a man in residence will make whoever is guilty think twice."

To his surprise, she reached out to take both his hands. "Oh, would you?" she asked, her eyes glowing. She felt as if an enormous weight had been lifted from her shoulders, just thinking of him here, protecting her and her mother— watching over them.

He smiled down at her, amused by her fervor. "I would," he said. "I'll be off now, but I'll return in time for dinner. Oh, I'll be bringing my man with me, and my groom, of course."

As she nodded, he went on, "I beg you not to tell anyone except your mother the real reason I will be here. The fire was most probably set by Mrs. Quigley, but until we know that for sure, everyone here at the Hall is suspect. *Everyone,* Miss Eaton."

Sarah promised she would not say a word, and as the two went downstairs, they chatted lightly of fabrics and wall coverings until Miles Griffin took a courteous leave of her.

Chapter 8

Upon reaching his home, the marquis gave the necessary orders, and shut himself up in his library until his baggage should be packed. As he did so, he marveled at how quickly he had come to Miss Eaton's assistance. And I've never been the type who rushed about looking for damsels in distress, either, he reminded himself wryly as he settled down in his favorite chair and selected a thin cigar from the leather case beside him.

But, of course, he had done so because the situation, not the tall Miss Eaton, intrigued him. A fire in the night and barely averted disaster, perhaps even death, made him eager to solve the mystery if he could. And if in doing so, he managed to save the shy, prickly Sarah Eaton and her darling of a mother, so much the better. It was sure to be more enjoyable than following the Prince of Wales down to Brighton, rusticating in Kent, or even traveling to Yorkshire to see the Earl and Countess of Darrin.

He considered then what Miss Eaton had told him, about the housekeeper first, then the footman. Either of them could have set that fire in the lady's armoire. Mrs. Quigley because she resented the girl acquiring such handsome clothes, which no doubt she felt should have been her due, and the footman because he could not like taking orders from someone who once had probably been even poorer than he.

But were either of them unbalanced enough to do such a thing? And how had they hoped to get away with it? Was that why the footman had worked so hard to put the fire out? So he would not be suspected? The marquis snorted a little as he contemplated the tip of his glowing cigar. For some reason he did not think the footman was guilty, and yet he had no facts to substantiate such a belief.

The discarded mistress, left out of the old curmudgeon's will and then dismissed by the new owner of the Hall, was so much more logical and satisfying. And she had probably been so incensed, she had not been thinking clearly of the consequences. He would call on her on his way to the Hall later.

He thought of Sarah Eaton then. It seemed too bad she had come home to face this disastrous beginning to what should have been a wonderful new life. And she had not seemed to him to be the kind of person who inspired animosity. There were some people, as he knew all too well, who positively begged to be disliked, but she was not one of them. Indeed, there was something about her that was quite winning and charming. Perhaps it was her old-fashioned air? He grinned. She had to be in her middle twenties, yet she had acted like an outraged nun when he had mentioned Mrs. Quigley had to have been her grandfather's mistress. And how imperious she had sounded when she had ordered him to leave her. At once! Now! she had said, her chin up and those hazel eyes flashing.

Miles chuckled before he drew another appreciative puff of his cigar. Well, he would go to the Hall and then he would see. He rose leisurely to select a few things in the library to take with him. His cigars certainly, although in deference to the ladies, he would smoke them outdoors. And a few books he had been meaning to reread, some papers he was working on, and letters he had yet to answer. His cousin Eliza had written only last week, wondering that he had not come to Yorkshire yet. He was afraid that was out of the question now.

Later, he climbed into his phaeton. His valet, Rogers, was beside him, and clinging to the perch behind, his head groom. They trailed a favorite riding horse. His baggage had left half an hour before, transported to the Hall by cart.

As he drove along, the marquis said, "There's a reason I'm going to Woodingham Hall, men. I'll rely on you both

to keep your ears open to any and all gossip you hear from
the servants there. You know of the fire, and it's my belief
there'll be more trouble, so keep alert."

"Certainly, sir," Rogers said, staring straight ahead at the
dusty country road.

"Nothing'll get by me, m'lord," Hal Wells said cheerfully from behind. "Bit of a thrill it'll be, won't it, Mr.
Rogers, trying to solve a mystery?"

Rogers pretended he did not hear, and Miles Griffin
smiled to himself. He was well aware of the rivalry between his two most trusted servants.

The former housekeeper's cottage was one of the larger
in the village, set off by itself in a pretty garden. A dark-
haired woman was weeding one of the flower beds, and as
the phaeton halted before her gate, she looked up in surprise.

The marquis studied her as he got down. She was in her
forties, and as robust as Miss Eaton had said. He could well
imagine a lonely old widower taking her to his bed, and
from what he could see of her new home, paying handsomely for the privilege.

"Mrs. Quigley?" he asked as he opened the gate and
walked toward her over the well-scythed grass.

"Yes?" she said, getting to her feet but keeping the
trowel in her hand, almost as if she intended to use it for a
weapon. The marquis told himself to stop being fanciful.

"I am the Marquis of Wexford," he told her, and she
dropped a shallow curtsy. "I would like to speak to you privately."

To his surprise, she did not hurry ahead to open the door
of the cottage for him. "We're private enough here," she
said, eyeing him coldly. "And I can't imagine what you'd
have to say to me, m'lord."

"It is about the fire at the Hall last night. You have heard
of it?"

She snorted. "Who hasn't? Nine days' wonder around
here it'll be, I'm sure."

"Fortunately it was discovered and doused in time,"
Miles told her. "It could have been very serious, even re-

sulting in several deaths. And in that case, it would have been a matter for the Crown. Did you know murder is punishable by hanging?"

"You mean you think it was set deliberately? My, my. But why are you telling *me* about it?"

"I just wanted to warn you, ma'am, for you are certainly a suspect in the matter. There are sure to be a number of witnesses to report how badly you took your dismissal from the Hall, the things you said to Miss Eaton, even how incensed you were. And there must be others who remember and could testify about another role than housekeeper you played there when the old gentleman was alive. True or not, I assure you it looks very damaging."

He paused then to study her face. She was looking away from him, obviously thinking hard. Her lips were set tightly, and she was clutching the trowel so tightly, her knuckles were white.

"I was here all last evening, and I don't go wandering around at night," she said at last, her voice defiant. "But since you're so good about giving warnings, you might consider one from me. There are things I know about the Hall and Jonah Eaton, lots of them, m'lord. And one in particular would be painful for Miss Eaton to have to face if it ever came out. I'm sure she'd never live it down. I've no intention of telling anyone, you understand, but I will if I'm forced to it. Be a shame to ruin her life, don't you think? M'lord?"

She stared up at him defiantly, and he was forced to nod. As he went back to his phaeton, he wondered about the woman. She had not seemed unnerved by his call, nor frightened. Was it possible she had not been the arsonist after all? Or could it be she felt the information she had was a powerful enough weapon to allow her to escape the consequences of her deeds? He told himself he'd give a great deal to know what that information was.

After Miles Griffin had left her that afternoon, Sarah had gone in search of Mrs. Bonnet to order a room prepared for their guest. To her surprise, the housekeeper had frowned a little and looked troubled.

"What is it?" Sarah had asked. "Is there something wrong?"

The older woman made an effort to smile. "Oh, no, not really, miss. It's just that this seems a bad time for company. I mean, the Hall still reeks of smoke, and probably will for some time. It won't be pleasant for the gentleman. And the servants are all upset; why, the maids are that jumpy today, they're apt to cry if a body just looks at them sideways. Then, too, I'm not sure Cook is up to preparing meals for a lord. Put her in quite a tizzy, it will, and as for Mr. Ferris, well! He'll probably have an apoplectic fit."

Sarah began to laugh. "Come now, Mrs. Bonnet, what a dire picture you paint. I'm sure the servants will be thrilled a marquis is to visit here. You'll see."

"But why is he? Visiting, I mean? Got a house nearby hasn't he?" Mrs. Bonnet dared to ask.

"He's agreed to help my mother and me plan new decorations for the Hall," Sarah explained. "He's an expert, you know, and he feels it would be easier to be on the spot, so to speak. There is a great deal to do."

She excused herself then to go and tell her mother of the treat in store, leaving a bemused Mrs. Bonnet behind her. But she had to delay her interview with Marion Eaton, for the curate arrived to beg a moment of her time, just as she was crossing the front hall.

"My dear Miss Eaton," he said as soon as they were alone in the large drawing room. "I cannot tell you how relieved I am to see you are all right after your experience last night. What a dreadful thing, to be sure! But servants can be so careless with candles unless they are constantly reminded how disastrous a fire can be."

Sarah was about to hotly deny any of the servants had been so negligent, when she recalled the marquis's instructions. "Perhaps you are right, sir," she said meekly instead.

"It is at all times disquieting, you and your mother up here in this vast place, with no man to guide and protect you," he went on, his handsome face set in a ferocious frown. "I worry about you constantly."

"It is very good of you, sir, but I beg you not to concern yourself. My mother and I are perfectly capable of taking care of ourselves. Indeed, after my father died, we managed the funeral, settled our affairs, and arranged for passage home without asking anyone for help. And although I've led a sheltered life in some ways, I am not a child. My father took great pride in overseeing my education himself. I daresay many men have not been so well schooled."

He smiled then. "I see I've made you indignant, Miss Eaton, and I would not upset you for the world. Of course you are intelligent and well educated. And, I see now, quite worldly." He paused then, the frown returning for a moment. Sarah wondered why he found being worldly so disconcerting. Did he consider it an unattractive trait in a woman?

"Forgive me," he said simply at last. "I am a man. I have always felt women were precious and should be protected." His rueful smile was engaging, and Sarah smiled back as she rose.

"You must excuse me now, sir. There is a great deal to do today after the fire, and my mother is waiting for me."

As they walked to the door, she added, "There is another reason you may be calm, Mr. Blake. The Marquis of Wexford is coming to stay at the Hall for a week or so. He has kindly offered to help us with new decorating schemes."

"Wexford? Coming here?" he echoed, sounding distressed rather than relieved. "Is that wise, my dear Miss Eaton?"

"Do you mean people might talk about it? Well, I don't see how they can when my mother is with me. There could be no more adequate chaperon than a parent, surely."

"Of course. And no one will dare making anything of it. If they try, you may be sure I shall correct them."

Surprised, Sarah nodded her thanks as she held out her hand in farewell.

Taking it, he said, "I do hope, however, that you will not be so busy with fabrics and colors and new overmantles, you will be unable to spare a moment for me, now and again."

Sarah was forced to say she would be delighted to see him anytime he cared to call before he would go away.

She had decided she would not tell her mother the real reason the marquis was coming unless she was forced to. She knew Marion Eaton would find it upsetting, frightening even, and she hated to spoil her newfound joy in her return to England and the luxury and ease that was now hers. Fortunately Mrs. Eaton was perfectly satisfied with the explanation she was given, and hurried off to the gardens to select a bouquet to brighten his room.

Betsy returned later that afternoon with a number of parcels and boxes containing new gowns and sandals, bonnets and gloves and shifts, petticoats, and hose. Sarah had already sent a letter to the London modiste, ordering more gowns, but it was comforting to get out of her mother's altered one and put on something new, even though it could only be black or white.

She and her mother were at breakfast the following morning when the marquis came down. As he greeted them before he went to the sideboard to select his breakfast, Sarah thought how comfortable a guest he was. Perfectly at ease himself, it was impossible for her to feel any awkwardness in his company. The previous evening he had entertained them at dinner with tales of London life, carefully edited, Sarah was sure, to be suitable for her mother's ears. And possibly even her own? she thought with a little frown as she put down her half-eaten toast. Later, he had not lingered over his port, but he had excused himself early, claiming he had to deal with some correspondence.

As Miles Griffin ate his breakfast, the three had a lively discussion about new furbishings for the breakfast room. Sarah favored light blue, Marion Eaton a sunny yellow. The marquis convinced them a combination would work well, and in the dark and dreary days of winter, be cheerful.

A letter arrived for Sarah just as they were finishing their repast. After asking permission, she tore it open eagerly, for she knew from the handwriting, it was from Daniel Horton. She skimmed the page quickly, then cried out in distress.

"What is it, my dear?" her mother asked, leaning toward her in concern.

"Oh, dear, how very sad," Sarah said before she looked up to see both the marquis and her mother regarding her. "Mr. Horton writes that his uncle—you do remember him, don't you, Mother?—died suddenly in his sleep last week. He has been much involved arranging the burial and with a press of business, now the firm has lost its senior partner. He says he will try to come to us as soon as he can, but he does not know when that will be. The poor, poor man."

"Horton," the marquis mused. "Of Horton, Horton, and Gavin?"

As Sarah nodded, he went on, "I know the firm well. It is much admired and highly regarded for its integrity. If your affairs are in its hands, you are fortunate indeed. But I must say I'm surprised to hear of the elder Mr. Horton's demise."

"Why is that?" Mrs. Eaton asked.

"Because he was not yet sixty." Wexford shrugged and put his napkin beside his plate. "Of course, death is at all times unpredictable.

"Enough of such gloomy subjects. Shall we stroll in the gardens, ladies, while we consider which rooms you would like to do over first?"

Mrs. Eaton excused herself so she might write a letter of sympathy to Daniel Horton, and the marquis and Sarah left the Hall by a side door.

"Perhaps I should have suggested a ride instead," Miles Griffin said as he took a deep breath. It was a day of bright sun and racing clouds, with a fresh breeze. Sarah held her skirts down with firm hands.

"Then, you would have had to go alone, m'lord," she said. "I do not ride."

He looked astonished. "But everyone rides. Or at least I thought so."

"I never had the opportunity to learn. When I was a

child, my father could not afford to keep a horse, and it certainly would have been impossible in India."

"Forgive me, I didn't think," the marquis said, disconcerted he had been so unfeeling. "But there is no reason you cannot learn to ride now, Miss Eaton. Yes, and drive as well. I believe you'll like it. And you'll find it gives you a degree of freedom that perhaps has been missing in your life. I'd be glad to teach you, if you are willing to trust yourself to me."

Sarah told herself she must not make too much of his generous offer. His voice had been light, teasing even, and she was sure he was only being polite.

"Of course, if you cannot trust me, there is always your head groom," he added when she did not speak.

Coloring up that he might think her rag-mannered, Sarah hastily assured him she would be delighted to have him as an instructor.

As they continued their stroll, she wondered that she was looking forward to it not only with dread that she might not acquit herself well, but with a secret, gleeful feeling of delight as well.

Chapter 9

The rapport between Miles Griffin and Sarah Eaton grew steadily in the next few days. Interspersed with their decorating sessions were several lessons for Sarah on handling the ribbons. At first she had been intimidated by the marquis's matched pair. They had seemed simply enormous to her, and it was hard to believe she would ever be able to control them. And she was even more disconcerted by the way m'lord sat so close beside her on the perch of his phaeton, even though she knew he did so only so he could grab the reins if she did something stupid.

Forrest Blake saw them one afternoon as he was riding between his parishes. He raised a hand in greeting, but Miss Eaton did not stop, and he frowned. She had not smiled at him, either. Of course Sarah had seen him, but she sensed the marquis had no desire to converse with the curate, and besides she was not sure she could stop the rig neatly. The marquis had told her she must never jab at the team's velvet mouths. As for smiling, she was too intent on her driving.

"Why are you holding the reins so tightly?" Wexford asked, touching one of her gloved hands with his own.

"I think I'm afraid I'll lose them if I don't," Sarah admitted.

He smiled. "Don't worry so. You're doing very well."

She did not dare turn even a little toward him, so he was treated only to her elegant profile. Idly he wondered what she would look like dressed for a ball. Perhaps in pale blue muslin? Or in a green silk to complement her eyes?

"You are kind to say so, sir, but I know very well your

groom takes the team out before we go driving. Would you call that 'taking the edge off'?"

He chuckled. "You wouldn't care to tool these high steppers if they had not had the edge taken off, Miss Eaton. But someday soon you'll have more confidence, more skill. I expect you'll be backing the team, maneuvering them even, in a week's time."

Later, as they walked up to the Hall from the stables, Sarah asked if he had discovered anything more about the fire.

He frowned. "Nothing so far. I've set my valet and my groom to some gentle prying among the servants, but it hasn't borne fruit as yet. They've only heard a few snippets of gossip about Mrs. Quigley and your grandfather, and the usual servant intrigues, but nothing whatever about the fire."

Sarah sighed. "I'm glad. I hated to think someone in my own household started it. What of Dennis Carten?"

"He seems well liked enough, although he can be sarcastic. He's no longer the bully you remember, however, even though the second footman is a mass of nerves. I suspect he would be wherever he found himself. My man tells me Carten is a hard worker. He's taken over most of the butler's chores, as well as his own."

He stopped then and turned toward her. "You do know you should retire that old man, don't you? He's practically moribund."

"Of course I do. I've been waiting for Daniel Horton to send a new butler to me. Of course, he's probably too busy to bother with that just now."

"Why not let Carten have the job? He's as good as the butler right now."

"I don't know. I never liked him as a child, indeed, I was terrified of him. He used to chase me yelling threats, or jump out from behind some bushes to frighten me, then laugh at me when I began to cry."

"Boys can be insensitive little horrors. I was one myself."

Sarah looked up at him. She knew he was not a handsome man, but every time she looked at him, he pleased her. And his smile made her feel warm and comfortable, and yes, safe. She could not imagine him ever bullying anyone, or taking pleasure in scaring a little girl, although she knew he could be sarcastic, even arrogant, on occasion. He was—he was a *fascinating* man.

"I have a smudge on my nose, Miss Eaton?" he asked lightly.

Sarah lowered her eyes. "Of course you don't. I'm afraid I was woolgathering."

She fell silent, and he said, "As for Carten, I think it safe to say he won't jump out at you again. And I don't think he'll be insolent if he's given the job. Perhaps he has acted that way because he knows he deserves it, yet he was never promoted."

"But what about the possibility that he set the fire?" Sarah asked.

"I've been thinking it over, and I don't see any reason he would. His job here at the Hall is too important for him to do anything to jeopardize it. Did you know his mother died some time ago, and he is responsible for his father's care? The man is blind. He cannot work. Carten's salary is all that stands between him and the almshouse."

"Oh, I didn't know," Sarah exclaimed. She remembered the elder Mr. Carten. He had been a big man with a long stride, and a way of looking at you that made you sure he could see inside your head. And now he was blind.

"You can always try Carten," the marquis continued. "If he doesn't suit, he can be replaced. And I suggest you ask him if he could recommend a suitable replacement for the second footman. Butlers often work best when their underlings are known to them."

Sarah agreed to the proposal, even though she still felt uneasy about it. Perhaps Dennis Carten had changed. Perhaps he would not bully the other servants. Miles Griffin seemed sure he would be a success, and to her chagrin, she found she was beginning to rely on him and his suggestions more and more. But he was such a positive man, so confident, unlike herself who still felt an impostor in the Hall.

"You saw the curate back there in the road, didn't you?" he asked next, changing the subject abruptly as he was so wont to do. "I can't tell you how relieved I was you did not stop to say good day. The man's a bore, as well as a pompous prig."

Sarah grinned to herself. "Yet he is so handsome, sir," she enthused, careful not to look his way.

"I cannot tell you how disappointed I would be to discover you are the sort of insipid female who goes into alt over an Adonis," he told her severely.

"I shall endeavor to control myself," she replied. "However, he is not only handsome. He has been most attentive and pleasant."

Miles snorted. "Of course he has. I'd wager he's having trouble sleeping for planning how he'll spend your inheritance. Beware, Miss Eaton, beware! Religious gentlemen are not always good, or particularly trustworthy."

"It's not fair to single out clergymen," she retorted. "I'm sure just as many of the nobility would also be suspect, would they not?"

He laughed, and she took a quick peep at him under her lashes. "Oh, we are at all times to be mistrusted, even held at arm's length," he said cheerfully. "There's many an earl or a duke who's no better than he should be. Er, for various unsavory reasons, Miss Eaton, which I have no intention of revealing. But remember what I've told you. And if the handsome curate goes down on one knee before you, run for your life!"

Now it was Sarah's turn to laugh at the picture he painted of Mr. Blake kneeling before an empty chair while she fled to the door, hands over her ears.

"This is a frivolous conversation, sir," she said, trying to make her tone disapproving.

"Why, so it is. But don't you think it good to be frivolous once in a while? Life is assuredly real and terribly earnest, but it can be faced a great deal more easily if its problems are tempered with laughter."

As they entered the Hall, he began to discuss a possible trip to Ipswich in a few days' time to inspect the wares of a particular cabinetmaker. "We can take the phaeton if the weather holds," he said, stepping aside to allow her to precede him up the stairs. "But stay. Do you think your mother would care to go? In that case we will have to take a carriage. The phaeton was not built for three."

"I'll ask her," Sarah promised, and told herself she was very bad to be hoping her mother would refuse the trip.

She would have left the marquis at the top of the stairs to go to her room and change her gown, if she had not seen Mathilda Dents coming out of it. Her gasp alerted Miles, and he moved forward with her to confront the girl.

"What were you doing in my room?" Sarah asked, eyeing what little she could see of the maid's pale face. The girl was staring at her shoes while she twisted her hands in her apron.

Mathilda did not reply, and Sarah didn't feel any pity for her when she saw a tear slide down her cheek.

"You will answer your mistress at once," the marquis ordered in the coldest voice Sarah had ever heard him use.

"She's not," Mathilda blurted out then with a flash of spirit. "Not *her*! It's her ma what's my mistress."

"Even so, you will answer."

Mathilda sniffed, and a tiny hiccup escaped. "I wasn't doin' no harm, honest. I just wanted ter look at her new gowns. An' that's all I did, I swear."

"We shall see," the marquis said, grasping her arm and hustling her back into Sarah's new bedroom. Still holding her lest she make off, he inspected the room. Sarah saw he was staring particularly hard at the fireplace, but she forgot all that when she saw one of her shifts lying over a chair, and a pair of hose puddled on the floor beside it. Oh, wretched Betsy, she thought. Why hadn't she put everything away? To think the Marquis of Wexford was seeing her undergarments. It was too humiliating.

As he moved with his reluctant captive to the adjoining dressing room, she said a small prayer that at least there everything would be in order. Following the pair, she noticed the door to the clothes cupboard was slightly ajar.

"Did you open that?" he demanded, shaking the maid a little.

"Yes, yes, I did," Mathilda admitted sullenly.

He released her then, and she made a show of rubbing her arm where he had held it. Sarah ignored her. She was watching the marquis. He opened the door wide and looked inside, even holding the gowns there to one side so he could inspect the bottom of the cupboard.

"I can see no evidence she did any more than she claimed," he said at last, almost reluctantly.

Sarah understood, even applauded his disappointment. It would have been so comforting if the arsonist had been Mathilda. She had never liked the girl, considering her both manipulating and unattractive, and she would have been delighted to send her about her business. Of course, her mother would have mourned her departure—although what Marion Eaton found to like about such an unprepossessing specimen, Sarah had no idea—but there were other maids, any number of them for her to befriend.

"Very well, Mathilda," she said instead. "You may leave us. But I want you to remember you are not to enter my room again, unless I ask you to do so specifically. Do you understand?"

The maid nodded, her eyes downcast again. Suddenly weary of the confrontation, and aware she would have to make a point of insisting before she got a verbal response, Sarah waved a dismissive hand. The maid turned and ran from the room.

The marquis and Sarah moved back to the bedroom. They did not speak, so they heard quite plainly the sound of a door slamming at the end of the passage.

"Insolent little brat," Miles murmured as he went to the door.

"Yes, she is not appealing, is she? I can't understand why my mother dotes on her so. Well, it is too bad she was not the culprit. I would have been delighted, not only to see the back of her, but to have the mystery solved at last."

"It is true we did not catch her in anything but trespassing, but that does not mean she is not the guilty party even so. She might have heard our voices and was trying to escape before she could make mischief. I wish I had thought to have her turn out her pockets. But tell me, does she have any reason to dislike you?"

Sarah shrugged, looking confused. "She knows I did not want my mother to engage her, but that's all. Would that be enough reason to try and burn the house down?"

"One wouldn't think so, would one? Still, there are those who enjoy setting fires, you know. I believe it is a compulsion they cannot resist. Perhaps this maid is one such person.

"Best you remain on your guard, Miss Eaton. And you may be sure I'll be keeping an eye on the unattractive—er, Mathilda, did you say her name was?—as well."

He left her then to go to his own room to alert his valet to this new development. Sarah had no sooner closed her door than she scooped up her shift and her hose and put them away. It was then she realized she could not scold Betsy for her carelessness, for if she did, the maid would know the Marquis of Wexford had been in her bedroom, and she had no way to explain such a socially unacceptable thing. She only prayed Mathilda would hold her tongue.

Later, before she joined her mother for a cup of tea, Sarah summoned Dennis Carten to the library and asked him if he would care for the position of butler at the Hall.

For a moment her old nemesis stared at her, his eyes narrowed, and Sarah wondered if she had made a dreadful mistake.

"May I speak plain, miss?" he asked finally.

"I wish you would, Dennis. There are things we must resolve between us, and we can only do so if we are honest with each other."

He nodded. "Are you offering me the job because of what I did the night of the fire?" he asked, his eyes never leaving her face.

"Partly, yes, of course. But Mr. Ferris is very old, and I've been made aware you are doing much of his work as well as your own. That was kind of you."

"Didn't expect it of me, did you?" he asked quickly, and Sarah thought she could detect a sneer in his voice.

"No, I didn't," she retorted, staring back at him. "I remember you as a bully who frightened me when we were children. Kindness was not something you were noted for in those days."

"Well, but I've grown up, haven't I? And I've changed. I'll admit I wasn't too pleased when I heard you were coming here, for I'd no mind to work for a *woman*. But I've come to see there's little difference. And you're fair. So, if you're sure I'd be satisfactory, I'd be pleased to have the position."

Sarah nodded, feeling relieved. It was not she personally he'd disliked. It was only because she was a female. And he had sounded sincere, almost meek, although she was aware he was not now, nor ever would be, a humble man.

They discussed the salary and what she expected from him, and came to an agreement easily.

"Mr. Ferris will be that pleased," the new butler said with a grin. "He's been fretting about not being able to go to his sister in Devon. I wouldn't be surprised if he left the Hall at daybreak."

"Please find out his plans so I can make arrangements to have him transported to the staging inn. His belongings can follow by carter later. And that reminds me. What would you like to be called? Carten? Mr. Carten? Dennis?"

"Just Carten will be fine, Miss Eaton."

"I must also ask you if you know of anyone to take your old place? And if you are content with the other footman's work?"

He took a moment to think before he said, "Well, Ned isn't much, but he does his work well if he's given proper direction. And there's a boy in the village, a cousin of mine, Sam Hatch is his name. He wants to go into service, and I promised to help. No need to fear he'll try to take advantage because we're related, Miss Eaton. I'll see he keeps his place."

Sarah was sure of that. She rose to signify the interview was over. "Very well," she said, smiling a little. "Have him come to the Hall tomorrow. And you'd better take some time to go to Ipswich to buy clothes more suitable to your new station. Have the bills sent to me."

He bowed and went to the door. Sarah wondered if it were just her imagination his step was jauntier than when he had come in. With one hand on the doorknob, he paused and turned back.

"You won't regret giving me this chance, ma'am," he said seriously. "You have my promise on that."

Chapter 10

After dinner that evening while the marquis was still in the dining room enjoying his port, Marion Eaton confided to her daughter that she had been giving a great deal of thought to how they might use some of Sarah's inheritance for good, and now she had arrived at the perfect scheme.

"It came to me when I discovered Mathilda cannot even write her name," Mrs. Eaton said, her needlepoint lying forgotten on her lap in her intensity. "It is terrible, Sarah, when any child, of whatever station, does not learn to read and write. And just think, she can never have the consolation of reading her Bible for guidance and inspiration. I'm afraid there are many such children in England, but now we are able to do something about it."

Sarah had a vision of her mother attempting to set up dame schools throughout the kingdom, and she hid a shudder. But to her relief, Mrs. Eaton's ambitions were more modest.

"I would like to start with a school right here in Woodingham Village," she confided. "A free school. That is, if you approve such a scheme, my dear. I am aware it would be your money that would finance it."

She sounded a little doubtful, as if she thought she was taking too much on herself, and Sarah rose to kneel before her and hug her close for a moment. Thinking what a dear, good person she was, her throat tightened with emotion.

"Of course you shall have your school, my dear," she said. "What a goose you are to think I would deny you. But we must make plans. You'll need a schoolhouse. I wonder if there is anything suitable vacant?"

"That is not a problem, Sarah. I've already discovered I can use our old cottage. It is only a short walk from the village proper, and the main room will be ample for the number of children we can expect."

"And who will teach this school?" Sarah asked.

"I would like to do so myself, but I don't have the training," Marion Eaton confided. "We must hire a teacher, and I will be her helper. Perhaps I could take charge of the younger children. And we'll need slates, and books and paper—all manner of supplies. And I was thinking we must serve the children a meal in the middle of the day, so they won't have to walk back and forth. You know, Sarah, some of them are poorly nourished. This is a way to be sure they get one good meal a day without their parents feeling they are accepting charity. You know how stiff-necked they can be. And . . ."

"Stop!" Sarah said, holding up her hands and laughing. "You go too fast, ma'am."

Her mother blushed and laughed with her. "It is because I'm so excited, of course. And Mathilda has promised to help, too. She does not have enough to do to keep her busy, just taking care of me."

Secretly delighted this scheme would remove the unpleasant Miss Dents from the Hall for a number of hours each day, Sarah asked her mother to tell her more.

When the marquis came in to join them, they were still in animated discussion. Apprised of Mrs. Eaton's plan, he smiled and nodded. "An excellent scheme, ma'am, and one worthy of your goodness," he complimented her. Sarah felt a pang that she had not thought of a school herself, then took herself to task for such foolishness. It hardly mattered what the Marquis of Wexford thought of her, and it never would. She must remember that and not begin making plans of her own. Foolish plans that had no hope of success.

Catching sight of her frowning face, Miles Griffin wondered at her displeasure. Could it be she did not approve a

school? He was aware there were many who would not, for
the elite of society were loathe to give those beneath them
any advantages, lest they get ideas above their station. For
as long as the peasants could not read, they could not benefit from radical thinking. And isn't that what had happened
in the United States? That declaration that said all men
were created equal? No wonder there had been a revolu-
tion.

Still, he was surprised to discover how disappointed he
was that Miss Eaton would feel that way, especially after
her own disadvantaged childhood. He had not thought her
so callous and unfeeling.

Sarah interrupted his musings to remark it would be better to open the school when the harvest was safely in. "For
you know, Mother, you'll not get a single pupil to come,
else," she added. "Their parents need the children's help at
that busy time of the year, and it's important the school
begin well."

While the marquis wondered if he had misinterpreted
Sarah Eaton's frown, her mother said, "I know. And of
course we will have to close early in the spring. But there is
a great deal that can be accomplished in the long winter
months."

She turned to the marquis then. "May I ask your opinion
of something, m'lord?" she said.

"Of course," he replied, wondering why he always felt so
protective of this fragile and faded little woman.

"I am concerned the parents will not let their children attend, no matter when we hold classes. I am sure you know I
am a Methodist. The villagers might think the school only a
trick of mine to convert the children. But I would never do
that. How am I to reassure them? Can you tell me?"

"Perhaps the curate might take a hand and assist you. If
you had his approbation, I am sure the villagers would welcome your school," Miles told her. He did not scoff at her
misgivings. He was well aware how real they were.

"Would you perhaps attend the village church again,
ma'am?" he asked.

"No, I could not," Marion Eaton said quickly. Her eyes

filled with tears as she added, "I would never be so disloyal to my dear husband's memory."

The marquis told her he was sure it would be unnecessary, but later, after Marion Eaton had gone up to bed and he and Sarah were alone in the drawing room, he was more open.

"Your mother is an astute woman, Miss Eaton," he said. "It is all too likely the villagers will think she intends to teach Methodism. Well, I'll have a word with the handsome curate."

"Perhaps if I spoke to him as well, m'lord?"

He smiled, a smile that did not reach his eyes. "Yes, I'm sure your pleading will be much more effective than any poor words of mine. But tell me, Miss Eaton, do you, like your mother, feel you can never attend Church of England services again? I only ask, you see, because it would be so helpful if you did. Everyone will know it is your inheritance that makes the school possible. As a communicant of the church, you would become one with the villagers, not a mistrusted outsider."

Sarah did not answer immediately. Finally she said, almost reluctantly, "It would not bother me. Not that I'd be able to worship there any more than I did in my father's church. I fear I have lost my faith, m'lord, but I beg you keep that to yourself."

She put her hands to her head for a moment. "But why did I tell you such a private thing? I don't understand myself. Do you, by any chance, have some unearthly power that makes people confess their innermost thoughts to you?"

He smiled again, and this time the smile did reach his eyes and warm them.

"I am not sure I would find such an ability any asset, Miss Eaton," he said. "People's innermost thoughts can be so, er, unsavory, don't you agree?

"But you need not worry. Your secret is safe with me. And do not feel you are a unique sinner, either. There are many like you who feel the organized church does not meet their spiritual needs. I am one of them, although I do not count myself an atheist by any means."

Relieved, Sarah rose. It was late, and she should not be sitting here with the marquis, pleasant as it had been. She looked around the drawing room and could not hide a shudder. Miles Griffin noticed it at once and asked her if she were chilled.

"No, I'm not cold. It's this house that makes me shiver," she told him. "Ever since we arrived, I've felt uneasy here. And no, it is not because I am unaccustomed to large, wealthy establishments. I feel there is something here I cannot see, something brooding, that crouches, waiting. Something almost malignant. Sometimes I wonder if I will ever be happy here and at ease, no matter how we change it. I pray you will not think me fanciful, sir. I have always been a most prosaic creature."

He stared down at her, his face serious. "I must admit I am at a loss, ma'am. If you sense something so strongly, it can't be a fancy. But I feel nothing myself except a vague distaste for its gloom. Give the Hall a chance. You'll see how improved it will be when it is freshly decorated. Trust me, it will."

Daniel Horton returned in the morning two days later. Sarah came to the hall to greet him, her hands outstretched and her face full of concern. As he took her hands, she thought how much older he looked, how careworn and sad, and her heart went out to him.

"I was so sorry to hear about your uncle, sir," she said, squeezing his hands gently before she withdrew her own. "Please come into the morning room. Would you care for coffee? Or some wine, perhaps?"

"Wine would be very welcome. The roads are full of dust," he said as Dennis Carten held the door for them and bowed. He was resplendent in a new suit of black clothes with a discreet vest and gleaming linen.

As he shut the door and Sarah took a seat, Horton said, "Can it be you have a new butler, Miss Eaton? I seem to remember that chap was only a footman when last I was here."

"He was indeed, but on the Marquis of Wexford's advice, I decided to try him as the butler."

"Ah, yes, Wexford. I seem to recall you writing he has been staying with you. Is he still in residence? I must say I find that a bit unusual."

Sarah remembered the marquis had told her not to reveal the real reason he was at the Hall to anyone, and for a moment she hesitated. Then she told herself he had never meant she must keep it from her solicitor, and she said, "He is here because of a fire we had a week or so ago."

Horton exclaimed, and Sarah told him the whole story. He did not speak until Carten had served him his wine and withdrawn. Then he said, "I am glad the fire was not serious. But I'm sorry I was not able to find you a new butler and two footmen. I know you understand why. Still, don't you think it would be better to hire different servants? Those that were here when your grandfather was alive cannot help but make comparisons. I fear that might be uncomfortable for you."

"The only one who did that was the housekeeper," Sarah retorted. "And as you know, she is gone now. I am trying to ignore her threats."

"Threats?" he echoed, his blond brows rising.

"Oh, yes. She said she knew a great deal about the Hall that I wouldn't want generally known, and she would tell if she had to. Or something like that. I do not remember what she said, word for word."

"But surely she has left the neighborhood by now," he remarked before he took another sip of wine.

"No, she has a cottage in the village. I wish she did not, but there is nothing I can do about it," Sarah confessed.

He smiled a little then. "Please don't concern yourself with her, Miss Eaton. I am sure it is just bluster, to pay you back for letting her go. As for the other servants, well, I still think it would be better to start with new, thus insuring their loyalty only to you. But that is your decision, of course."

Struck again with how worn he looked, Sarah said, "Forgive me, but may I say how sorry I am to see you looking as you do? I fear your uncle's death was a great sorrow."

"Yes, it was. We were close, for my own parents died some time ago, and Uncle Willis was all the family I had left. Then, too, I have been so busy that Charles Gavin, the other partner in the firm, insisted I come to the country for a rest. He will see to the day-to-day business until I return. Eventually we must acquire another partner, but I cannot think of that now. I only hope you do not think me overbold to impose on you without prior notice."

"Of course I don't. And you will stay at the Hall as long as you wish, sir. I insist on that," Sarah told him. He smiled at her again, and she thought what a nice-looking man he was with his butter-blond hair and keen blue eyes. Not, to be sure, the Adonis Forrest Blake was, but someone much more comfortable to be with, someone more appealing. Just to have him here again made her feel good.

When she offered him another glass of wine, he rose to pour it himself. Again she thought it was a shame he was not taller as she began to tell him of her mother's plans for a school. He listened carefully, only now and then interjecting a comment or a suggestion.

At last he said, "I am glad to see you and your mother are going on so well here. It has been a worry for me, thinking of you here helpless and alone. But of course to reveal my concern is to insult you, for you are a discerning young woman with a great deal of sense. Tell me, does the curate continue to call on you?"

Sarah thought she detected a teasing note in his voice, and was quick to say, "Why, yes, he does. He left some tracts for me to read only yesterday. Unfortunately I was not here at the time, for I was out driving with the marquis. He is teaching me to handle the ribbons."

"It is very good of him to indulge you. Not many of the nobility would be bothered. But that reminds me. I did look into his finances while I was in London, as I said I would." He paused then, as if he were choosing his next words carefully. "I do not want to alarm you, Miss Eaton, but there have been rumors about the Marquis of Wexford."

Sarah stiffened. "Indeed? What rumors, sir?"

He held up a hand, smiling a little. "No, no, ma'am, not *that* kind of rumor! Although it is true he has perhaps overindulged in gambling and racehorses and his mistresses. I beg you not to fault him for that. They all do it. He is in no way unusual, and he certainly has the wealth to spend any way he wishes. No, I meant there have been stories recently that he has invested heavily in a hare-brained venture that has little hope of success. Have you heard of something called a steam engine? Or what is just starting to be known as an iron horse? No? Well, I am not surprised. It seems incredible to gamble on the possibility man might someday travel throughout the country in carriages on rails, pulled by an engine instead of horses. I would never risk your money on something so bizarre, yet that is what the marquis has done, if the rumors are correct, and I rather think they are."

He paused again, one hand caressing his jaw before he went on, "I hope you remember what my uncle warned you about, Miss Eaton, and will forgive me for what I am about to say. It may not even be true, for a man of Wexford's rank generally marries a woman of his own station. But he might be tempted to recoup any losses he might incur on this investment he has undertaken, by trading his title for your own considerable wealth. After all, he is in his mid-thirties. It's more than time for him to be setting up his nursery. And, you know, it would not be at all a *bad* match for you. I did not mean to imply that. No doubt you would enjoy being a marchioness . . ."

Sarah made herself smile even as she wondered why she felt so hollow. "I do assure you, sir, the marquis is not interested in either me or my wealth," she said. "We are only the most casual of acquaintances. Any affection he has is given only to my mother."

"Ah, that is understandable. She is a lovely woman. I'll always cherish the letter she wrote to me when my uncle died.

"But forgive me for saying what I did. I am probably too apt to look on the dark side of things at this particular time. It is just that I want only the best for you, and I do not want you to be hurt.

"But come, let's discuss something more cheerful, shall we?

"Have you had a chance to study those new proposals I suggested? And have you decided what you want to do about them?"

Chapter 11

Sarah excused herself from her driving lesson with Wexford that afternoon. She was feeling a little ambiguous after what she had learned about him from Mr. Horton that morning, and she felt some period of time away from his increasingly disturbing presence would be time well spent.

Of course, she told herself, what the solicitor had told her was not a bit surprising. At first it had been reassuring to know the marquis was wealthy, although she regretted his gambling and especially his mistresses. She wondered how many he had had, before she brought herself up short. What did it matter? One was as bad as a hundred. Well, perhaps not *quite* as bad.

And she supposed anyone could make a bad investment on occasion. Perhaps this wasn't one. Perhaps there would come a day when people could travel by rail—she did not know. And neither did Daniel Horton, she reminded herself.

What he had said about Wexford probably intending to marry a lady of his own station was certainly realistic. Only see what had happened to her father for stepping outside his own circle and marrying a lowly cabinetmaker's daughter, and his family had only been wealthy country squires.

She remembered, too, what the marquis himself had said about the nobility—how they were not to be trusted. "Held at arm's length," he had said, for various reasons so tawdry he would not tell her. Did he class himself with his peers? It seemed he must if he were honest with himself. And somehow she knew, for all his faults, Miles Griffin was an honest man.

Yet as she looked out one of the windows in her room, she could not help but remember how much she was beginning to like m'lord in spite of herself. No doubt that was what Daniel Horton was warning her against, forming a friendship with a man who would probably leave Essex in a week or so, never to be seen again. One who might well be whiling away a tedious stay in the country, amusing himself by saying he wanted to help them. He might not even care what happened to them. He might only be intrigued by the mysterious fire and the sullen former housekeeper.

Sarah sat up straighter. But of course, Mrs. Quigley!

She thought for a moment. It was a beautiful late August day. She knew her mother had taken her maid out in the dogcart. No doubt they would stop at the cottage. Sarah did not expect to see her mother till teatime. Daniel Horton had excused himself to rest, so he was accounted for. What Wexford was doing, she had no idea, but that didn't matter. She intended to cut across the park and enter the village by one of the back gates near the Home Farm.

As she rose to tie on a wide-brimmed straw hat, she told herself she would not be intimidated even if Mrs. Quigley was as brutal as she had been before. She would bear it because she had to, to discover the secrets the woman supposedly was hiding. Perhaps if she offered her money, Mrs. Quigley would reveal those secrets?

As she hurried down the stairs and across the empty hall to the front door, she wondered if knowing those secrets would make her new home more appealing. Turning to look back at what she could see of it before she closed the massive front door, she grimaced. And as she hurried down the front steps, she told herself that horrid suit of rusting armor near the stairwell was going to be dispatched first thing in the morning. Why she had not thought to banish it earlier, she couldn't imagine.

The Marquis of Wexford spent some time wondering about Sarah Eaton's request to be excused, before he changed into riding clothes and ordered his horse brought up from the stable. He knew Miss Eaton's solicitor had just arrived. It was entirely possible there were matters she had to discuss with him.

He paused for a moment to have a few words with his groom. "Anything, Hal?" he asked quietly as he pretended to adjust the cinch.

"Nothing, sir. They aren't given to gibble-gabble, none of 'em. Could be it wasn't one of the servants at all."

"Yes, entirely possible. I suspect we must discard that theory and look further abroad for our culprit."

He stared at the groom. Hal Wells was a strong-looking young man with sandy hair and an impudent grin.

"Something wrong, m'lord?" he inquired.

Wexford shook his head. "I'm afraid you're entirely too young and good-looking to be effective," he said.

Wells's face lit up in a smile. "For what, sir? Give me a go at it!"

The marquis gained the saddle with one quick move-ment. Looking down at the eager groom, he said, "I doubt you'd want that 'go' when you hear I only meant you're not at all believable as an admirer of Mrs. Quigley."

Wells's mouth dropped open. "Gawd," he said under his breath. "I should hope not."

"I'll ask Rogers to approach her. If he can gain her confi-dence, she might tell him a thing or two."

"Won't she know he's your valet, m'lord?" Wells asked.

"Of course, but Rogers can pretend he's dissatisfied with me and looking about for another place. He can even tell her a few wild tales about me to whet her interest. Ficti-tious, of course."

Wexford rode away, leaving the groom chuckling behind him. He could not help smiling himself. He knew the task he was going to set his valet would be unpleasant, but there was no other way. Obviously, this Mrs. Quigley was never going to tell him anything.

As he turned out between the gates and trotted down the village street, he caught sight of someone who looked sus-piciously like Sarah Eaton. Slowing his horse to a walk, and sheltering behind a large wagon, he followed her. His brows rose when he saw her hesitate for a moment before

Mrs. Quigley's gate, then take a deep breath and tilt her chin before she unlatched it and stepped inside. So, Miss Eaton was not closeted with her agent after all, was she? She was calling on the woman who just recently had insulted her so badly. For what reason? he wondered as he rode past the cottage. And if he taxed her with it later, would she tell him?

He was beginning to admire Sarah Eaton. It was true she barely knew how to go on, but like her mother she had an innate dignity, and she was valiant in her efforts to do the right thing. She had an intriguing smile as well, one that lit up her face the same way the flare of a newly lit candle disperses the dark. And the little chuckle she gave when she was amused, and which he had heard all too seldom up to now, was endearing. He realized he had tried to be as entertaining as possible, to provoke that chuckle.

She had common sense, too, something a great many women of his acquaintance were missing. And she was not consumed by a need for endless clothes or jewels or possessions. Was that because of her Methodist background, or the poverty she had known?

He smiled. To think he would find the prim-and-proper daughter of a missionary attractive was so ludicrous he had to laugh out loud. And how his cousin Eliza would mock him if she knew. Perhaps he had been in the country too long? Perhaps it was overtime for him to return to London, or make for Kent or Brighton. Perhaps he needed to see Harriet, Duchess of Glynn, or failing her, any rounded little armful with a pretty face and a winning way, both in bed and out.

Yes, of course. He was not falling in love with Miss Eaton. He was only missing the feminine company he was accustomed to enjoying. How could he have thought otherwise?

But he knew he couldn't leave Woodingham Hall just now. He had to stay to unravel the mystery if he could, and make sure that dear old Mrs. Eaton was all right. He knew she had gone out in the dogcart with her maid and he suspected he knew their destination. He would stop at the old cottage later and see if he could assist the lady, or at the very least, dissuade her from trying to do too much herself. Later, he planned to return to the village and call on the curate, although whether the man was in Woodingham or at another of his parishes was anybody's guess. Somehow he was sure he would be here, as close to the heiress's skirts as possible. He grimaced in distaste.

Sarah knocked on the door of Mrs. Quigley's new home. She looked about her as she waited. The cottage was a pretty place, surrounded by rose bushes and flower beds. The hum of the bees was very loud as they dipped into one flower and then another. A little distance away, a long chair was set beneath an apple tree, a workbasket on the table beside it. A pure white cat was curled up in the chair in a patch of sunlight.

When no one replied to her knock, Sarah turned away, disappointed. As she reached the gate with its hooped trellis covered with clematis, she came face-to-face with the woman she had come to see. Mrs. Quigley's eyes narrowed, and she looked beyond Sarah as if to make sure she was alone.

"What are *you* doing here?" she demanded as she opened the gate and stepped in. "What do you want?"

Sarah stepped back instinctively to let her pass. Mrs. Quigley had a large shopping basket on her arm with some packages and a loaf of fresh bread in it. Under the packages, Sarah could just make out the squat rectangular shape of a dark bottle. Could it be Mrs. Quigley *tippled?*

"I asked what you wanted. Speak up, then," her unwelcoming hostess demanded, putting an end to Sarah's speculations.

"I wanted to ask you about the Hall," Sarah began. She was interrupted by Mrs. Quigley's coarse laughter.

"Well, you've some nerve, ain't ye? Turn me off, then come down here, cool as cool can be, expecting me to tell you all I know. It'll be a cold day in hell before you hear anything from me!"

She shifted her basket from one hand to the other. "That fire must really have scared you," she said in derision.

"Yes, yes, it did," Sarah agreed. Anything to keep her talking. "But it wasn't only that. There's something strange about the Hall, something, oh, I don't know how to describe it, something *threatening*."

Mrs. Quigley had turned away, but now she stopped. "What do you mean, threatening? It's just a house. There's nothing there. There's not even a stray ghost." She smiled, as if amused.

Sarah spread her hands. "I told you I couldn't explain. But I thought you might be able to help. I—I'd be glad to pay for whatever information you can give me."

For a moment she thought Mrs. Quigley was going to strike her, and she stepped away quickly. The former housekeeper's round face was red, and her eyes snapped with anger.

"*Money*, is it? Your *money* isn't going to do you a bit of good, not with me, it won't. I don't need it. Your randy old grandfather saw me right, as well he should have. Be off with you! I've nothing more to say."

Sarah hesitated for a moment, then turned to go, her shoulders drooping a little in her disappointment. She had just reached the gate when Mrs. Quigley spoke again.

"Ah, I must be getting soft," she said. "I guess I still feel sorry for you, you poor little nobody. I'll tell you one thing. People aren't always what they seem. Even the ones you think are the best can't always be trusted. Do well to remember that, you would."

Sarah longed to ask questions, beg her to say more, but Mrs. Quigley had started walking briskly up the path. A moment later the door to the cottage slammed shut behind her.

As she trudged down the village street, keeping to the side to avoid the worst of the dust, Sarah wondered what the housekeeper had meant. Who wasn't what they seemed and couldn't be trusted? And who had she meant by "the best of them"? Had she meant the Marquis of Wexford?

No answers came to mind, and she looked up to discover

she had reached the old stone church set at the end of the green. She was wondering if she dared call at the manse and ask for the curate, when he came out of the church and saw her there.

"My dear Miss Eaton," he said as he swept his hat from his carefully combed black curls and bowed. "Dare I hope you have come to tell me you will attend services here again? Rejoin the rightful Church?"

Sarah made herself smile. "Is there somewhere else we can go to talk, sir?" she asked. "It is so public here."

He held out his arm and when she took it, covered her hand with his own. He led her through the graveyard next to the church until they reached the lych-gate. This homely little roofed shelter, where the bearers rested the coffin until the clergy came to conduct the burial service, was old and mossy. Still, Sarah did not hesitate to take a seat there when Forrest Blake suggested they do so. Sarah looked around. Behind them, the old graveyard drowsed in the sunlight. Some of the stones were so ancient you could not make out any lettering on their surface at all, and some of them leaned precariously in one direction or another. Even though they were just a few steps from the busy village street, it was a lonely spot. She realized they were as isolated there as they could have been anywhere, and she wondered if Forrest Blake had chosen it for that reason.

"I am encouraged you have read the tracts I left you so promptly, Miss Eaton," he said. He had seated himself beside her on the bench, too close for her comfort. She could even smell the lotion he used on his hair.

Sarah told herself she must stop being so ridiculous every time a man came anywhere near her. She was not a silly little thing, she was a woman grown. And she was determined this interview would be more successful than her meeting with the former housekeeper.

"Alas, I must confess I have not had the chance as yet, sir," she said as lightly as she could. "I have come to talk to you for quite another reason."

"Of course. You know I'll do everything I can to help

you," he told her, his intent eyes burning down into hers. "Tell me," he said simply.

Sarah described the school her mother intended to start. She was as persuasive as she knew how to be, but when she reached the end of the story, and asked him to assist them by giving his approval to the venture, she was not surprised to see he was frowning.

"I do not see how such a thing is possible," he said. "Your mother, no doubt an excellent woman in every other way, is a Methodist. How could I, a curate of the Church of England, recommend her to my parishioners as a suitable teacher for their impressionable young? My vicar, the bishop—why, they would be horrified."

"But she is not going to teach anything, never mind Methodism, I promise you that, on my honor. She intends to hire a teacher, and merely be her helper with the younger children. The school will be a free one where children can learn to read and write and do their sums. And you know there is a great need for such a school in the village, indeed, throughout England."

"Are you, by any chance, becoming a reformer, Miss Eaton?" he asked. He sounded amused, and Sarah had to pause until she could control herself.

"The school is entirely my mother's idea, but I do agree with her that it is needed," she said.

"I am not the only one who does not encourage education for the lower classes," he said next. "You see, it gives them ideas they should never entertain. All of us on earth were born to our proper places in life. The lowly should not try to better themselves. That is to go against the natural order of things."

"No, that can't be right," Sarah protested, trying to keep the distaste she felt from showing. "I was born to poverty. Are you saying it was wrong that I was able to leave it?"

He took her hand in his, bending toward her earnestly. "You must know I do not. You are Jonah Eaton's granddaughter. You have simply returned to your proper position."

"I cannot tell you how what you say reassures me,"

Sarah said dryly as she withdrew her hand from his clasp. She was so disappointed for her mother she felt she must cry, and she had to concentrate on keeping the tears at bay.

"I am sorry, very sorry I cannot help you in this. But I cannot compromise my own ideals and standards, any more than I daresay you could. I pray you will understand and not think the less of me for that, Miss Eaton."

Sarah heard the pleading in his voice, the humbleness as well as the conviction, and she began to like him more than she ever had before. It was not his fault he could not endorse the school. His hands were tied. And even though she thought him an intolerant man and a rigid one, she had to admire the way he stood up for his principles.

"But perhaps there is a way after all," he said slowly. "A way that will be acceptable to all."

"Please tell me what it is," Sarah begged. "I would do anything, *anything* to assist my mother in starting her school."

For a moment he stared down at her. Sarah could hear a wagon going by in the street, some children laughing nearby, and she wondered what Forrest Blake was thinking. At last he shook his head a little, as if to clear it before he said, "If both you and your mother were to attend church here again, it might just work. Then, you see, I would be able to lend my support and welcome your return with open arms. That return has been the object of my most fervent prayers ever since you came home, Miss Eaton."

"My mother does not feel she can betray my father's memory by abandoning his beliefs," Sarah admitted. "However, I might well do so. Would that be sufficient, sir?"

When she saw Blake pondering her remarks, Sarah thought she had won, but at last, and with a rueful shake of his head, he said, "I am afraid it would not suffice. It is not to be your school, but your mother's. So even though you return, and I beg you hold fast to that resolve, it cannot affect the outcome. The villagers are ignorant people, full of prejudice for anyone different from themselves. They will shun the place."

"I see," Sarah said carefully as she rose and smoothed

her gown. She knew what he had said was true, yet she
dreaded having to tell her mother that her dream could not
come true after all.

The two walked in silence back through the graveyard to
the street. When she said good-bye and curtsied, Sarah saw
Forrest Blake was pale and serious, his handsome mouth in
a stern line, and again she felt a rush of liking for the man
that he could feel her disappointment so keenly himself.

Much later, back at the Hall, she met the Marquis of
Wexford in the foyer as he came from the stables. Beyond
them in the drawing room, Sarah could hear her mother and
Daniel Horton conversing, but before she could join them,
the marquis detained her with a hand on her arm.

"You look uncommonly serious, Miss Eaton," he said.
"What is wrong?"

Sarah did not even try to dissemble. "I have seen the curate, m'lord. He tells me there is no way he can give his endorsement to the school. I dread having to tell my mother
that. She will be so disappointed."

His dark brows rose as if in astonishment. "But how can
this be?" he asked. "I myself left the very same man only a
few minutes ago, and he promised he would give his support, starting with an announcement in church this coming
Sunday. Oh, only if you are there, of course, in the Eaton
pew. I took the liberty of promising you would be. I hope I
did not overstep my authority by doing so?"

"What do you mean?" Sarah demanded, stepping closer
to him so the others would not overhear them. "You got
him to agree? But how did you do that, m'lord? In spite of
all my most fervent pleas, he was adamant he could not
compromise his standards. Yet now you tell me he is willing to do just that? Why would he do such a thing?"

Miles Griffin smiled down at her, his dark eyes teasing.
"Even at the risk of being thought rude—however many
times that unfortunate trait is laid at my door— I do believe
that how I convinced the handsome curate to see things our
way must remain my secret for now. You must not repine,
Miss Eaton. In spite of what I said earlier, men sometimes

do have more means of, er, persuasion, than even the most passionate lady."

He bowed a little before he went up the stairs, leaving a confused Sarah Eaton staring after him. On the one hand she was extremely grateful for his intervention, and yet, on the other, equally indignant that he had succeeded where she herself had failed. And to think he would not even tell her how he had done it. Well! And it was said *women* were difficult.

Chapter 12

Dinner that evening was a pleasant affair. The marquis was his most entertaining, and Daniel Horton set aside his air of sad abstraction to join in the conversation. Sarah was glad the marquis did not mention the school, or the curate's unexpected capitulation, for she wanted to tell her mother when they were alone of the condition he had insisted on.

She was able to do this after the two of them had left the men to their port. Marion Eaton cried a little when her daughter told her she herself must return to services at the village church, but she did not argue it.

"I do see it is the only way, Sarah," she said as she wiped her eyes. "I shall be able to bear it, for after all, John Wesley only meant to reform the Church of England, not leave it. Does Mr. Horton approve as well?"

"Why, yes, wholeheartedly. I do hope he will stay with us for some time, Mother. He seems so depressed."

"Yes, I have noticed that, too. The poor man, to lose his uncle so."

She could say no more for the gentlemen were coming in to join them. Tonight, the marquis did not excuse himself, but sat a little apart from the others where he could see everyone's face. Sarah wondered what he was thinking as her mother talked of the school to Daniel Horton and listened to his suggestions.

"I am sure there will be no trouble finding a suitable teacher, ma'am," he said. "I shall send word to my partner to be on the lookout for one. You said you hope to begin after the harvest is in? A wise decision."

"Mother, where is this teacher to live?" Sarah interrupted. She knew she should offer the Hall, but somehow she could not like such a thing. Suppose she did not care for the teacher? Suppose he or she wasn't a pleasant guest?

"Do not worry about that, my dear," Marion Eaton said quickly. "M'lord stopped by the cottage this afternoon just as Mathilda and I were able to leave. He suggested we expand the cottage to provide living space."

Relieved she was not to be saddled with a permanent housemate, Sarah nodded, and until the tea tray was brought in, the four discussed the project.

But as they were drinking their tea, the Marquis of Wexford turned the subject to the death of Daniel Horton's uncle. Sarah wished he had not done so, for Mr. Horton's face sobered at once, and his hand shook a little as he returned his cup and saucer to the tray.

"Yes, it was very sudden, m'lord," he said in answer to his question. "And most unexpected. Uncle Willis was, or so we all thought, a healthly, vigorous man for his age. But the doctor assured me these things do happen."

"It was his heart, then?" Wexford insisted.

Daniel Horton stared at him for a moment before he answered. "Yes, his heart. He passed away in his sleep."

"Surely the easiest way to go if you must, with no pain or any long illness to suffer," m'lord said carelessly. Sarah tried to catch his eye, to implore him to change the subject, but she was unsuccessful.

"If only everyone was so lucky," Marion Eaton said softly. Sarah knew she was remembering her husband's painful death from fever, and felt a pang till her mother added, "But come. Let me pour you another cup of tea, Mr. Horton. And one for you, m'lord?"

Thinking what a gallant woman she was, and every inch the lady the marquis had named her, Sarah smiled in relief. Wexford declined a second cup and excused himself. Sarah walked with him to the door. She wanted to ask him why he had persisted in questioning Mr. Horton about his uncle's death, but she knew she could not do so now.

"I understand tomorrow will be fine, Miss Eaton," he

said as they reached the door. "Shall we drive to Ipswich as we planned earlier? Your mother tells me she has no desire to come at this time, although she has given me some commissions. I did ask Mr. Horton if he cared to come as well, but he denied me. He says he intends to see your agent tomorrow. How providential he is so tireless on your behalf. It must give you a great feeling of reassurance."

"It does. He has been wonderful to me, and to my mother," Sarah said, not even wondering why she felt so happy that both her mother and the solicitor were otherwise occupied.

"I suggest an early start. We'll take the phaeton, of course, and if you are good, perhaps I shall even let you handle the ribbons."

"I am always good," Sarah told him before she thought. He bent a little to gaze into her eyes, and what he saw there made him chuckle. Sarah was conscious of a blush as she turned away. She hoped it was not still visible when she rejoined the two near the fire.

As she was telling her mother of tomorrow's expedition, she was aware Daniel Horton was watching her, but when she turned to include him, he had looked away, his face somber again.

Sarah was ready well beforehand the next morning, dressed in a black carriage gown with a short capelet attached. She wore a large bonnet, one she had hesitated to purchase, for it seemed to make her more conspicuous than she cared to be. Still, she had known it was stunning, and she had not been able to resist it.

She had to wait in the foyer for Wexford, and she spent the time questioning her new butler about how things were going for him.

"Just fine, Miss Eaton," he told her, his face serious, as befitted an upper servant. "My cousin Sam has taken to the work well, and even Ned seems more competent now he's first footman. There's only one thing that bothers me a bit . . ."

He frowned, but before Sarah could question him, she

saw Miles Griffin coming down the stairs, pulling on his driving gloves.

"I cannot linger now, Carten," she said. "But I shall want to hear what concerns you when I return this afternoon."

As he bowed, she turned to greet the marquis with a smile. He held out his arm. "I like that bonnet," he said in his blunt way. "It draws the eye."

"That's what I was afraid of," Sarah confessed as they went down the steps to where the marquis's groom held the team in readiness. "I was sure such a hat was not at all the thing for someone in mourning, but I purchased it anyway."

He squeezed her hand a little. "I'm glad you did. It becomes you," he said.

Miles Griffin did not offer to let her handle the reins on the drive to Ipswich. Sarah was glad, for she could see the horses were frisky this morning. Even the marquis had his hands full, and he did not speak until he had settled them down to a mile-eating canter.

"Mr. Horton intends to stay at the Hall for some time, Miss Eaton?" he asked first, to Sarah's great surprise.

"Why—why, yes, I believe so. Why ever do you ask?"

"Only because it is unusual for a man of business to devote so much time to one client. Oh, I know you are probably his most important one, but even so . . ."

"He is being kind to me, for he knows how ignorant I am about business. I imagine as soon as I am more adept, he will not feel he has to indulge me with so much attention.

"But that reminds me. May I ask you something, m'lord?" When he nodded, she went on, "Why did you question Mr. Horton about his uncle's death last evening? It upset him, for he feels it so deeply. I tried to catch your eye to warn you, but I could not."

"Commendable of him, I'm sure. As for why I did it, it was nothing but vulgar curiosity, Miss Eaton. However, I shall not mention it again, since he is, as you say, so sensitive.

"I saw you in the village yesterday," he said, changing the subject again. "You were about to call on Mrs. Quigley.

That was a surprise, after the way she has treated you. Why
did you do it? What did you learn from her?"

"You are inquisitive, m'lord," Sarah said coldly.

"Didn't I just say I had more than my share of vulgar curiosity?" he said blandly.

Smiling now, Sarah said, "Very well. If you must know,
I went to ask her what she knew about the Hall that I would
not want revealed. But she wouldn't tell me anything. In
fact, she scoffed at me."

"Which you certainly must have expected, after the way
she treated you earlier," he remarked.

"Of course I did. But just as I was leaving, she did say
something. Something I did not understand."

"And that was . . . ?"

"That people aren't always what they seem, not even the
best of them. And she warned me to remember it."

"An excellent piece of advice, even if it was cryptic. I
wonder who she had in mind?"

Recalling she had considered it might be the marquis
himself, Sarah said nothing.

"Perhaps she meant the curate," he continued, staring
straight ahead at the road before them. "Or she might even
have meant me, although I do not see how that can be. I
never knew your grandfather, and I certainly never visited
the Hall."

"Surely Mr. Blake cannot be suspected of anything . . ."

"Except pompousness and conceit."

". . . For he is a man of God," Sarah concluded, as if she
had not been interrupted. To her surprise, Wexford put
back his head and laughed.

"And you think because he has taken the Church as his
profession, it naturally makes him a good man? You disap-
point me, Miss Eaton. I thought you more astute than that.
Surely you know the side a man shows the world is not
necessarily his true self. And I am almost convinced the
handsome Mr. Blake is acting a pious part."

"I do believe you are jealous of him," Sarah said. "You
never speak of him without mentioning his looks."

He chuckled now. "No doubt you are right," he agreed,

so humbly she looked at him sharply to see if he were mocking her. "But you must admit, it is the first thing that comes to mind."

"He cannot help being handsome," Sarah said, wondering why she was defending the man so vehemently.

"No, but he does not need to present himself so, er, elaborately. Those well-tailored coats, hairstyling that cries of London, his glowing boots and skintight . . . Er, forgive me, Miss Eaton. I almost forgot you are a young lady of tender sensibilities."

Sarah felt a lump in her throat. He had sounded cold and sarcastic. What had she done to displease him? She was glad when later the outskirts of Ipswich appeared ahead.

By the time they had left the rig at one of the inns and she had returned from the private room Wexford had engaged for her to freshen up, he seemed to have regained his good spirits. After offering his arm, he led her down the street to the cabinetmaker. From there they went to a cloth merchant and a shop selling fine china before they returned to the inn for a brief respite and some refreshment.

Sarah was dazed. She had spent more money that morning than she had ever once imagined she would have. Even knowing there was a great deal more could not erase her feeling of guilt.

"Do not tell me you are regretting the armoire, Miss Eaton," the marquis said as he cut her a slice of cold sirloin. "I recommend the salad. It is excellent."

"Well, yes, I was thinking about that, among other things," Sarah admitted, remembering the handsome piece of mahogany furniture the marquis had insisted she order to replace the one that had been burned. And then there had been the new tables for the drawing room, and a pair of armchairs in the style of Sheraton. She had even commissioned a satinwood four-poster for her own use, for she had not been able to resist its delicate lines, so unlike her grandfather's massive bed. "I simply can't believe I have spent so much money, and all in one morning, too."

"But you have it, so therefore, why not spend it?" he asked as he buttered a roll. "What good is it otherwise?"

Sarah served herself some salad. "I can think of several things it would be better spent on than furniture I do not really need, a new set of china, and expensive wall hangings. The poor, for example, or the orphans."

He waved a hand in dismissal. "Of course you should contribute to their welfare, if your heart moves you to do so. But to give all your money away is not only foolish but unnecessary. Come! Do you think the poor or the orphans would do as much for you if the tables were turned? Not very likely. Take the money and laugh in your face, they would. At least *try* to remember what you know of human nature, Miss Eaton."

He sounded so acerbic, Sarah had to laugh herself. They finished their repast in perfect accord and returned to the shops. Now Sarah bought slates and primers and a set of globes while the marquis ordered chairs and tables to be made of sturdy, plain construction. He also ordered a large stove to heat the cottage, and a desk for the teacher.

"Of course the school will need a great many more things," he said as he handed her to the phaeton later for the ride home. "But at least we have made a start."

The streets of Ipswich were crowded, and Sarah sat silently as Wexford maneuvered around a large dray, passed a wagon full of hay, and halted to allow two ladies to cross the street. She was glad she was not driving, even though she was a little disappointed he had forgotten his promise. And she had certainly been "good" all day.

"You must not worry, Miss Eaton. I did not think you would want to take charge of the team in town. As soon as we have gone a few miles, we will change seats," he told her. Once again Sarah wondered if he could read her mind. He seemed to know her thoughts the moment they occurred to her, and this ability of his was not only uncanny, but uncomfortable.

He halted the team on a straight stretch of road a few miles farther on. Handing her the reins and telling her to slide over, he got down to go around the back. Sarah took a deep breath and concentrated on the team, willing them to behave. It was the first time she had been in sole charge without the marquis seated beside her, and even though she knew it was only for a minute or so, she could not be easy. Just then, a large hare darted out of the bushes on the side of the road, almost running over the horses' hooves in its hurry to reach the other side. The horses snorted and moved restlessly, and when a large dog came chasing after the hare, they bolted.

Sarah gasped in alarm as the phaeton careened down the road, even as she tried to remember everything the marquis had taught her. The team thundered on. She gave them their heads, mainly because she had no idea what else to do. She knew she was not strong enough to rein them in, not in their present agitated state. She only prayed they would not meet another carriage, or come upon some livestock crossing the road.

It was several miles later before the team began to slow of its own accord, and minutes later still before she could turn them. Feeling rather proud of herself now, she set them to a trot, back the way they had come.

When she reached the place where she had inadvertently left Wexford, she found him seated on top of a stile in a field a little distance away.

The marquis got up and ambled toward her across the muddy field with all the insouciance of a man who has never had to clean his own boots. To Sarah's disgust, he did not look a bit concerned for either her welfare or his precious horses. As he took his seat, he said, "Yes, I rather thought you'd be coming back just about now. How far did they get before you could pull them in?"

"I have no idea," Sarah said shortly, disappointed he had not thought to compliment her on her level head, her bravery. Piqued, she added, "But weren't you worried? Didn't you think I might come to grief?"

"Of course I didn't," he scoffed. "No one *I* teach ever does."

Sarah had to halt the team again, for she had begun to laugh so hard she was afraid she would set them off again, and she did not feel at all capable of another wild ride to nowhere. Not thinking, she collapsed against the marquis's shoulder.

Miles put his arm around her and hugged her to him, and still she laughed. At last, when she was only chuckling weakly, he said, "But where is your bonnet, Miss Eaton?"

Confused, Sarah dropped the reins to feel her head, and he deftly gathered them into his free hand. "Why, I had no idea I had lost it," she exclaimed. "It must have blown off. Oh, dear, I must look a fright."

Miles smiled down at her, still holding her tight in one arm. Her brown hair had come down and was streaming over her shoulders. A few little ringlets curled around her face, now rosy with embarrassment.

"Nonsense. You look delightful," he told her.

Suddenly Sarah realized how improper her position was, enclosed in the marquis's strong arm, and she attempted to sit up and move away. He immediately released her. "Shall I take the reins now, Miss Eaton?" he asked.

"Please do, sir," she said. "And this time I'll go around. If we should see my bonnet, I am not at all sure I could manage to stop the team again."

As she took her seat on the other side of the perch, he said, "But you did so just now. And before, you turned them as well, did you not?"

It was quiet for a moment before Sarah confessed, "Well, I did not precisely *back* them, m'lord. I waited till we reached a crossroads where I could drive them in a wide circle."

He laughed as he set the team in motion. Sarah made herself smile in response, although she was feeling not only confused but breathless. She seemed able to feel his arm around her still; the same sensation of homecoming she had experienced when she had arrived in London. Yet she knew it had been wrong of him to put his arm around her, and wrong of her to permit it, even for a second. She put her hands to her head again, trying to twist her hair into its customary chignon. If she were to return to the Hall looking like this, she knew what everyone would think. She had only a few hairpins left, but she did the best she could. Fortunately they discovered her bonnet by the side of the road a mile or so farther on; once she had recovered it, and tucked her hair up under it, she felt much better. Still, she did not forget that inadvertent lapse of manners, and doubted she ever would. She stole a sideways glance at Miles Griffin, but she could read nothing in his carved profile, nothing at all. He looked almost indifferent with those sleepy lids half hiding his dark eyes. But of course he was a man. A very experienced man. He could hardly know how momentous a moment it had been for her who had never had a man's arm around her before.

They reached the Hall again quite late that afternoon. Sarah was both glad and sorry to see its oppressive walls as they came up the drive. She thought she had acquitted herself well on the remainder of their journey, chatting lightly on a number of subjects, and never letting the marquis know how he had affected her. But now she knew that although she would be glad to leave him to go to her room to recover her poise, part of her was sorry their time alone together was over.

His groom was there to take the tired team in charge, and Miles Griffin himself came around to lift her down. Did he clasp her waist tighter, lower her to her feet more slowly than necessary? Perhaps it was only her imagination.

Stammering her thanks for a pleasant day, and all his assistance, she ran up the steps into the house, so unnerved, she completely forgot she had promised to speak to Dennis Carten on her return.

Chapter 13

Miles Griffin lingered to exchange a few words with his groom before he followed Sarah into the Hall. There was no one in the foyer, and he went quickly to the stairs. For some reason he had no desire to see either Marion Eaton or Horton just now, and was looking forward to a period of calm reflection.

His valet was in his room, however, putting away some freshly laundered cravats, and he set himself to calm the man after Rogers saw the condition of the once-glowing, pristine boots he had helped him into only that morning.

"And it was not possible for you to wait in the road for Miss Eaton to return the rig, m'lord?" the valet asked as he set the boots aside to be cleaned and polished.

"What? Stand about a dusty road like a yokel? That would probably have ruined my coat, and then you'd have had something to say about that."

As Rogers helped him remove this garment, he sniffed. "I daresay. Of course I shall not comment on the seeds and chaff that are clinging to it, nor the spot of mud here near the bottom of the sleeve."

"What did you find out in the village today?" Miles asked, well aware it was not so much the state of his clothing that was annoying Rogers, as it was the commission he had been set.

The valet sniffed again, more loudly this time. "I met the woman. Quite chatty she became when I admired her garden. Had me in to inspect it, and offered me a cup of tea. Of course, this was after I mentioned I was dissatisfied with my present position and was looking for another one."

His colorless voice spoke volumes, and Miles's dark eyes glinted in amusement. "I can imagine the lurid stories you told her about me. You should be ashamed of yourself."

"I did not have to make them any more, er, lurid, than they already were, sir," came the careful rely.

"Did she tell you anything?"

"Nothing of any import. I did not press her, for although she is a woman of the commonest sort, she is not stupid. I invited her to join me for a pint tomorrow night at the inn. She accepted."

"Going to ply her with strong drink, are you?" Miles asked lazily as he untied his cravat and let the valet assist him into the loose jacket he favored when he was alone.

"Yes, it might loosen her tongue. From the whiff I got of her breath, I gather she drinks rather heavily."

Rogers took the mistreated clothing to the dressing room, holding the dirty boots at arm's length. Miles settled down in a chair near the fireplace to think as the door closed behind him.

Strangely, instead of considering the enigma that was the housekeeper or the mystery of the fire, his thoughts turned at once to Sarah Eaton. He was still amazed at how strongly he had been attracted to her today, how much he had wanted to run his fingers through that long, glorious fall of hair, as warm and glossy as any chestnut newly burst from its shell. And without her bonnet, her prim hairdo, she had seemed another woman. Even the natural, easy way she had collapsed against him as she laughed uncontrollably had been endearing. Lord knows he had not meant to put his arm around her; somehow it had just happened. He recalled how hard it had been not to bend and kiss her laughing mouth—hold her closer still, caress the smooth column of her throat, so white against the black of her gown.

He rose suddenly, kicking a footstool out of his way. Was he *insane*? He had no intention of getting entangled with any woman, not permanently, at any rate. And any further liberties he took with Miss Sarah Eaton, daughter of a Methodist missionary, would most certainly result in a long walk up the aisle, his bride on his arm. There was no other way. Not with someone like her.

He must remember there were any number of lovely women who would welcome his advances with no thought of any permanent liaison in their minds.

As he returned to his seat and picked up the book he was reading, he wondered why the thought of all those women was not more appealing.

In the drawing room a flight below, Sarah was seated with her mother and Daniel Horton. She had changed to a white muslin afternoon gown, and had Betsy redo her hair. And while she had not endured the lecture on the state of her clothes the marquis had suffered, Betsy let her know by her silence that the stunning bonnet would need major work to return its black plumes to respectability.

Carten entered the drawing room with a card on his silver tray. Studying his grave face, Sarah suddenly remembered she had promised to speak to him when she arrived home, and for a moment, she was impatient. Was she never to have a moment to herself? Was she always to be hedged about with tedious details—household problems—disgruntled servants?

Hiding her little sigh, she studied the card. "And who might General Sir Harold Fisher be, Carten?" she asked.

"The general was a great friend of your grandfather's, Miss Eaton," he told her. "He often visited here."

"And now he has come to call on me?" Sarah asked, her expression doubtful. Surely this general was aware of Jonah Eaton's dislike of his son's family; how he had thrown them off. Why would he have anything to do with them now?

"He has brought his grandsons with him, miss," Carten added, staring at the wall behind her shoulder, his voice carefully expressionless.

As Daniel Horton coughed, Sarah glanced at him where he sat beside her mother on the sofa. His knowing look, the little nod he gave her, told her everything she needed to know.

"Please show the gentlemen in, Carten," she said. "Bring wine and biscuits."

She did not dare look at Daniel Horton now lest she betray herself by laughing. When Carten announced the visitors, she had herself well in hand. With the white-haired general, still vigorous and erect after over sixty years, came a pair of young men as alike as the two horses that comprised the Marquis of Wexford's famed team. She certainly did not doubt they were just as frisky when she saw the merry look in their eyes as they bowed over her hand in turn.

Sarah introduced her mother and Daniel Horton, and asked the guests to be seated.

"Horton, is it?" the general barked as he sat down. "Thought I recognized you, sir. Come down to help the young lady with her inheritance, have you?"

Mr. Horton nodded, but he did not speak.

"Hmmph!" the general said before he turned away to ask Marion Eaton a few questions about India. As the conversation progressed, it appeared to be the only part of the world where he had not served at one time or another.

Owen Fisher—or was it Nelson?—asked Sarah how she was enjoying Essex while his twin inspected the drawing room closely. With an eye to its possibilities as his future abode? Sarah wondered before she scolded herself for being so cynical.

The young men seemed lazy, gregarious sorts about her own age or a little younger. They often finished each other's sentences as they enumerated all the things to be enjoyed in the area.

"She's in mourning, you silly ninnies," their grandfather snapped, interrupting his conversation with Marion Eaton for a moment to set his grandsons straight.

"Right you are, guv, but mourning doesn't last forever . . ." said one.

"Indeed not. Soon be dashing about and up and doing, what, Miss Eaton?" concluded the other.

"Excellent Madeira, excellent," the general said after

Carten had served them. "I remember how often Jonah and I shared a glass or two."

His face got very red, and he had to take out his handkerchief and blow his nose loudly. "Dreadful thing, his death, dreadful," he said as he emerged from its snowy folds. His faded blue eyes were wet. It was obvious how much he had loved his friend.

"I never would have suspected he had any problems with his health. He was one of those tall thin men, all sinew and muscle and not an ounce of fat on him. That type generally make old bones, yet the day after I called here last, he was gone. You remember it, don't you, Horton?"

"Indeed I do, sir," Daniel said quietly. "It was a horrible shock to us all. My uncle was most distraught."

Carten entered the room again, this time with Forrest Blake's card. As Sarah rose to greet her newest guest, she wondered when this impromptu party would end, and prayed Miles Griffin would not swell its ranks. She could well imagine the sport he would have with the Fisher twins, and what he must think of the old general.

The curate paused at the threshold to inspect the company. Sarah could almost imagine an actor doing the same as he came onstage, to be sure his audience was aware of his importance.

"Ma'am, Miss Eaton. Your servant, ladies," he said as he smiled and swept them a bow.

"You are acquainted with General Sir Harold Fisher and his grandsons, sir?" Sarah inquired.

"I am indeed. I trust I find you well, sir?" he asked as he spread his bottle-green coattails before he took a seat.

The Fisher twins seemed rather subdued now the curate had made one of the party, and hardly said another word. Mr. Blake and their grandfather more than made up for any lapse on their part. It seemed to Sarah both men were intent on outdoing the other with civilities and anecdotes and compliments. During this conversation, she discovered the Fisher estate was next to the Hall on the western side. Sir Harold assured her they would be delighted to come over anytime she felt the need for assistance. Mr. Blake promptly told him he must not trouble himself, since he was only moments away at the manse in the village, a statement that had the old gentleman glaring at him.

After half an hour when Sarah was wondering how to end this confrontation, Marion Eaton rose. Immediately all five men jumped to their feet.

"It has been so kind of you to call, gentlemen," she said firmly, yet with a smile. "I must ask you to excuse me and my daughter now."

Mr. Blake cleared his throat. "I beg the indulgence of a few minutes with Miss Eaton," he said at his most pompous. Seeing the general coloring up, he added, "A matter of church business."

"I am afraid that is impossible at this time," Marion Eaton said politely yet in a cool voice. "I must ask you to call another day."

With that ultimatum, Mr. Blake had to be content, although his handsome face was dark with his displeasure. In contrast, the general positively beamed as he waved his grandsons before him as they all left the room.

There was silence in the drawing room until the front door closed behind the guests.

"I say, well done, Mrs. Eaton," Horton complimented her. "I thought they would never leave."

"They were so funny, were they not?" Marion Eaton said. "However, I cannot like the way Mr. Blake assumes that simply because Sarah has agreed to attend his church again, he has some hold on her. He presumes too much."

She sighed before she added, "I'm afraid we are going to be seeing a great deal more of the lot of them. It is too bad."

"Just deny them when they call. The butler will handle it," Horton told her. "At least I hope he is capable of that. But if they manage to get through his guard, I beg you will consider letting him go for someone more practiced, Miss Eaton."

"You remind me, I meant to have a word with Carten. If you will both excuse me?"

She found her new butler in his pantry, counting out the

plate needed for dinner. He seemed flustered she was there in that homely place, and asked her if she wouldn't be more comfortable somewhere else.

"Certainly not," Sarah said. "I do apologize for not seeing you as soon as I reached home this afternoon. Do you remember our talk this morning? How you said something was bothering you?"

"I remember. It's the new housekeeper. I don't know how to explain it. It's more a feeling I have than anything else. But she doesn't seem right to me somehow. It's as if she's just pretending to be a housekeeper, if you follow me."

He was frowning now as he polished a teaspoon over and over. Sarah remembered she had had some qualms about Mrs. Bonnet, too, qualms she had forgotten to discuss with her mother.

"She does her job well, doesn't she?" she asked. "There are no problems in the servants' hall?"

He shook his head. "No," he said slowly. "There aren't any problems that I know of. And yes, she's able enough. It's just—aw, well, maybe it's just I was used to Lena Quigley and her ways, and Mrs. Bonnet's some different."

Relieved the problem was not bigger, and her chat with Carten seemed to have reassured him, Sarah went to the door of the butler's pantry. "You will let me know if anything else occurs to you, won't you, Dennis?" she asked. "I rely on you to tell me how things are going in the Hall, you know."

He nodded, but as Sarah went away, she carried with her a picture of his grave face.

She went to the library to select a book. The library was the one room in the Hall that pleased her, for her grandfather had amassed an extensive collection of books. Some of them she had trouble understanding, but others she was finding fascinating.

She surprised Daniel Horton there, reading one of the London journals. He put it down as she came in, and rose to smile at her.

"I trust you are aware of the honor Sir Harold bestowed

on you this afternoon, ma'am," he began, the corner of his mouth twitching a little in amusement. Sarah was delighted he was in better spirits.

"I was almost overcome, sir," she said.

"I have to admit I never thought the old martinet would ever acknowledge you and your mother. He was well aware of your grandfather's sentiments; indeed, I suspect he agreed with them. But your fortune made it impossible for him to cut you. Tell me, Miss Eaton, which of the boys do you prefer? I am sure they are both available."

"Would it matter? They are so alike."

To her surprise, Horton continued to pursue the subject. "From a practical point of view, it would be an excellent match. The estates adjoin. To combine them would make you wife of the largest landowner in the county. Of course, I fear whichever young gentleman you chose would also saddle you with his twin. They appear to be inseparable."

"How fortunate I do not have a tendre for either. And not even to acquire so much land could I be persuaded."

He nodded. "Well, it is early days, and after all, you do not know them well as yet. You might also consider the curate, Miss Eaton. I can tell he is in a fair way of being smitten. Surely you agree he is a handsome man who thinks just as he ought? There could be worse husbands."

Disturbed by this lecture, for lecture it appeared to be, Sarah went to the window. The late afternoon sun cast long shadows on the lawns and gardens. It was almost time to dress for dinner.

She turned back to face the solicitor and said, "Is it so important I marry, sir? I fear I have no inclination for it."

"Not now, you don't," he agreed. "You are newly arrived home; still mourning your father. But someday soon you will want a husband, children. I only want you to choose the man best suited for you, one who will treat you well, feel some affection for *you*, as well as for your vast wealth."

He had come closer as he spoke, much too close, but Sarah did not step away.

"Then there is the Marquis of Wexford," he added softly.

"He is titled, wealthy—a man revered by the ton, if such things are important to you. He might very well be the man you choose."

"Are you married yourself, Mr. Horton?" Sarah dared to ask.

"Why, no, I am not," came the swift reply. "And I doubt I ever will be. The woman I would choose is far beyond my scope. I do not forget I am only a solicitor."

"Perhaps that would not matter to some women, sir," Sarah said.

His smile was warm and gentle, but he said no more. After a moment, Sarah went to the bookshelves. When she turned around a little later, she discovered Daniel Horton had quietly left the room, and she did not even wonder why the books in her grandfather's library had suddenly lost their appeal.

Chapter 14

Miles Griffin wondered at Sarah's preoccupation at dinner that evening. Several times her mother had to speak to her, until at last, as if suddenly aware of her bad manners, she set herself to be pleasant.

Marion Eaton amused Miles with an account of the afternoon's visitors. He wondered if her daughter's mood had anything to do with them. As the butler poured more wine and the footmen cleared the table before the savory was served, she concluded, "Mr. Horton has assured me we will not have to suffer them constantly, however. We have merely to ask Carten to tell them we are not receiving."

She gave a little laugh. "How grand that sounds. I feel somewhat like the queen.

"But enough of that. Tell me, m'lord, what you and Sarah accomplished in Ipswich this afternoon. Did you have a pleasant excursion?"

Miles sensed Sarah's discomfort, and he did not look her way as he told her mother of the purchases they had made for the school. Only when Horton commented did he glance at her, but by then, she had herself well in hand. Surely she had not thought he had any intention of revealing he had embraced her, had she? Why, if she knew, Mrs. Eaton would be well within her rights to insist he marry her daughter without delay, and that was more than enough reason for a prudent bachelor to hold his tongue.

When he and Horton were left alone later with their port, the solicitor excused himself almost immediately.

"Please extend my excuses to Mrs. Eaton, m'lord," he

said as he rose. "I am not feeling well this evening. I intend to go early to bed."

He bowed and left the room. Certainly Miles did not mind. Although he would grant the man was excellent in his profession, he had very little interest in him or his conversation.

When he had finished his port, he went out on the terrace. He often did this after dinner to enjoy a cigar before he joined the ladies. As soon as he had one alight, he strolled down the terrace steps, then beside a tall hedge. There was only a quarter moon, barely enough light for him to see his way, but he was becoming so familiar with the grounds, he did not need additional illumination.

Suddenly he heard the murmur of voices somewhere ahead of him on the other side of the hedge, and he moved closer, his head cocked to listen.

"But there's nothing I can tell you. No one knows who lit that fire."

Miles recognized the butler's voice, and his brows rose. Surely Carten should be supervising the footmen, or counting the plate before he washed it and put it away. What was he doing out here instead in the warm dark August night? And why? And who was that with him?

He strained to hear the answering voice, but he was to be disappointed. The speaker was whispering harshly, and he could only catch a word or two. He could not even tell if the whisperer was a man or a woman.

". . . To know . . . family . . . be careful . . ."

"You're seeing trouble where there's none," the butler interrupted. "And didn't I tell you I'd let you know as soon as I knew anything myself?"

". . . Danger . . . I warn you . . ."

Miles went a little closer to the hedge, very slowly and carefully so as not to alarm the two conspirators. All at once the whisperer said, "Quiet! . . . there's someone . . ."

Miles stopped moving immediately, but it was too late. The others rushed away. He heard the butler heading for the house, so he did not need to watch where he went. Instead, and moving as quickly as he could now, he started for the end of the hedge. As he stared and cursed the darkness now, a thick dark figure, hunched way over, scurried past the opening to disappear in the gardens beyond. Miles could not even be sure if the figure was male or female, and in only a moment more, the gardens were silent and empty.

He began to stroll in the direction the whisperer had taken. As he did so, he wondered how he had been discovered. He could have sworn he had not made a sound. As he puffed his almost forgotten cigar, he grimaced. Of course! Its aroma must have traveled through the hedge, effectively announcing his presence as surely as if he had called out his name. What an idiot he was.

Putting aside his disgust at his carelessness, he walked on, pondering what he had heard. And not heard, for surely there was little of substance to a few whispered words. At least he knew one of them had been Carten. He wondered who the other had been. Surely not an inmate of the Hall, for if it were such a person, there was no need for them to meet in the dark garden. Who else then? An old crony of his, come to gather what gossip he could? Or could it be Carten had a lover? He was young and virile. Did he have some girl in the village he crept out to meet every chance he got?

The little smile on his laps faded as he considered whether there could be a more serious reason. Could it be Carten was involved in the fire that had been set? Perhaps even set it himself? He had told Sarah Eaton he did not think the man had had anything to do with that misfortune; why, he had even recommended she elevate him from footman to butler. Perhaps he had placed her in danger by doing so. He frowned. Such a thing was most unpalatable to think about. He wondered if he should warn her, or would that be more upsetting for her than just watching the butler himself? But of course he could tell Rogers; enlist his aid. He decided he would not mention that he had even been in the gardens tonight as he threw away the remains of his cigar and turned to go back to the house. But as he did so, another plan began to form in his mind, and he consid-

ered it carefully as he made his way up the steps, across the
terrace, and back into the Hall.

The next day was Sunday, and Sarah went dutifully to
church. She went alone, dressed in her most subdued black
gown and plain hat. In her gloved hands she carried her
grandfather's prayer book. She had found it next to his bed,
and it seemed fitting, as his heir, she take possession of it
now. It was only a short distance from the Hall to the
church, but still she summoned the carriage. I might just as
well play this part to the hilt now I'm the lady of the manor,
she told herself as Carten helped her to her seat, and the
groom closed the door carefully behind her. And no doubt
the villagers expected her to come by carriage. It might
even make it easier for them to accept her, and the school.

She heard the whispers, the rustles, as people already in
church turned to watch her as she walked down the aisle to
take her seat in the Eaton pew situated right below the pulpit at the front.

Mr. Blake was already seated to one side of that pulpit,
intent on his Bible, and he did not lift his head. Thankfully
Sarah closed the door of the pew and sank down on the
faded velvet cushion, glad the high walls that formed it hid
her from any further observation.

The old familiar rituals of early childhood came back to
her easily, and she did not falter. She rose and knelt with
the others, and tried not to think of her mother's regret or
the disapproval her father would be sure to express if he
were here.

When Mr. Blake climbed to the pulpit, Sarah stared at
him. A ray of sunlight touched his dark curls and brought
them to glowing life. He looked impossibly handsome in
his white surplice. Sarah wondered how many young village girls behind her were secretly in love with him, even
as she had been at their age.

His homily that morning was based on the Sermon on the
Mount, and she let her mind wander as he spoke. At least
he had had the kindness not to preach on the return of the
prodigal daughter. At the conclusion, he mentioned the new

school with lavish praise, and extolled Sarah's goodness until she wanted to squirm.

At last the final hymn was sung, the benediction given, and she was free to escape. The villagers stood aside for her, some of them smiling shyly as they bowed and curt-sied. Mr. Blake waited for her at the door of the church. Aware of the many eyes on them, Sarah only intended to pause for a moment, but the curate detained her.

"I must see you, Miss Eaton," he said. "We have much to discuss."

As she nodded reluctantly, he continued. "Shall we meet this afternoon? Somewhere private?"

For some reason Sarah did not feel she could bear to spend any time with Forrest Blake, not today at any rate. Wasn't it enough she had had to sit beneath him and listen to him preach? Surely she deserved some time to herself before she had to endure his sermons again.

"I'm afraid that will not be possible today, sir," she said firmly, remembering to smile. "Could you come tomorrow at two? There is a gazebo in the gardens. I shall meet you there."

His disappointment was obvious, but he nodded and Sarah escaped to her carriage.

The Hall was quiet, the foyer empty, when she entered it. She wondered where everyone was as she went to a mirror to remove her hat and rub her aching forehead. She had not noticed how tight the band was when she had purchased it.

Hearing a little sound behind her, she stared into the wavy old glass to see the Marquis of Wexford coming down the stairs.

"I see you survived the prosy preacher's pompous pontif-icating," he said, but he did not smile. Sarah turned to face him, surprised he was so grim.

"Come along, Miss Eaton," he ordered, holding out his arm. "There is something I must say to you."

Sarah longed to deny him as she had the curate, but some-how she could not do that, not to the Marquis of Wexford.

"Well, for a moment or so, m'lord," she said, trying for a compromise. "I have the headache and would rest."

"I don't doubt it, after having to listen to him carry on. Did he mention the school as he promised?"

"Yes, enthusiastically. To hear him, you would have thought the whole thing his idea in the first place."

Miles shook his head as he opened the door to the terrace and led her down the steps to the gardens. He did not speak now. After one glance at his thoughtful face, Sarah fell silent as well.

They walked on. There was no one about, for the gardeners did not work on Sundays. The marquis took her to a marble bench in the rose garden. They were some distance from the Hall now. Sarah wondered what he had to say to her. He looked so serious, his long face grave. The heady scent of roses was all around her, and she could feel the heat of the August sun on her hair, her face. Somewhere a bird was singing sweetly. But today the gardens did not soothe her. Instead she began to feel apprehensive, unnerved, and she took a deep breath to calm herself.

"I overheard something last night," the marquis began abruptly, and her sense of dread increased until her heart seemed to flutter in her throat. "At first I did not mean to tell you of it, but I've come to see it is far better you know."

He went on then, revealing Carten's rendezvous in the dark garden with some unknown person. Sarah's hand crept to her throat. Even on this beautiful day, eminently safe because Miles Griffin was beside her, she was afraid. Dreadfully afraid.

"They were discussing the fire, and from the few words I was able to hear, the stranger was warning him to watch his step. Carten scoffed a bit at this, but he did promise to let his confidante know any future developments."

Sarah seemed to hear a faint echo of Dennis Carten, assuring her she would not be sorry for appointing him butler. Now her disappointment made a bitter taste in her mouth.

"Then, Carten is the one who set the fire, m'lord?" she asked when Miles paused.

"We can't be sure of that. There is still no evidence he did it."

"Perhaps if I confronted him with what you have told

me? Insist he reveal his crony's identity?" Sarah persisted, although facing Carten with this information was the last thing she wanted to do.

"No, you must not do that," came the swift reply. "He will only refuse to tell you anything, and it would put him on his guard. He knows I was in the garden, of course. That wretched cigar! But he cannot know if I heard anything of his conversation. I intend to pretend I did not. I may even ask him, winking as I do so, if he has a sweetheart somewhere nearby. Then, he will think I heard nothing of value, and perhaps lead us to this other person.

"There is something more, Miss Eaton," he added, staring down at his clasped hands for a moment and frowning. "I am beginning to be greatly concerned for your safety. We have no idea what this stranger intends, nor why he is interested in the Hall, and in you, its heiress. Not even why he resents you and wishes you harm, as we may assume he does. But there is one thing I do know. You are in danger. Grave danger.

"I think it would be best, therefore, if we were betrothed."

"What?" Sarah asked weakly, as if she could not believe she had heard him correctly.

He lifted his head to stare at her. "Come, come, Miss Eaton. *Betrothed.* If we were, it would be easier for me to watch over you, keep you safe, for I would be able to be with you more often without causing speculation and gossip."

"But—but you don't love me," Sarah protested.

"Of course I don't," he said so swiftly her heart sank. "No more do you love me," he went on, as if aware his statement had been much too abrupt, to say nothing of vastly impolite. "We would only be pretending, for expedience's sake."

"Well, but then, sir, besides being trapped in a loveless betrothal, eventually we would have to contract an equally loveless marriage. And as much as I appreciate your concern for my safety, even to ensure that safety, I could not marry you."

"No, no, there will be no marriage," he explained.

"When all this is over, the culprit discovered and punished, we shall find we do not suit. You may cry off, you know. No stigma will attach to you in such a move. Being changeable creatures, women do it all the time. You need not be concerned about what the ton will say."

She laughed bitterly. "I do assure you, m'lord, that what the ton says is the least of my worries. I shall, in all probability, never even make its acquaintance. But I do worry about my mother's opinion, those of the servants and the villagers—everyone here. This is to be my home. What you suggest is to make me out the fickle jilt."

"Ah, yes, but an alive one," he muttered.

"There is that, of course," Sarah agreed reluctantly.

"I would ask you not to tell even your mother our betrothal is only a sham," he went on, as if so sure he could persuade her to his point of view there was no need for him to argue it further. Fuming, Sarah thought him the most arrogant man she had ever met.

"It will be a difficult deception because you are so close, but that dear lady could so easily let it slip. Perhaps she would only tell her maid, the winsome Mathilda, but from her to the rest of the servants is a very small step. And then it would all be for naught, and we would be back where we started. You do see I am right, don't you, Miss Eaton?"

Sarah said nothing. She was going over everything he had said, searching for flaws, misconceptions, even a way to escape, but there was nothing. At last she looked at him and said, "I really do think you should begin to call me Sarah, Miles. 'Miss Eaton' is such a terribly formal address for a newly engaged man, is it not?"

He smiled at her then, that confiding smile that always warmed her. He picked up her hand, and as he kissed it, Sarah said sharply, "There must be no lovemaking, sir. I may trust you in that?"

"Oh, I shall endeavor to be the perfect gentleman, ma'am," he said as he restored her hand to her lap. "Of course, it may be necessary once in a great while to show some small signs of affection in public. You will permit those, to preserve our little deception?"

Sarah nodded, still reluctant. She could not think of another thing in the world to say, and she rose from the bench feeling somehow that in a mere few minutes, her life had changed in some irrevocable way.

As the two walked back to the Hall, she thought to tell the marquis her mother had never learned the real reason he was here.

"I never told her you were investigating the origin of the fire. I didn't want to upset her," she said. "I think she has forgotten all about it. I don't want her fretting, now she is so happily involved with plans for her school."

"There is no need for her to know. We can, between us, keep her safe and content."

He stopped then and put his hands on her shoulders to turn her to face him. "You may believe I will do everything in my power to make this as painless a thing as I can for you," he said softly. Sarah stared up at him, searching his face, those half-hidden dark eyes. Yes, he seemed sincere. The little ice that had begun to form somewhere deep inside began to melt.

"Do you have any other concerns, my dear?" he asked.

"No, I can't think of any," she said as he let her go and they walked on. She smiled a little then and chuckled. As he looked a question, she said, "At least there will be some good come of this betrothal. Besides keeping me safe, I mean. It will deter not only Mr. Blake from pursuing me, but those silly Fisher twins as well."

As he grinned at her, she added, "Mr. Blake is to call on me tomorrow at two. I agreed to meet him in the gazebo then, for he insisted, saying we had much to discuss privately."

"Is that so?" Miles remarked, his voice bland. "Then, my first official act as your betrothed will be to send the handsome curate about his business. I cannot remember when I have looked forward to anything with quite as much anticipation."

Chapter 15

But by the next afternoon, Sarah had persuaded the marquis to let her talk to Mr. Blake alone first. He had been disappointed, but at last he had agreed. They had discussed it just before they sought their respective beds that night, when Marion Eaton left them alone together to say good night, blushing deeply as she did so.

Sarah had not been able to tell from her mother's reaction to the announcement that had been made at tea, whether she was pleased by the betrothal or not. At first she had looked troubled, until Miles had assured her there were to be no plans for a wedding until the full year for mourning Sarah's father had passed. Furthermore, he had said the betrothal would not be announced during that time, either.

Mr. Horton had also looked grave, but he had been quick to congratulate the marquis and wish Sarah every happiness. She thought she saw regret deep in his eyes, and she was sorry for it. She liked Daniel Horton a great deal. Surely there would come a time when she could explain the hoax. She hoped he would not take umbrage at being deceived.

Later, after a festive dinner that evening, she found herself alone with her mother in the drawing room. Even though she had been dreading it, she had not imagined the interview would be so difficult. But Marion Eaton was not to be put off with a few vague remarks. She wanted to know everything. *When* the marquis had proposed, and *what* he had said. *How S*arah had felt, and what he had done. Sarah began to spin her a tale of kisses and promises, a tender embrace and even more tender words of love. And as she did so, she was ashamed, for she had never lied to her mother in her life.

At last Mrs. Eaton sighed and took out her handkerchief to wipe her eyes. "Oh, my dear, it is so affecting," she said softly. "And it does bring back happy memories of your dear father's proposal, down on one knee. He was so fervent.

"I admit I did have my doubts when you first told me; I would never lie to you about that, Sarah," she had added, making Sarah squirm under her smart gown. "Because, you see, the marquis, well, he is titled and from a proud family. And I didn't want you to have the life I was forced to live because your grandfather Eaton refused to acknowledge me. But I see there is no comparison. M'lord is thirty-five and an only child; his parents are dead. There can be none to say nay to his choice of bride, not now. Oh, my dear, how very happy you will be. I have always liked him, you know," she confided in a whisper as she darted a glance at the dining room doors. "He tries so hard to be cool and sarcastic, always ready with a quip or a jeer. But underneath there is a sensitive man who will love you always. You'll see."

Sarah had never been so relieved when the two men rejoined them and the tête-à-tête was, of necessity, concluded. Not, she thought gloomily, that her mother would not refer to it again, over and over. Pray this business was done quickly, and the culprit who threatened her and the Hall found.

The following afternoon, Forrest Blake was prompt to their meeting. Sarah was waiting for him in the gazebo when he came bounding up the steps, a sheaf of papers in his hand.

"My dear new parishioner," he said, beaming as he took a seat beside her and stretched his arm along the railing behind them. Sarah told herself there was nothing to worry about. He would not turn loverlike. He never had before. Still, she leaned forward a little to avoid any inadvertent contact with that arm.

"Mr. Blake," she said coolly. "What is it that we have to discuss, sir?"

"So businesslike," he replied, his voice teasing. Then he sighed. "But very well. I have brought you some additional tracts to read and pray over. There are some uplifting sentiments I am sure you will feel worth your time and study. Later we can discuss them, and I shall be happy to explain anything that might be too difficult for feminine comprehension.

"And, naturally, there is the school to discuss."

"I am so glad you saw your way to agree to it," Sarah said, choosing her words carefully. "I was most disheartened when I left you the other day."

"I know," he confided, bending closer. He was not touching her, but still Sarah felt trapped, stifled. "I think it was the sight of your face, so troubled and disappointed that did the trick. I assure you, I prayed long and hard, long and hard indeed, dear lady. But all is well now. We may proceed."

Even knowing he would hardly mention he had been coerced by the marquis, Sarah was indignant at this pious pose.

"What I wanted to suggest is that I take a hand in the religious education of the children," he went on. "To do so would also serve to still any doubt of your mother's intentions. And, although as I am sure you are aware, I have little time with three parishes to serve, I shall strive to do my best."

He stared off into the distance, treating her to a view of his handsome profile, and Sarah struggled to control herself. She found the assumed idealism of Mr. Blake, when he was at his most noble, very amusing. His next words, however, sobered her at once.

"Of course," he said, "if I had a wife, a dear helpmate, she could take over the children's religious training. Alas, I am not so fortunate, although I can tell you, dear girl, I have great hopes in that direction."

He paused, as if to give her a chance to comment, but Sarah only pretended to be busy waving a bothersome insect away, and he went on, "I also have an unpleasant duty I must perform, Miss Eaton."

"Indeed? And what might that be?"

"I have to warn you to be on your guard with the Marquis of Wexford. As your spiritual adviser, I am most distressed he continues to stay at the Hall. I fear he can be up to no good. He is a vain man, and a proud one, no fit companion for you or your mother. I cannot tell you how distressed I would be if I thought you were the type of woman who set great store in a man's wealth, his position in life, and ignored the festering evil that lies in his soul. I tell you, Miss Eaton, in God's eyes a title is nothing, a mere bagatelle. Furthermore, if you are thinking he might be brought to consider matrimony, you will be sorely disappointed. The marquis knows his worth too well. He would never marry a woman such as you. Why . . ."

Furious now, Sarah lashed out before she had time to consider her words. "Do you think so, sir? How very unnerving then for you to learn the marquis is indeed considering matrimony, and with me, no less. He proposed yesterday afternoon, and I accepted."

There was a stunned silence in which Sarah took herself to task for being so rash and quick to anger. When at last she looked at the curate, she gasped. His handsome face was contorted, and his gray eyes aflame with fury. As she watched, he raised a fist and shook it in her face. Shrinking back, she was sorry she had not let the marquis handle the man as he had suggested. But surely he would not strike her! He would not do that!

"You—you tell me you have accepted that godless reprobate?" he demanded through clenched teeth. "You are that careless of your soul that you will risk going to hell with him? For I tell you, girl, he is most certainly bound for hell."

"Oh, I do hope not. But how can anyone be sure? Even you?" came a careless voice as the marquis came up the steps and paused on the threshold to inspect the two of them. "Darling," he said in a caressing voice that made Sarah shiver with more than fear, "I cannot allow you to

entertain other men like this. I am, I'm afraid, in spite of
Mr. Blake's opinion of me, too conventional for that."

He held out his hand, and gratefully Sarah rose and went
to him.

"You will excuse us, won't you, Mr. Blake?" he said
carelessly as he put his arm around Sarah and held her tight
against his side. "Oh, and you might as well take those
tracts with you. Sarah is going to be much too busy with,
mmm, *other things* to read them."

He took her down the steps, leaving the furious, but fortunately silent, curate behind them. Sarah did not say anything until they were out of earshot. Then she shivered and
said, "Thank heavens you came. He became violent when I
told him we were betrothed."

"Yes, I saw his face. He looked angry enough to commit
murder, did he not? We must keep an eye on him. There is
no telling what he might be up to."

"Do you think he could be the one?" Sarah asked, then
answered herself by adding, "But how silly of me. Mr.
Blake wouldn't slip into the Hall to start a fire if he's been
intent on gaining it for his own ever since our arrival."

"Why did you tell him of the betrothal, Sarah?" Miles
asked.

She looked away for a moment before she admitted, "He
angered me. After hinting he was hoping for a particular
wife, he went on to warn me against you, saying you were
no better than you should be . . ."

"He was certainly right there."

Sarah remembered what else Forrest Blake had said
about the marquis; that he was too proud to marry a woman
like her, and swallowing, she changed the subject and
asked if they might not go for a drive.

When she had gone to change her gown, Miles gave the
necessary orders and retreated to the library to await both
Sarah and his rig. Sprawling carelessly in a comfortable
chair, he was soon deep in thought. He devoted no more
time to the curate. Instead he wondered if he should tell
Sarah what he had learned from Hal Wells that morning;
that her butler had gone to Mrs. Quigley's cottage yester-

day afternoon, and spent over an hour there. And, the groom had said, he had as much as sneaked into the place, cautiously looking over his shoulder often to make sure he was not observed.

His valet had also reported on his meeting with the woman. She had downed several glasses of daffy, but the gin had not made her careless, no matter how he had questioned her. Instead she had become belligerent, demanding to know what he was about, until he was forced to give it up. Shuddering, Mr. Rogers said she had invited him in when he saw her home, but he had pretended he was feeling ill and made good his escape.

Miles frowned as he studied the faded turkey carpet under his feet. This business of Mrs. Quigley and Carten was worrisome. What connection could there possibly be between them? And for what reason had they met? He was too young a man to be interested in her in an amorous way, yet still he had sought her out. Well, there was nothing for it but to have his groom continue to shadow the man. Perhaps something would come of it.

As he helped Sarah to the phaeton later, Daniel Horton came out on the steps to watch them and call a compliment to the marquis on his team before he wished them a pleasant drive.

Sarah waved back to him and smiled. "Isn't he a dear?" she asked. "I am so fond of him."

"Are you? And here I was going to suggest you send him on his way. He has spent entirely too much time here, and I have noticed the two of you seldom discuss any business. But I am sure it is only a minor gaffe on your part. You could not know that being friendly with someone like him is just not done. I like my man of business, too, even admire him for his acuity, but I have never sat down to a meal with him, and I have never given him the run of my house, as you have with Mr. Horton."

"You sound terrible," Sarah was quick to tell him. "So— so insufferable! I do not choose my friends because of who they are and what they do. And I most certainly do not hold myself so high I would look down on a man who has made my interests his primary concern. Not done, indeed!"

There was a little silence before Miles said meekly, "No doubt you are right, and it is certainly democratic of you. And, of course, what you do and who you know are not my affair. Dear me, I wonder if I am beginning to take this sham betrothal too seriously, to be preaching to you as I would no doubt to a real fiancée? What an appalling thought. You must forgive me."

Sarah changed the subject, but inwardly she continued to seethe. She was only able to forget when Miles revealed Carten's trip to the village; his suspicious visit to Mrs. Quigley's cottage. Although they discussed this at length, neither could explain it.

Miles told himself there was no need to sully her ears with an account of his valet's attempts to storm the woman's defenses by plying her with gin. Such doings were not for anyone like Sarah Eaton who had such tender sensibilities. Instead he changed the subject by asking her how she liked the new wallpaper the workmen had just today begun to apply to the drawing room walls. It was an innocuous topic and a safe one, for beginning to know Sarah as well as he did, he could tell she was still upset by his arrogance. He even wondered why he felt so sorry it should be so.

Chapter 16

As awkward as Sarah found her connection to the Marquis of Wexford—now all the world and his wife thought he was to be her future husband—she found dealing with her butler much more unsettling. Even giving him an order or discussing the most commonplace household matters, she could never forget how deeply involved he was in the mystery here at the Hall. And he had lied to her when he told her she would not be sorry she had made him butler, something she found especially repugnant. She watched him covertly whenever she could, wondering about him and the kind of man he had become. She should not have let the marquis sway her judgment in this instance; she should have remembered the horrid bully he had been as a child and acted accordingly.

She could not understand why he visited Mrs. Quigley, unless the two of them were involved somehow in the doings at Woodingham Hall. But how could that be? None of it made any sense.

For the last few nights, she had had trouble getting to sleep no matter how tired she was when she sought her bed. She would lie there in the dark, staring up at the canopy over her head, trying, *trying* to fathom this puzzle.

It was on Wednesday morning, while she was at breakfast with her mother and Mr. Horton that she heard a commotion beyond the baize door that led to the back of the house and the kitchens a floor below. Surely she had heard a scream? People calling out?

Before she could inquire, a young housemaid hurried into the room, bearing a fresh pot of tea. As she set it on the table, her hands shook, and when she would have retreated after only a token curtsy, Sarah detained her.

"No, Fanny, please stay. I want to know what all that noise we just heard was about."

The maid twisted her apron in her hands, her eyes lowered. She was very pale, and when she tried to speak, her voice came out a croak and she was forced to clear her throat before she could go on.

"Oh—oh, Miss Eaton, it's Mrs. Quigley, ma'am."

"What about her?" Sarah asked, puzzled.

"She's—she's dead, ma'am!" Fanny wailed before she burst into tears and had to run from the room.

"Goodness gracious," Mrs. Eaton said faintly, dropping her fork. It clattered on her plate, and Daniel Horton reached over to pat her hand.

"There now, ma'am," he said in a steady voice. "We must have more information than that."

"You're right," Sarah said. "I'll ring for Carten and see what he knows of this." Secretly Sarah wished the marquis was there to handle the interview. She was afraid she would not ask the right questions.

But Carten did not appear. Instead Ned Haskell, the first footman, came in and bowed. The state of his nerves was evident by the way his Adam's apple rose and fell rapidly in his long, thin neck.

"Where is Carten, Ned?" Sarah asked, surprised he was not there.

"He begs to be excused, ma'am. We all just heard about Mrs. Quigley, and Dennis, well, he's some upset."

"Fanny told me she was dead. Can it be true?" Sarah persisted.

The footman nodded. Without his tray, he did not seem to know what to do with his hands, and he almost hopped from one foot to the other in his agitation.

"Yes, it's true all right. A neighbor found her early this morning after she heard the cat crying outside the cottage door."

"And how did she die?" a deep voice from the doorway

inquired, startling everyone in the breakfast room considerably.

"I beg your pardon, Mrs. Eaton, Sarah," Miles Griffin said as he came forward. "Well, come on, man, tell us. How did she die?"

A miserable Ned Haskell looked around the table at the filled plates, the bowls of jelly and fresh butter, the silver basket of scones and muffins. On the sideboard behind him were chafing dishes steaming gently as they kept warm the shirred eggs, oatmeal, kippers, and ham. He swallowed hard before he said, "It was awful, or so they say. She'd been ill, very ill before she passed away, and . . ."

"That will be all," the marquis said firmly as Mrs. Eaton gagged a little and buried her face in her napkin.

"The authorities have been notified?" he asked next.

"Aye, to be sure. Ah, I mean, yes, m'lord. General Sir Harold Fisher is the local justice. He lives quite near."

Miles waved a hand, and gratefully, the footman bowed and disappeared.

"I'll go to the village now and find out all I can," Miles said. Although he addressed both women equally, his gaze lingered longest on Sarah's face. "May I suggest you remain indoors together until I return?"

"I'll join you, m'lord," Mr. Horton said as he rose from the table. His voice was steady, but there was an undertone of horror and revulsion in it for what he had just heard.

"As you wish," the marquis tossed over his shoulder. He was already moving toward the hall. In a moment both men were gone.

Marion Eaton sat quietly, her head bowed and her eyes closed. Sarah knew she was praying, praying for Mrs. Quigley's soul.

Closing her own eyes, she began to think. The fact that the former housekeeper had been so ill led Sarah to suspect she had not died a natural death. And that meant she had not died by her own hand, because what person would choose to poison themselves and suffer such a painful, difficult death when there were so many other ways? A pistol, for example . . .

She shuddered. What was she doing to even be thinking of such things? Besides, Ned had not been himself. She was well aware how things get distorted and exaggerated as any story traveled from person to person. Perhaps what he had told them had not been so. Well, Miles would discover the truth.

Mrs. Bonnet came in then, her face red from toiling up the stairs. She looked concerned.

"I beg your pardon, Miss Eaton, ma'am," she said as she sailed up to the table and curtsied. "I just had to make sure you ladies were all right, and didn't need anything. I'm afraid it's no good asking the servants, that upset they are. And as for Carten, well! I never would have suspected the man was so sensitive. I always thought him as arrogant as a lord.

"But I'm talking too much as usual. Now, is there anything I can get you?"

"No, thank you, Mrs. Bonnet," Sarah said as she rose and went to help her mother. "I don't believe either of us care for any more. You may clear."

Mrs. Bonnet curtsied again, but was still frowning her concern. Irrelevantly Sarah wondered if she would appear in the morning room shortly, decanter in hand, and insist they have a tot of brandy for the shock.

The two women sat quietly for some time. There was no conversation. Sarah was anxious to discuss the death, but she knew it would be better to wait to hear what Miles had to say, and she did not like to interrupt her mother, who was reading her Bible now.

Down in the village, the marquis and Daniel Horton pushed their way through the little knot of villagers clustered at the cottage gate, and strode up the path. As they approached the door, now wide open to the morning sunlight, the elderly justice appeared. For a moment he paused there holding onto the jamb, his white knuckles showing the force of his grip.

"General Sir Harold Fisher? I am Miles Griffin, Marquis of Wexford in Kent, and justice there as you are here, sir."

"Wexford," the old soldier got out. Then he straightened

up and squared his shoulders. "Beastly thing, beastly. I've seen any number of horrible deaths in my time, had to listen to wounded men scream with pain, waded through what seemed like rivers of blood, but I've never seen anything like—like *that*."

He jerked his head back toward the cottage. "May I go in?" Miles asked, Daniel Horton hovering at his elbow.

"If you must," the general said. "I wouldn't advise it, however, because . . ."

But he only spoke to empty air, for both men had entered the cottage. Horton reappeared almost at once. His face was shining with sweat, and he had to keep swallowing as he moved a little distance away into the gardens, keeping his back turned to the onlookers. Miles Griffin, on the other hand, remained in the cottage for several minutes. When he came out at last, his long face was white, but he had himself under control.

"Have you made a determination of the cause of death?" he asked the justice.

"Had to have been poison," the general barked. "No sign of anything else, no knife or bullet wounds. Did you notice the plate on the table, that portion of mushrooms on toast?"

As Miles nodded, he continued, "She must have been eating supper, for it was half consumed. Probably a toadstool got mixed in with the mushrooms she had gathered for her meal."

"So you are calling it an accidental death?" Miles persisted.

The older man stared at him, his eyes keen under their white brows. "Nothing else it could be, what? Unless you have some other theory?"

Miles looked around at the villagers whispering at the gate, a shaken Daniel Horton drawing near again, and the stern old face of the man beside him. "I agree she was poisoned," he said.

Mr. Horton excused himself from returning to the Hall with Miles. He admitted he was feeling ill after what he had seen, and intended to visit the pub for a glass of brandy.

"While you're doing that, keep your ears open," Miles told him.

"You mean you don't believe it was an accident, m'lord?" Horton asked, clearly unsettled by the idea.

"Did I say so?" Miles demanded at his most haughty. "I just wonder what the villagers will make of it. The woman was an enigma. Interesting to get their opinion."

Horton nodded. As he went up the street, Miles Griffin stared after him, his sleepy eyes almost closed as he considered what he had just seen in the pleasant little cottage. Or the once pleasant little cottage, he amended, as he set off for the Hall.

He found the place little changed from when he had left it. True, there were no more disturbances from the servants' quarters, no noisy crying to rend the air, but neither were things back to normal. He had to let himself into the foyer, for no butler or footman appeared in answer to his knock. It was very quiet, and for a fleeting moment he could almost sympathize with Sarah Eaton and her feelings about the Hall. It did seem to be waiting for something. Brooding, almost.

Shaking his head, and putting such ridiculous thoughts down to the gruesome scene he had just observed, he went to the library to ponder Carten's relationship with the woman again. He knew he should have mentioned it to the justice, and how he had visited her only a few days before. But the old soldier had already decided it was accidental poisoning. Perhaps it was even so, although such a neat solution offended him somehow. It was too easy, too pat. Yet he could hardly suppose anyone as suspicious as Mrs. Quigley had been willingly sitting down to consume a plate of poisoned mushrooms someone had either picked or prepared for her. It just did not fit what he knew of the woman. And that meant the general was right.

Sarah found him there some time later when she came in and shut the door behind her. "What did you discover?" she asked, sitting down next to him.

Miles roused himself from his abstraction to give her a

carefully edited version of the death, as well as the justice's conclusion.

"But I can see you don't believe that, do you?" she asked.

He looked amazed. "How on earth could you tell? I thought I hid my opinion very well."

She smiled at him. It was only a little smile, but he was glad to see it, for her face had been somber during his tale.

"I have no idea. How do you always seems to know what I'm thinking?" she asked. Not giving him time to answer, she said quickly, "But what of this death?"

He rose then to pace the room, his head bent in thought and his hands clasped behind his back.

At last he stopped and looked up. "I think she was murdered," he told her in a quiet voice. As Sarah gasped, he went on, "I know all the evidence points to an accident. After all, there are so many poisonous mushrooms, some of them masquerading as their innocent cousins. But still, I find it hard to believe. Mrs. Quigley was a countrywoman. She would have known the good from the bad. Then, too, she was so unappealing, so prickly. A woman who perhaps had many enemies. It is just a feeling I have, but it is one I cannot discard. I do beg you to keep this to yourself, Sarah. If she was indeed killed, it would put you in danger. We must, both of us, pretend we believe it was an accident."

"Have you had a chance to interview Carten?"

Used to his abrupt change of subject, Sarah did not hesitate. "I asked to see him, but I was told he had had to go to bed, he was so upset." She frowned. "That certainly doesn't fit the picture I've always had of him, but I am told it is undeniably true. I'll see him tomorrow, or whenever he reappears, but, Miles"—she paused and held out her hand to him. As he came to her and took it in his own, she went on, "I know it makes me a coward, but would you be there with me when I interview him? I am afraid of him now. I don't want to be alone with him."

"Of course I will be there. You see what a good idea becoming betrothed was?" he said, trying to tease her.

She could not even smile in response. "But wouldn't it be best to discharge him?" she said.

"No, you can't. We need him under our eye until we are sure of either his guilt or his innocence.

"I wonder what the handsome Mr. Blake was up to last night?"

"Surely you do not suspect him," she protested. "Oh, I know you said he looked ready to do murder when he learned of our mock betrothal, but you can't really believe he would commit one. Besides, why would he murder Mrs. Quigley? We don't even know if they were acquainted."

"Very true. And I'd wager anything you like she was not a churchgoing woman. But you must remember, Woodingham Village is not London. There are not hundreds of people about who would be capable of dastardly acts. What has happened, both here and in the village, could only be committed by one of a small group of people. And so I shall continue to ask questions, try to determine where everyone was. That way, at least we can eliminate some of them."

"Isn't that work for the justice here?" she asked, for what he was proposing sounded dangerous. The murderer, if indeed there was one, could not risk being exposed. He or she might try to do the marquis harm, and the very thought of it alarmed her.

"Sir Harold has already decided she died of accidental poisoning. He will look no further."

"I don't think you should, either," Sarah said stubbornly. "I—I am afraid for you.

His stern expression softened. For a moment there was silence in the library. Then he said, "Thank you. I can't remember the last time someone really cared what happened to me."

Sarah felt her face grow warm at his intimate tone, and she hurried to say, "But if you ask Carten—anyone—where they were last evening, all they would have to do is deny they were anywhere near Mrs. Quigley's cottage."

"I don't have to ask Carten. My groom has been following him whenever he leaves the house. He'll know if he went to the village. And my valet has been watching as well. You remind me, I must see them both at once. Excuse me."

Miles found his valet in his room. As Rogers hung up his robe, he asked him about the butler and the other servants.

"Yes, there was quite a to-do this morning. I happened to come down for a cup of tea just as the news was brought to the house by one of the grooms who had gone early to the village. The maids behaved typically, crying and clutching each other in their distress. Women! Hmmph!"

The marquis did not comment. He was well aware of his valet's general opinion of women.

"Carten's reaction was surprising. He didn't say a word, but he went quite pale. I noticed it especially. Then he had to sit down at the table. Cook pressed him to have a cup of tea, but he only waved her away. At last, still without speaking to anyone, he went to the back stairs. He moved like a blind man in a strange place, m'lord, so tentative he was, his gait so awkward."

"What do you make of it?" Miles asked.

"I've no idea," Rogers said, frowning as he straightened the coverlet on the bed. "It seems an excessive reaction for a man. I know Mrs. Quigley was the housekeeper at the same time Carten was footman here, but she was not especially likable. Why would her death cause him so much anguish?"

"I've no idea, either. Keep listening and watching. I depend on you."

The valet's bow was stiff, for he was offended his master thought he needed reminding, but Miles did not notice. He was already on his way to the stables.

He was to be disappointed there. Hal Wells admitted sheepishly he did not know if Carten had gone to the village the previous evening.

"I know he was here at the Hall all yesterday afternoon, m'lord," he said eagerly. "But as for the evening, well, I can't say for sure. I was busy in the stables. One of Miss Eaton's mares was foaling, and her head groom asked me to help."

Miles hid his disappointment. As he walked slowly back

to the Hall, he thought how unfortunate it was he could not confirm the man's whereabouts. Surely that malaise he had suffered when hearing of Mrs. Quigley's death was most suspicious, most suspicious indeed.

Chapter 17

Carten returned to his duties by early afternoon. Sarah summoned him to the library, where she interviewed him in company with the marquis. The butler was pale but composed, and he answered their questions readily. Unfortunately they could get nothing from him of any value. Yes, he had left his duties and he was sorry for it; Miss Eaton could be certain it would not happen again. He had not been feeling well that morning—perhaps it had been something he had eaten—and the combination of that and the bad news had made him feel faint. And yes—staring straight at the marquis, who had asked the question—he had called on Mrs. Quigley a few days ago, but only to bring her a few things she had left in the housekeeper's room. They could ask Mrs. Bonnet if it wasn't so. She was the one who had asked him to do the errand.

At last Sarah dismissed him. She thought his bow insolent, and she could not like the burning look of accusation he gave her, that she should even consider him implicated. She knew his remaining at the Hall was going to be a problem, but Miles had said he could not be dismissed, and she concurred. At least for now.

To distract her, Miles insisted she come and inspect the drawing room. The new striped paper was up and the woodwork freshly painted. It was a great deal more cheerful, especially now the dark brown draperies had been removed. New royal blue velvet ones with a rich gold braid trim were being made to replace them. Some workmen were busy recovering the furniture, and Sarah could see the

drawing room was going to be a vastly different place in
only a week or so.

Not content with that, Miles took her upstairs to her
grandfather's old room. This too was almost completely
transformed. The charred door to the dressing room had
been replaced, the dressing room itself completely rebuilt.
All the depressing oil paintings were gone, and the smell of
paint and wallpapering was strong. The massive four-poster
had been dismantled as well, and carried up to an attic to be
stored out of sight. The room looked empty without it, but
Sarah knew the new bed would be delivered shortly. As she
walked about, admiring everything, she was surprised at
how much more at ease she was in the room now. Perhaps
Miles had been right. Perhaps all the Hall needed was re-
decorating to rid it of its brooding darkness, that feeling she
had it was waiting for something it knew was going to happen. Something awful. She shivered just thinking about it,
before she forced it from her mind. She had never been fanciful or silly. She certainly did not intend to become that
way now.

That evening, at the conclusion of dinner, Daniel Horton
still looked pale. Sarah had no idea when he had returned
from the village, for she had not seen him all afternoon.
When she questioned him, he said he had gone for a long
walk to help clear his mind of the tragedy.

"I did not know the woman well—only as well as any
guest here would know the housekeeper. I did see her when
I had occasion to visit your grandfather on business matters, Miss Eaton. Still, her death was upsetting, especially
coming as it did on the heels of my uncle's demise."

Mrs. Eaton commiserated with him, but he could not
smile.

"And now I have something I must tell you," he went on.
"Something I am afraid will upset you especially, ma'am. I
am so sorry. If there were any way to avoid it, I would."

"What can it be?" Marion Eaton asked, the remains of
her pudding forgotten.

"This afternoon, as I returned from my walk, I surprised
your maid—Mathilda Dents, I believe?— near one of the

garden sheds. She was trying to light a little pile of twigs
and paper she had placed against one of the walls."

"Oh, no!" Marion Eaton cried.

Sarah looked up to see Carten and the two footmen had
stopped even pretending to be busy at the sideboard, and
she was quick to dismiss them.

No one spoke until the doors closed behind them.

"I can't believe it. Are you quite sure, sir?" Mrs. Eaton
asked pitifully, tears in her eyes.

Horton spread his hands. "There can be no doubt it was
she, ma'am, even though she ran away as soon as she saw
me watching her."

Mrs. Eaton wiped her streaming eyes on her napkin.
"The poor, poor child," she said. "She is so young, and she
has known nothing but misfortune all her life."

She lowered her napkin then to stare at them. "But—but
does this mean she started the fire in Sarah's dressing
room? Why would she do such a thing?"

"She knew I did not like her," Sarah said. "You remember, Mother, how I wanted you to let Mr. Horton find you a
maid rather than take her on?"

Mrs. Eaton nodded, looking thoughtful.

"I believe we should have her come down now," the
marquis said. "The butler and footmen heard Horton accuse
her. It will not be long before she knows of it herself. And
there are some questions we should ask, things we have to
know."

Sarah rang for Carten and asked him to fetch Mathilda
Dents. Lost in their own thoughts, no one spoke until she
appeared. As she slipped into the dining room, looking
frightened at this unusual summons, Sarah thought her no
more appealing than she had been at first meeting. True,
she had gained some weight, but she was as pale as ever,
and her lank hair hung about her face in limp, colorless
strands. Sarah was glad the marquis undertook the questioning. She did not have the heart to do it herself, not when
she knew how her mother was suffering.

"Mr. Horton says he saw you trying to set fire to one of
the garden sheds this afternoon," he began.

The maid's mouth dropped open; her eyes bulged. Sarah had not realized she was such an accomplished actress; why, anyone would have sworn she was struck dumb by the accusation.

"Well, what have you to say?" Miles went on relentlessly. There was no pity in his voice. It lashed out at the girl as coldly as the iciest winter wind that sent you scurrying to the comfort of a blazing hearth.

"No, I never, I never did it," Mathilda said at last, her voice shaking with her feelings. "I wasn't there! You can't make me say I was!"

"You would have us believe Mr. Horton is a liar?" Miles demanded. "Be very careful, girl. You can be punished for bearing false witness."

"But I didn't do it! I never set no fire," she persisted. "Mrs. Eaton, ma'am, you got ter believe me. I would never, never do anything that would take me away from you. I been good ever since you took me in, I have, I *have*! Oh, please, ma'am, please don't listen to them. That one, he's lying. He's got ter be lying! And no one here likes me. None of 'em. Yer the only one what's ever cared what happened to me. Oh, please, ma'am, please!"

"I think it might be a good idea to have a look at where she sleeps," Daniel Horton suggested in a calm, controlled voice. "Right now, it is only my word against hers, although, I do assure you, she is the one who is lying. Still, I . . ."

"I'm not either! Mrs. Eaton learned me not to lie!"

"Be quiet," Miles told her, and such was his tone, she fell silent at once.

"As I was saying, I would feel easier if we could find additional proof," Horton concluded.

"Fine, 'cause there's nothing there," Mathilda insisted, brave even in the face of Wexford's order. "I sleep in Mrs. Eaton's dressing room, and she knows that's true, don't you, ma'am?"

Marion Eaton bowed her head. "I want to believe you, Mathilda. You'll never know how much. But Mr. Horton's account of what he saw cannot be discounted. Please, gentlemen, go and search the dressing room. Mathilda, sit over there against the wall and keep silent until they return. I—I cannot take much more."

The girl did as she was bade. Sarah leaned back in her chair and closed her eyes. She could not bear to look at her sorrowing mother, nor the frightened, yet angry and defiant face of the homely maid.

It seemed a long time, but in reality, it was only a few minutes before the marquis and Daniel Horton returned. Sarah looked only at Miles, and when she saw him tight-lipped, so stern and implacable, she knew they had found the culprit at last.

"So there was something," she said.

He held out a small bottle. "This is a Pocket Luminary. It is all the thing in London now. The wooden splints in it are tipped with sulfur. When struck against a rough surface, they ignite, eliminating the need for flint or steel. It was under her mattress."

"No, that's not mine," Mathilda said, rising and shaking her head in denial. "I never saw that before. *He* put it there! I tell you, it's not mine!"

"You will hold your tongue," the marquis told her. Sarah saw how the girl was shaking, watched the tears running down her face as she twisted her hands in her apron and looked pleadingly to her mistress. Sadly Marion Eaton shook her head before she turned away.

At once, all the fight left the maid. Her shoulders slumped, and she bowed her head. Only an occasional muf-fled sob could be heard instead of her impassioned defense of her innocence.

"We must prosecute," the marquis told them. "The best place for her is in prison. Since she has this compulsion to light fires, she will be a danger to anyone near her, and I could not have that on my conscience."

He looked steadily at Marion Eaton. At last she raised her head and nodded. Everyone knew she could not speak just then.

Carten was summoned and asked to lock the girl away somewhere until morning. After he had taken her from the room, Daniel Horton said regretfully, "I am so sorry I was the one to discover her guilt. It has been most upsetting."

"But just consider how much more upsetting it would have been to wake up some dark night to find your bed on fire," Miles reminded him. He turned to Marion Eaton and added gently, "Yes, it is too bad, and we are all sorry your trust in her was so misplaced, ma'am. But at least we have solved the mystery of the fire in Sarah's dressing room, and now we can all sleep easier."

Mrs. Eaton nodded as she rose. "I would go to bed," she said. "I am afraid I will not be pleasant company tonight."

As Sarah made to come with her, she added, "No, don't come up, dear. I prefer to be alone tonight."

She smiled valiantly, to show she could manage, and left the room. But Sarah watched her from the dining room door. Her mother looked old, as old and defeated as she had before preparations for the school had begun. Hopefully, Sarah thought, she would forget Mathilda Dents quickly. Hopefully the restoration and expansion of the cottage would keep her busy. And perhaps another girl, someone in need of love and care, would come along for her to take under her wing. Sarah prayed it might be so, for she knew that now she was grown and independent, Marion Eaton needed someone else to mother.

The next morning early, when Miles Griffin went to the room where the maid had been locked up for the night, he found the door wide open, and Mathilda Dents gone. He sent for Sarah, for it was not his prerogative to question her servants. But before she could come down, Marion Eaton arrived. She looked exhausted, and the blue circles under her eyes bespoke a sleepless night.

"Mrs. Eaton, you should not have left your bed," he scolded her gently as he came to take her arm. "This unfortunate business has been such a trial for you."

"Yes, but I did not want you and Sarah bullying Carten, when it was not at all his fault," she replied as her daughter, looking less than her usual tidy self, came down the hall to join them. "I made him give me the key to this room, even though he didn't want to. I was the one who set Mathilda free. You see, I could not bear to think of her in prison. Prisons are such horrid places, are they not? And the authorities might well have sentenced her to Bedlam instead. No, no, I could not take a chance on that. She is only a child, and I daresay she has learned her lesson. I gave her my Bible. She has been learning to read, and it will be a comfort to her."

"You let her go," Sarah repeated, afraid to look at the marquis. She was sure he was furious.

"Please don't be cross with me, Sarah. Or you, either, m'lord. I *had* to. I gave her enough money so she could take the stage to London and have enough to live on until she can find a new position. I told her she must never come back. She was still insisting she was innocent, but I would not listen. Indeed, I made her promise she would never light another fire, ever."

"And did she promise you that?" came the marquis's even question.

Marion Eaton looked up at him. "Yes, she did, and I believed her," she said with gentle dignity.

The marquis looked at Sarah over her head, his expression unreadable. He did not like this a bit, but he knew he could do nothing about it unless he followed the girl and hopefully caught her up before she disappeared into the warren of squalid tenements and dark back alleys of the metropolis. And it was probably too late for that. She had several hours head start. Well, he thought, whatever happened now, he had done his best.

Sarah had no idea where the marquis disappeared to later that morning. They had made no plans for the day, and seeing Daniel Horton talking to her head gardener, she went out to join him. She felt vaguely guilty of neglect where the solicitor was concerned, even though she knew, as the marquis had pointed out, she was not responsible for his entertainment.

When she suggested a walk, his face lit up in a warm smile and they set off together at a brisk pace. It was a warm day, and Sarah was glad when they reached the leafy shelter of the woods.

When they came to the little pond Sarah had discovered earlier, they stopped by mutual consent.

"You should keep a boat here," Daniel Horton told her. "I'd wager there are trout in that pond."

As if in response to his remark, a fish jumped, leaving widening ripples on the water's surface, and they both laughed.

"Shall we sit here for a while and enjoy the view?" he asked.

Obediently Sarah sank down on the grassy bank. "It is a lovely spot, isn't it?" she asked idly, as she began to pick some daisies starring the grass near her black skirts.

"It is indeed," he said, staring out across the water. The sun, lighting his blond hair, turned it to silver. Sarah was glad to see his face had regained its normal color from his stay in the country, and the listless, sad demeanor he had sported was no more. Suddenly she felt an urge to tell him her betrothal to the Marquis of Wexford was only a sham. Surely it would not matter if Daniel Horton knew. But something stayed her tongue. Miles had told her it must be their secret, and she was most reluctant to disobey him, even though he could hardly punish her for it. She wondered why she was always attracted to forceful, decisive men. The marquis was certainly one, as were Forrest Blake and Daniel Horton. And then, in a flash of insight, she knew she was drawn to them because they were everything her dear but incompetent, ineffectual father had not been.

"I assume Wexford saw to it that the maid was turned over to the authorities this morning?" her companion asked, recalling her to the present. "I hope it was done before your mother came belowstairs. She was so distraught last evening, and who could blame the dear lady? I will always regret my part in the discovery."

"I forgot you did not know!" Sarah exclaimed, dropping her daisies to put her hands to her face. "He did try to, but he discovered my mother had set her free."

"What?" Horton asked, looking stunned. "She let her *go*?"

When Sarah nodded, he continued, "This is unfortunate.

I am sorry she was so rash. Of course she was sorry for the chit; we all were. But as Wexford so rightly pointed out last evening, she is a dangerous person. Heaven knows how many people will die because she has this compulsion and is now at liberty to indulge it."

"I agree, but you will never convince my mother of that. She says Mathilda promised her never to light a fire again."

He snorted. "And if you believe that, I might be able to interest you in buying a nice bridge that crosses the Thames in London.

"Does she have any idea where the girl has gone?" he asked next.

"To London, she says. She gave her all the money she had, for Mathilda was like another daughter to her. She even gave her her Bible to read for comfort and instruction."

"Your mother is too saintly a person to live in the real world as we know it, Miss Eaton. We must hope London can survive Miss Dent's arrival. It has sustained a number of tragic fires in its history. I suppose we can only hope she does not start another one."

Sarah wondered at his sarcasm, but she forgot it in a moment when he said next, "I must say I was surprised when you announced your betrothal to Wexford. Rather sudden, was it not? Why, only the day before you assured me you had no inclination for marriage."

As Sarah wondered desperately what she was to tell him, he chuckled a little. "Swept you off your feet, did he? Refused to take no for an answer? Well, he's a fascinating fellow, and he is a lord. Oh, you don't have to answer. It is really none of my business, except I am fond of you, as fond as I would have been of any sister."

"You are kind, sir," she managed to get out.

"It is a shame the wedding must be delayed until your year of mourning is over. That will be next March I believe?"

"Early April," Sarah corrected him.

"I hope the marquis, when he takes over your lands and

investments, all your vast wealth, will think me suitable to continue as steward," he continued, sounding humble.

Sarah could only nod. She was positively aching to tell him that it was not true, and he would certainly remain her man of business when Wexford went his merry way, but she could not.

She was relieved when he changed the subject by calling her attention to a pair of fox cubs, come to the water's edge on the opposite side of the pond for a drink this warm summer afternoon.

Chapter 18

Miles Griffin returned to the Hall late that afternoon. He had spent the day searching for Mathilda Dents, even though he was sure she was shrewd enough to stay away from the nearest staging inn. If she had gone there, he would have found her easily, and she had enough animal cunning to know that. But although he had traveled many a dusty road, asked any number of people if they had seen her, he had no luck at all. She had disappeared, leaving no trace.

This is a bad business, he thought as he walked up to the house after Hal Wells had taken charge of his tired horse. And however Christian and kind Mrs. Eaton was, in this instance she had been wrong. The girl should not have been freed to continue her mischief. Someday soon, a lot of innocent people were going to suffer for it.

There was no one about in any of the ground-floor rooms. He paused in the drawing room for a moment, to exchange a few words with the workmen, before he went to the terrace doors and looked out over the garden.

Sarah was there, some distance from the house. He saw she was alone, and, eager for her company, he went out to join her. As he walked toward her, he noticed a particularly lovely rose. It was a delicate peach color with a golden heart, and thinking it might please her, he bent to pluck it. As he did so, a shot rang out, and instinctively, he dropped to the ground, his heart beating at trip-hammer pace.

"Get down, Sarah," he called.

He dared not raise his head to see if she obeyed. Lying there on the soft grass, he wondered where the gardeners

were, before he realized they had probably stopped work
for the day. He listened, but there wasn't a sound anywhere. Even the birds, no doubt startled by the loud noise
the firearm had made, were quiet.

"Are you all right?" Sarah asked, and he hoped she was
safely down and out of sight.

"Yes, don't move," he told her. "I cannot be sure whoever fired that shot has gone away."

Thinking how close a call he had had, for he had felt the
bullet humming over his head, he thanked whatever powers
there be he had thought to pick that rose. He looked for it
where he had tossed it as he went down and saw it was
ruined now, its stem snapped. Still, it had saved his life, for
he did not doubt whoever had fired the shot had intended to
kill him.

Who? he asked himself. Who would do such a thing?
And why? He immediately discarded the notion it could be
an angry Mathilda Dents, returned to seek revenge. No, for
he was sure the maid could not be the expert shot who had
just fired. He thought hard. The shot had come from the left
boundary of the wall that surrounded the gardens. As far as
he knew there was nothing beyond but an orchard and the
gardening sheds. Still, he knew there were many arched
openings in the wall, spaced at regular intervals for easy ac-
cess. The gardeners used them all the time to bring in their
wheelbarrows and implements.

"I say, m'lord, are you all right?" he heard Daniel Horton
call, and he turned his head to see the man hurrying toward
him from the house.

He waited for a moment, but when no one fired at the solicitor, he got cautiously to his feet. His eyes scanned the
left wall. There was no movement there, no sign of any in-
truder.

"Are you injured, m'lord?" Horton panted as he came to
his side.

"Fortunately I am not. But not for someone's want of
trying," Miles said dryly. "Someone fired a shot a few minutes ago. Did you by any chance hear it, sir?"

Horton shook his head. "No. I must admit I was dozing

over today's paper in the library until just a moment ago. It was only by chance I glanced out and saw you sprawled here. That was a shock I'd sooner forget."

"And I," Miles said absently, still searching the gardens. It was then he remembered Sarah, and he called to her to get up, for it was quite safe now.

Some distance away, her wary head peeked up over a bed of brilliantly colored dahlias. The two men went to her side.

"What on earth?" she asked, taking the hand Miles extended to help her up. "Who would do such a thing?"

Miles saw she was shaking, and he put his arm around her to pull her close. "It's all right now, my dear," he told her softly. "There's nothing to worry about now."

"I was so frightened for you," she whispered. Both of them had forgotten Daniel Horton. It was as if he were not even there. Miles hugged her closer, wondering at the lump in his throat.

"But who do you suppose fired the shot?" she persisted, content to nestle in the safety of his arm.

"I've no idea, and Mr. Horton never even heard it," he told her. "But I'm afraid we shall have to discard any notion our problems at Woodingham Hall are over."

"This terrible house!" she exclaimed. "There has been nothing but trouble here ever since I arrived. Oh, I know you told me it isn't the Hall's fault, Miles, and deep down I suspect you are right, but I cannot conquer this helpless feeling I have. It seems as if we are caught in a web we cannot escape. And something we have no power to prevent, something dreadful, is going to happen."

The two men stared at her before they looked up at the Hall beyond. Its bulk was dark against the pale blue of the sky. Miles had never thought it a particularly handsome building with its deeply recessed narrow windows, its cold gray stone exterior, but to him it was just a structure. He could not understand this antipathy Sarah had for it. How could it threaten her?

He whirled, putting Sarah behind him as another shot

rang out some distance away. Beside him, Daniel Horton looked wildly around.

"Go into the house, Sarah," Miles ordered. "Stay away from the windows."

"No," she said, shaking her head. "You mustn't go out there. It's not safe."

"Horton and I will go together," he told her. "There's nothing to worry about now. Whoever just fired is not the man who shot earlier. I'd wager on that. Go on now, there's a good girl."

He turned her about and gave her a little push before he set off quickly in the direction the shot had come from.

"He'll be all right," Daniel Horton reassured Sarah. "I'll look out for him."

Sarah watched the two until they went through one of the archways and disappeared into the orchard beyond. Only then did she make her way back to the Hall.

The grass under the apple trees had been scythed recently, and the two made good time. At the end of the orchard, there was a large field planted to wheat. As Miles paused to consider which direction he should take, a hunting dog burst out of the tall wheat and ran to them, tail wagging madly. Its long pink tongue hung out of its mouth as it panted from exertion.

Horton bent to pat it. "Now, where have you come from?" he asked the dog. "And do you have a master somewhere about, I wonder?"

"Ruddy, where are you, Ruddy? Blast that animal! Come here, boy," a voice called from somewhere across the field.

"How opportune. Now Ruddy can lead the way," Miles said as the dog turned to run back the way it had come.

Several minutes later, the two pushed aside the last of the wheat and found themselves face-to-face with one of the Fisher twins. The young man beamed at them.

"I say, didn't know anyone was about," he said. Miles noted he was holding a handsome flintlock musket pointing down as was correct when not actually preparing to shoot.

"Saw you the other day, didn't I, sir? Mr. Horton, ain't it?" the young man asked. "Sit, Ruddy!" he added as the dog pranced about his legs. "He's not much of a hunting dog yet, but I've great hopes of him," he confided.

"Who are you?" the marquis asked. "And why are you trespassing on Miss Eaton's property?"

"Why, I'm Nelson Fisher, Sir Harold's grandson," he explained. "As to why I'm here, well, I suppose it is a bit brash of me when I don't have the lady's permission, but the old 'un, Jonah Eaton, let us hunt here anytime we liked. *He* didn't hunt, heaven knows. I say, you don't think I've made a botch of it, do you? Will she be angry? I mean it's not as if I were an ordinary poacher, y'know. Neighbors . . . all that."

"Tell us, is your twin somewhere about?" Daniel Horton asked.

"No, he had to run an errand for Grandfather in Ipswich today, so I came out alone. Fancied a rabbit pie, and I thought I might be able to bag an early duck or two. Not that Ruddy is very good about fetching them yet. Or anything else," he added with a rueful glance at his dog, who was now stretched out at his feet, yawning in complete indifference to this less than glowing assessment of his accomplishments.

"Did you hear anyone else shooting today?" Miles asked.

Nelson Fisher nodded. "Surely did," he said. "And since I didn't fancy being mistaken for a deer, I started for home."

"You didn't see whoever it was? Near the garden or in the orchard?" the marquis persisted.

"Can't say I did. I wasn't all that close, and to tell the truth, I was more interested in getting my game than wondering who the chap might be."

"I don't see any game," Miles persisted.

Fisher reddened. "'Fraid I didn't bag any," he said sheepishly. "Bad luck, what?"

"I suggest you stay away from Miss Eaton's land, Mr. Fisher," Miles told him. "She may not care for strangers wandering about on it."

"Not a stranger, sir! Met her t'other day. Neighbor, don't

you know? And hope to be a great deal more." He winked at them and grinned.

Daniel Horton cleared his throat. "Allow me to introduce the Marquis of Wexford, Mr. Fisher," he said, his voice expressionless. "He is Miss Eaton's fiancé."

"Never say so!" Fisher exclaimed, before he was quick to add, "Must forgive me . . . heartiest congratulations, m'lord . . . well done, er, I mean . . ."

Shortly thereafter, a dejected Nelson Fisher headed homeward to the unenviable task of acquainting his grandfather with the news the wealthy Miss Eaton was already spoken for. Horton and the marquis set out for the Hall.

"Somehow I cannot see that young man as the marksman," Horton remarked. "It does not seem at all his style."

"You wouldn't think so, would you?" Miles agreed. "Still, he was extraordinarily disappointed Sarah was no longer on the Marriage Mart, wasn't he? But if he disposed of me, that problem would be solved."

"Surely he didn't even know that until I told him," Horton protested. "Unless you think him an expert actor, m'lord? I must admit he does not seem the type.

"I've no doubt he'll have to endure a lecture from the old general about letting someone else nip in before him, but shoot to kill? No, no, sir. If he is guilty, I am sure it was only an accident. But we'll never know, for he'll not admit to it."

Sarah was pacing up and down the terrace when they came back to the Hall. Horton excused himself at once, and wisely, Miles did not reprimand her for ignoring his direct order to wait indoors. It was getting harder and harder for him to remember she was not his to order about for her own good.

"What did you find?" she asked, coming to stand close.

"Only your neighbor, one of the Fisher twins, out with his dog for some sport."

"Do you think he shot at you? Oh, Miles, how dreadful."

"No, of course he didn't. He has very little wit and not a mean bone in his body from what I can tell. His grandfather may regret our engagement, but as for the boy himself, I don't think it matters to him one way or the other."

"Thank you," she said coolly. "It is so good to know what you think of my charms, sir."

His smile was a little forced. "No, whoever took that shot at me was not Nelson Fisher. That person was serious. He wanted me dead. And if I had not stooped to pick you a rose, I would have been."

Her expression brightened a little. "But won't they try again?" she said after a minute. "Oh, I am so frightened."

"I intend to go armed from now on," he said. "And I'll take Hal Wells with me whenever I leave the Hall. He'll be armed as well. But come, we must dress for dinner."

"Is there any way we can keep what happened from my mother?" Sarah asked as he held one of the terrace doors for her. "She is so very sad about Mathilda's departure. I don't want her to hear any more bad news."

"I'll have a word with Horton, tell him to keep mum about it," Miles promised as they moved to the foyer. A stiff Dennis Carten bowed to them before he disappeared to the back hall.

"I'd give a great deal to know if he was on duty all afternoon," Miles said softly.

"Do you think he did it?" Sarah whispered back.

"I am sure any number of people dislike me for one reason or another, but who else hates me? Of course there is the handsome curate. You do remember how furious he was when he learned of our betrothal."

"But was he furious enough to commit murder? It seems unlikely."

She paused, frowning a little. The marquis had the strangest urge to smooth that frown away with one gentle finger.

"Is it possible it might be someone we have not even suspected?" she asked slowly. "A stranger?"

He did not threat her suggestion lightly. "All things are possible, of course. But if it is a stranger, he has to be a maniac."

"Considering the way Mrs. Quigley died, that is more than likely," Sarah said with a shudder.

"This conversation becomes gruesome, and it is getting late," Miles said as they reached the stairs. "By the way, Sarah, it might be a good idea to ask Mr. Blake to dinner tomorrow. I would like to question him about his whereabouts today, and I can do so over the port."

"What if he won't come?" Sarah asked as they climbed the stairs side by side.

"Oh, I imagine he will find a way to swallow his distaste and accept. He will not want to lose your patronage. Mark my words, the handsome curate will come in all smiles and compliments."

"What hypocrites men are," Sarah said indignantly. Miles wisely refrained from making any answering remark.

Dinner that evening was a quiet affair. Sarah felt she had seldom worked harder to make everything appear as normal. Mrs. Eaton was still depressed, and Wexford preoccupied, so it was up to her and Mr. Horton to maintain some semblance of normality.

Horton excused himself immediately after dinner, as had become his wont. Tonight he claimed the afternoon post had brought a number of letters he must attend to at once.

Miles finished his port before he went out on the terrace to enjoy a cigar. He did not do so expecting Carten and the whisperer to be so accommodating again; he only wanted to be alone to consider. As he paced the length of the terrace and back, he thought this entire business was becoming not only perplexing but bizarre. And he was sure all of it revolved around Sarah Eaton. She was at the center of the vortex, drawing everyone and everything to her. And that had to be because she was the heiress. Still, it had been Mrs. Quigley who had been poisoned, and he himself who had been fired at. At least the mystery of who had started the fire had been solved. Be thankful for even small blessings, he reminded himself.

But it was entirely possible Mrs. Quigley's death had nothing whatsoever to do with Woodingham Hall. It might be a completely separate thing. The woman had been abrasive and difficult. Her enemies were probably legion.

As he turned once more at the balustrade, he heard a whisper of sound, and his eyes grew keen as he tried to pierce the blackness around him. There was a little more moonlight tonight, but hardly enough to show him the gardens plainly. He felt vaguely uneasy, and he wondered if coming out here had been the smartest thing to do.

Sarah must have felt the same way, for she came through the terrace doors just then and hurried to his side.

"You promised you would not come outside alone," she scolded. "Yet here I find you not far from where the shot was fired. And if you have a pistol in that exceedingly well-fitting evening suit, sir, I cannot imagine where you keep it."

Miles smiled down at her as he tossed his cigar into the gardens. "Would you care to search for it, Sarah?" he teased.

She looked shocked for only a moment. Then she put her arms around him. Surprised, for he had not expected her to accept his challenge, Miles stood very still. Her hands went over his back to his waist, where they lingered before they crept up his chest to his shoulders. "I knew you weren't carrying one," she said in a little voice.

Miles stared down at her. Her eyes were half closed, her lips parted.

He groaned inwardly, remembering his promise that there would be no lovemaking. It was obvious Sarah had no idea how she was affecting him.

What am I doing? Sarah thought wildly. How could I behave so boldly? And what must Miles be thinking of me? Still, something she had no control over kept her from stepping back and returning the scene to normalcy.

Her hands moved with a will of their own to take his face between them. Standing on tiptoe, she pulled that face down to hers, her eyes intent.

At the first contact of her soft lips, Miles lost his restraint to gather her close in his arms. Those lips opened under his seeking ones, moving and caressing his in a way that made him dizzy. And to his great surprise, she pressed closer still, locked against him the entire length of their bodies. Even his growing tumidity did not frighten her away. And this was Sarah Eaton, the prim little Methodist? Unbelievable! She was all fire and passion in his arms. He kissed her eyes, her throat, and she buried her hands in his hair and moaned her delight.

When reluctantly he raised his head at last, he found it difficult to speak. In the faint moonlight, he could just make out the little smile she wore.

"So that is what it is like to be held in a man's arms and kissed," she said. "What a very good thing it is girls do not learn how marvelous it is until they are betrothed."

She opened her eyes then, startled back to reality. "Oh, I did not mean, that is, you must not think . . . oh, dear. I did not kiss you to entrap you, m'lord," she said with dignity as she stepped back, then back again while he stalked her. He was as intent on his prey as any tiger hunting his supper.

"Entrap me?" he asked in a husky voice. "No, no, rather you have bewitched, bedazzled, and beguiled me, love. There is one thing, though," he added as she backed into the balustrade at the other end of the terrace and he took her in his arms again.

"Yes?" she asked breathlessly.

"I am afraid I have the gravest doubts we are going to be able to wait for an April wedding," he told her as his fingertips traced her lips, then whispered their way up her jawline to begin to loosen the pins in her hair.

She laughed as she buried her face in his cravat. "But don't you think if we both put our minds to it, we might be able to, er, arrange something?" she asked demurely.

The two of them stayed on the terrace for some time, and when they finally went inside, arms around each other, the man who had been watching them put the pistol he was holding back in his pocket. He was below the terrace in the dark garden, where he had had a perfect view of the marquis. The gleaming white linen of his shirt and cravat had made a perfect target, even in the faint moonlight. He had been ready to fire when Miss Eaton had come out. And then, of course, he had had no shot, for she had been as close to the man as his own skin from then on.

Another missed opportunity. He grimaced in disgust as he silently left the garden. But it didn't matter. Wexford would be dead soon. There was plenty of time left.

Chapter 19

The next morning, Forrest Blake responded to Sarah's invitation immediately, sending back word with the groom who had delivered it, he would be delighted to dine at the Hall that evening. Once the task had been accomplished, Sarah and Miles, accompanied by Hal Wells, went to Ipswich to shop. It was late afternoon when they reached the Hall again, and Sarah ran up to her mother's room immediately, to report on her purchases. She had brought a book on educating the young with her, thinking to cheer Marion Eaton by giving her thoughts a new direction. As she had hoped, her mother threw off her air of sad distraction, and began to leaf through the pages eagerly.

Alone in her room later, Sarah wondered whether it had been the fact Miles Griffin was accompanied that day, or he had left Woodingham Hall that had prevented his unknown assailant from trying again. She did not know. She only knew it was hard, loving him as she knew she did now, to think of such things. That he might be shot—killed—was enough to start a surge of panic rising in her breast. He had to live, for she would never be happy living without him.

So, even though she longed to be alone with him, they must continue to have Hal Wells accompany them whenever they left the Hall. Today, with the groom right behind them on the perch, they had not been able to talk openly. Only their eyes had spoken, sometimes so fervently, Sarah had felt herself blushing. She could tell Miles was as deeply in love as she was herself, while at the same time bemused, as if he were wondering what on earth had happened to him. She smiled to herself in the mirror, the same smile women have employed in like situations since time's beginning. But to think she had discarded her prim modesty and reserve like an old coat she had outgrown and could not wait to throw away was still unbelievable to her. That she had been so eager and passionate; that she looked forward to being that way again, just as soon as it could be contrived—what had he done to her?

When she thought of all the things she and Miles had to learn about each other, the life they would share, the love-making they would enjoy, she was so ecstatic she felt if she spread her arms she would be able to fly. And as for that April wedding, well, she was sure she could convince her mother a year of mourning was an outdated custom, and her father would have wanted her to marry and be happy as soon as possible. Well, at least by early December, she amended. That was two thirds of a year.

Remembering again how bold she had been the evening before, how she had as much as made him kiss her, she blushed again. But somehow, as she seemed to sense so many things about Miles, she had known he wanted her as much as she wanted him. She was looking forward to re-peating the kiss and a dozen more like it tonight.

Of course there was still the evening to endure. She sighed then. She had almost forgotten dinner with a sure to be seething, resentful Forrest Blake.

But Sarah was to discover he was no such thing. Instead, he was all smiles and compliments, just as Miles had pre-dicted. He even made dinnertime a happier occasion, draw-ing Marion Eaton out to discuss her plans for the school, asking questions of Daniel Horton about the City, congratu-lating the marquis on his good fortune, and telling Sarah she was sure to grace the title of marchioness as it had sel-dom been graced before. Sarah was careful not to look at Miles when he said this. She was sure if she did the two of them would disgrace themselves by dissolving in laughter.

It seemed forever to Sarah before she was alone with Miles at last, for even after the curate had bowed himself away, Marion Eaton and Daniel Horton lingered.

The door had hardly closed behind them before Miles

had her in his arms. "It's been so long," she gasped when he stopped kissing her for a minute.

"An age at least," he muttered, kissing the soft skin above the neckline of her gown. "You have the most beautiful skin. I couldn't take my eyes off it all evening."

Sarah cradled his head against her breast, and bent to kiss the top of it. "What will you do when I can wear more fashionable clothes, then?" she asked. "This is such a modest gown . . . now, Miles, don't! What if someone should come in?"

His hand stilled for only a moment before it slipped under her gown to caress her breasts. As he began to pull the gown off her shoulders, he said simply, "They wouldn't dare. Surely they know I'm making love to you."

Sarah wiggled away from him. "No, my dear, we must not. Not now. There are so many things we must discuss." She paused, then added, "Have you thought of anyone who might have been your assailant?"

Frowning, he straightened and moved away from her as if a little distance between them would make it easier for him to get control of himself. "I've thought about it, yes, but I've come to no conclusions. However, I am almost sure Mrs. Quigley's death has no connection with either the fire or the scare yesterday.

"Incidentally, what did you make of the handsome curate's bragging about his hunting prowess at dinner?"

"I was shocked. But would he make such a point of how accurate a shot he is, if he were the guilty one? And he did say he had spent all yesterday afternoon in his study at the manse."

"Who can vouch for him? He also said he had asked not to be disturbed, for he was writing this week's sermon. The manse is not that far from your gardens. He could have approached them by way of the woods, and no one would have seen him. Besides, he could have mentioned his skill as a ploy to mislead us."

Miles ran an impatient hand through his hair. "Damn it, Sarah, there are any number of ways everything that has happened could be twisted. Which one of them therefore can we believe?"

"Sometimes I'm afraid this will never be over," she confided. "I've even considered dismissing the servants, closing the Hall—even selling it—going somewhere else."

"You still feel so strongly the evil is only here in this house?" he asked. "You don't think it might follow you wherever you went?"

"Can it be you think, as I have come to, that all these things are happening to me because I inherited my grandfather's fortune?" she asked, sliding along the sofa into his arms. "Hold me, Miles, please hold me. I am so frightened, for you, for me—for both of us."

"I won't let anything happen to you, darling," he told her as he tipped up her chin. "You are too precious to me. And I'll take good care nothing happens to me, either. We have a lifetime to share together."

He kissed her then, a kiss that demanded every bit of passion she was able to give him. In his arms, Sarah was finally able to forget the darkness she felt coming closer to her with every passing day.

The next morning, when Sarah was closeted with Daniel Horton discussing some business matters, Miles invited Marion Eaton to join him for a spin in his phaeton. He knew she had not ordered the dogcart since her maid had fled the Hall, and he hoped a drive at a spanking pace would bring some color back to her cheeks. He did not think to turn her mind from her absent maid; he knew it was too soon for that, indeed, he was quite prepared to listen to her talk about the girl, if that was what she cared to do. True to his promise to Sarah, he had his groom accompany them.

For a while, Marion Eaton did talk about Mathilda. "Oh, I know Sarah never liked her, nor, I imagine, did you yourself, m'lord," she said gently. When he would have denied it, she put her hand on his sleeve in protest.

"There now, there is no need to dissemble with me, sir. I

know very well Mathilda was not appealing. It was for that very reason she was important to me."

When he inquired why that might be, she added, "It is the unattractive, unlikable people in the world who need to be treasured. Everyone can love a pretty little girl with golden curls and a charming smile. But that child doesn't need everyone's love. The one people turn away from, sneer at, ignore; now there is where love should be lavished. I have seen it any number of times. And when someone begins to care about these children, show them they are important and valuable, too, why, then they blossom. They even begin to be able to return affection, something they were incapable of before. Unfortunately, there is only a short period of time when they can be reached, and a definite point beyond which they cannot be redeemed. That is when they become too embittered, too inured to indifference and distaste to be saved. I pray every day Mathilda will remember my love and concern for her. That she will not slip back once again into the state in which I found her.

"But heavens, forgive me, m'lord. I did not mean to preach you a sermon.

"Oh, there is the cottage ahead. Would it be possible to stop for a bit, m'lord? The workmen finished the addition last week, but I have not felt like inspecting it till now."

Relieved she had changed the subject, for he was nowhere near as sure as she appeared to be, that people like Mathilda Dents could ever be lovable, he halted the team. While his groom ran to hold the bridles, he helped his companion down.

The gate to the cottage screeched just as it always did.

"I wonder the workmen didn't oil that for you," Miles remarked as he shut it behind them.

She smiled. "Sarah hated that gate from the time she was a child. She said it sounded like an old witch, cackling at her. But we could never fix it for long, no matter what we did. I thought of it every now and then in India, and smiled."

She paused to look around the small yard. The gardens

had been weeded, and the place looked much more respectable.

"It was strange," she mused, as if to herself. "The day we stopped here soon after we arrived in Woodingham, Sarah would not even step over the threshold. She seemed frightened, and I wondered why. But she was probably just mourning her father."

She sighed a little before she started up the path again. She was reaching for the key above the frame when Miles saw the door was slightly ajar. Pushing it open, he stepped inside and halted abruptly. He was glad he had gone first, his tall frame successfully shielding the interior from the fragile lady hovering behind him.

He turned then and put his hands on her arms, still hiding the sight from her. "What is it? What is wrong? And why are there so many flies?" she asked, trying to twist around him so she could see.

"No, come away, ma'am," he said kindly but firmly. "This is no place for you now."

When she made no move to go, he picked her up under the elbows and turned her about, then put an arm around her to help her back to the rig.

"But what is wrong in there, m'lord? You must tell me or I shall imagine the most dreadful things!" she implored.

"I will tell you just as soon as I return to the Hall, I promise," he said. "Hal, take Mrs. Eaton back as quickly as you can, then drive to Sir Harold Fisher's home and ask him to come immediately. I'll wait here for him."

"Aye, sir. Have a care for yourself," Wells reminded him as he climbed to the driver's place. Beside him, a pale Marion Eaton huddled on the seat. It was as if she suddenly knew what the cottage held, knew and yet could not bear to face it.

The marquis watched until the phaeton was out of sight before he entered the cottage again. His face hardened as he did so, and he went past the body sprawled on the floor to some cloths the workmen had left behind. He spread them carefully over Mathilda Dents's half-nude body, her discolored face, and protruding tongue—and the cord around her neck that had been used to strangle her.

It was a long time later before he returned to the Hall, for he wanted to see to the disposition of the body before he left. He arranged for it to be placed in a coffin, and that coffin nailed shut before it was brought up to the Hall, as soon as Sir Harold was satisfied death had occurred yesterday by strangulation, after the girl had been sexually assaulted.

Carten told him Mrs. Eaton was in her room, eyeing him uneasily as he did so.

"Where is her daughter?" Miles asked next through lips that were stiff and pale.

"Miss Eaton is still in the library with Mr. Horton," Carten said.

"Tell her to come upstairs as soon as she can. Her mother is going to need her," Miles said over his shoulder.

He found Marion Eaton sitting in a chair by the window. Her needlepoint was in her lap, but she was not working on it. As he came and knelt at her feet, tears began to fall down her white cheeks.

"It was Mathilda in the cottage, wasn't it?" she whispered. "She never did go to London, did she?"

"No, she must have decided she could not bear to leave you, ma'am. No doubt she thought you would come to the cottage soon, and she could plead with you to keep her near," Miles told her, keeping a tight rein on his own emotions.

"She is dead? Murdered?"

"Yes."

She sighed and wiped her cheeks with the backs of both her hands, one after the other. "I suspected as much when you would not let me look. I have been praying for her. Please don't tell me about it. I don't want to know how she died."

He held out the book he carried then. "Is this your Bible, ma'am? I found it near her, and I thought you might like to have it back."

As she looked at it, something seemed to snap inside Marion Eaton, and she lost her tight composure and began to wail. Quickly Miles rose and gathered her up into his arms. Sitting down in the chair she had used, he held her close, her head cradled on his chest, and he rocked her just as he would have rocked a small child, lost or in pain.

They were still together like that when Sarah found them a few minutes later.

Chapter 20

That afternoon, Woodingham Hall was very quiet. Everyone knew about Mathilda's death by now, and not only the other maids, but the footmen as well exchanged whispered confidences while looking over their shoulders as they did so. It was almost as if they were afraid they might bring this curse down upon themselves somehow by talking about it.

When Marion Eaton could not be quieted, Sarah had had to summon the doctor. He had given the distraught woman a sedative for the shock, and ordered her put to bed. Sarah sat beside her, holding her hand tightly until she fell asleep. Mrs. Bonnet relieved her then, whispering Miss Eaton was not to worry about her mother, for she would not leave her.

Sarah went looking for Miles only to discover a pale Daniel Horton in the library, holding a journal he was not even bothering to pretend to read.

"Miss Eaton, are you all right?" he asked, getting to his feet quickly to come to her. "What a terrible thing."

"Yes, it is awful isn't it?" Sarah agreed. "I never liked the girl, but I would not wish such a ghastly end for anyone."

"Have the authorities any idea who did it?" he asked, but Sarah could only shake her head before she excused herself.

She found Miles in the drawing room. As soon as they had clung together for comfort, she begged him to tell her what Sir Harold had decided.

He smoothed her hair back. "What anyone would. The girl was new here. She had no enemies. He believes it must have been a tramp who just happened to be passing through the area. You know the roads are thick with laborers now, hoping to find work bringing in the harvest. And she was alone in the cottage, unprotected."

He stared over her shoulder, and from his grim look, Sarah knew he was reliving the scene in the cottage.

"Yes, it could have happened that way," he added slowly.

"But you don't believe that, do you?" she said, her hands tightening on his arms.

He seemed to have to force himself to focus on her face. "No, I don't," he said. "Oh, I have no other theory for what happened. It is just an unknown rapist and murderer seems too simple a solution. Yet I would have come to the same conclusion if all these other things had not been occurring lately.

"But if she was not killed randomly, why was she killed at all? What had homely little Mathilda Dents to do with all this? Why was she a danger to the killer?"

Sarah's hands tightened still more, but he did not notice. "Yes, we have never thought of it that way," she said eagerly. "Perhaps even Mrs. Quigley was poisoned because she knew something the killer did not want exposed. Remember, Miles, how she said there were things she knew about the Hall that I wouldn't want revealed? Maybe that knowledge made her death inevitable."

"I believe you've hit on something," he said, his dark eyes intent. "But why then, if we are assuming the two were killed because they were dangerous, did he try to shoot me? I don't know anything that would implicate him. God knows, I wish I did."

Sarah let him go to take a turn about the room. Coming back, she said, "There has to be something, perhaps something you know but don't yet see as a threat. Think, Miles, think."

Then she said quickly, "As if my ordering you to do so will produce answers. I shall go away and leave you alone. But please, my dear, come and tell me if anything occurs to you. Promise?"

Miles nodded and threw himself down in one of the newly upholstered chairs as she left. The drawing room was a lovely place now, elegant and bright with its blue and gold and white decorating scheme. Still, the way the marquis felt, it might just as well been its old depressing shades of brown.

It was well over an hour later before he went to find Sarah. She was just coming out of her mother's room after checking to see she still slept peacefully.

"You have thought of something?" she asked eagerly as she shut the door.

"I don't know. It might not be so. But I must go up to London tomorrow before I can be sure."

Sarah searched his grim face. "London?" she repeated. "Oh, Miles, must you leave me?"

He took her hands in his. "I would never do so if I thought you were in the slightest danger," he told her. "But if what I believe is correct, that is far from the case. Indeed, you are the safest person at Woodingham Hall."

When he saw she still looked distraught, he added, "I know how you have been fretting about me. Just think how safe I will be, once I am away from here."

"There is that to say for it," she said reluctantly. "Will you be gone long?"

"Trust me to be as quick as I can. Two or three days, no more. It all depends on whether the information I seek can be easily obtained."

"You are being very mysterious," Sarah complained as they went down the stairs side by side. "Why can't you tell me who it is you suspect? And what this information is?"

"I am not trying to be difficult, Sarah. But neither can I accuse anyone when they might not be guilty. And then there is the matter of proof. You see my dilemma. There is only the merest chance what I suspect might be true."

"Of course," she said. "I did not mean to . . . but, yes, I *did* mean to pry. Oh, Miles I do so hope what you find will end all this for good."

He shut the door of the morning room behind them and took her in his arms. "I wish we could leave the Hall right now," he said. "I wish we could find some place to be alone for the rest of the day." He smiled down at her ruefully then. "But it is probably just as well for your continued virtue, ma'am, we cannot. I can promise you a great many things, and keep those promises, but I cannot guarantee I would be able to control myself in such a situation."

As he bent to kiss her, she whispered. "Who said anything about wanting you to?"

By evening, Marion Eaton had awakened from her drugged sleep, and if still in great distress, at least she was seemingly resigned to her maid's death. Still, she had not been hungry and Sarah did not press her to get up for dinner. Instead she ordered a tray of delicacies, hoping to tempt her to eat something before she went down to dinner herself.

It was a subdued affair that evening, which Sarah did not even try to overcome. Both she and Miles, Daniel Horton as well, were sunk in their own peculiar apathy. Sarah tried not to stare at Miles too often, although she was already feeling sad and he had not even left her yet.

Their leave-taking, when they were finally alone, was long and tender. And when Sarah came down the next morning, she discovered the marquis and his groom had left at dawn. Mr. Rogers remained at the Hall, and somehow that made her feel a great deal less bereft, as if this little connection to Miles kept him closer than he was, when with every mile he traveled he was getting farther and farther away from her.

Mr. Horton was already at breakfast, and he rose to hold her chair while Dennis Carten filled a plate for her.

"I understand the marquis has gone to London?" Horton asked as Sarah poured herself a cup of tea.

"Yes, he left early," she said.

"You will miss him. I trust he will not find it necessary to be gone long?" Horton persisted.

"I don't believe so," she said, trying to smile in the face of his sober expression. "It is just a small matter of some estate business in Kent he said he has neglected for too long."

He nodded, and she wondered why she had lied to him, and about such a simple thing as well.

"Of course, I myself must be thinking of returning to town shortly," her companion said as he cut his ham. "I have imposed on your hospitality for much too long, Miss Eaton, and I have other matters that await my attention. But, I hesitated to leave while so many dire things were happening. And if the justice had not determined your mother's maid was killed by a vagabond, I would not be thinking of it now. Still, just to be on the safe side, I beg you not to go out alone."

As Sarah assured him she would not do so, she realized she could not ask him to remain. He had been here for quite a while, and she could not expect him to place her interests above all the others he was responsible for.

"And your mother? How is she faring this morning?"

"She seems much the same," Sarah said with a little frown, all her appetite for her breakfast gone. "I am afraid Mathilda's murder has affected her greatly. And as unappealing as I found the girl, my mother was very close to her. I have not seen her so distraught since my father died."

"It is entirely too bad," Horton said. "I do hope the murder will not give her a distaste for the cottage, or that the villagers will take it in their heads to stay away from the school because of it. You know how superstitious country folk can be."

"That possibility never occurred to me," Sarah admitted.

"No reason why it should, so much as you have had on your mind lately, dear lady," he told her. Laying his napkin beside his plate, he rose and bowed. "I'll leave you to enjoy your meal while I take a brisk walk before I settle down to the morning post. Be sure to summon me if there is anything at all I can do for you, or your dear mother."

Sarah thanked him absently, and a moment later she was alone with her butler. It was not a happy situation for her, thinking she might well be alone with the murderer. As she stirred sugar in her tea, she reminded herself Miles had assured her she would be safe. And even if Carten was the killer, he could hardly slay her in her own breakfast room and hope to get away with it. Still, she had to admit she was glad when he went away.

She remained at the table for some time, toying with her breakfast and drinking several bracing cups of tea. And as she did so, she thought hard about everything she knew. Miles had announced he was going to London right after he had asked how Mathilda Dents could possibly be a danger to the killer.

Suddenly she lowered her teacup, her hand shaking so badly it clattered noisily against the saucer. Mr. Horton had accused the maid of trying to start a fire near the gardeners' sheds. She had denied it vehemently. Was it possible he had done so to make sure she left the Hall and never came back? And then when he had found out somehow she had only gone as far as the cottage, he had felt he had to kill her?

But why would he have done that? Could Mathilda have seen something that would put him in jeopardy? From what? Sarah shook her head. Surely this was a ridiculous line of reasoning. To even think the honorable, universally admired Daniel Horton of Horton, Horton & Gavin had murdered anyone was insane. Besides, there was the Pocket Luminary Miles had found under Mathilda's mattress. But that could easily have been put there sometime when both she and Marion Eaton were out, she realized. Everyone knew they spent every pleasant afternoon driving the dog-cart, and often stopping at the cottage. And there were all those walks Mr. Horton was so fond of taking, all those times he drove out to see her agent. After he learned Marion Eaton had freed Mathilda, might he not have stopped at the cottage and found her there? Sarah suddenly remembered how stunned and amazed the maid had been when she had first been accused of trying to start a fire; perhaps she had not been acting?

She shook her head. No, what she was thinking had to be wrong.

But even knowing that, she continued to probe it, much the way a dog attacks a meaty bone. Daniel Horton had been here when everything had occurred. Except for the

fire in my dressing room, she amended, glad to be able to
find something he could not have done.

But he could have killed Mathilda Dents. And he could
have poisoned Mrs. Quigley because she, too, knew something dangerous to him, although what that could be, Sarah
had no idea. But why would he have tried to kill Miles? Besides, Miles had said he had come running out of the house
shortly after the shot had been fired, and she could vouch
for that herself, crouched as she had been behind the
dahlias. No, she thought, taking a deep, reassuring breath.
He couldn't have done it. Furthermore, he had no reason.
He wasn't jealous of Miles, for he had never tried to play
the lover with her, even when she had as much as invited
him to do so. No, he had smiled and wished them well.

But so had Forrest Blake, Sarah reminded herself, and he
was a hypocrite if she had ever met one. Might not Mr.
Horton be one as well? For if he were guilty, he would certainly be careful to behave in a way that was entirely normal.

Reluctantly she decided there was nothing for it but to
add him to the list of possible suspects. Carten, Blake—
Horton. It had to be one of them.

There was a little knock on the door, and Betsy Borden
came in. To Sarah's surprise, she was dressing for traveling.

"I'm that sorry, Miss Eaton, indeed I am, but I can't stay
here another minute," she began, twisting the strings of her
reticule in her hands and not meeting Sarah's eyes. "These
murders, well, I'm that scared, I am. So I'm off to London
today if I have to walk to the staging inn."

"Of course you'll not walk," Sarah assured her. "Don't
be so silly. But really, Betsy, nothing has happened here in
the Hall, and . . ."

"Not yet, it hasn't," Betsy said darkly.

"And it won't. Your going away puts me in a most awkward position. I suppose all the other maids will want to
leave as well, and then where will I be?"

"No, they're all local, and they're set here at least for
now. And Fanny won't budge no matter what," she added

darkly. "I asked them. I didn't want to leave you short, miss."

When Sarah saw she was adamant, she led the way to the library to give her her wages, although she knew she would be perfectly within her rights to deny them, since Betsy had worked for her little more than a month. She also wrote her a reference, which had Betsy all smiling gratitude.

Sarah went with her to the foyer to await the carriage. Suddenly there didn't seem to be anything to say. As Betsy curtsied at last and tripped down the front steps, Sam Hatch carrying her portmanteau, Sarah envied her. How wonderful it would be if she too could get away from here, she thought. Far away.

She saw Carten staring at her as she reentered the Hall, and she stiffened. "There was something you wanted, Carten?" she asked.

"No, miss. I was just thinking it's too bad all these things have happened. Seems as if ever since old Mr. Jonah died, the Hall has been under a cloud, like."

It was impertinent, but Sarah could hardly reprimand him, when to her mind he had spoken nothing but the truth. As she turned away, the knocker sounded and she paused while Forrest Blake was admitted. He came and took her hands in his.

"My dear Miss Eaton," he said. "What a terrible, terrible tragedy. I was at St. Matthew in the Meadow yesterday conducting a funeral, but I came as soon as I could. Your dear mother? She is bearing up?"

"Do come into the library, sir," Sarah said, very conscious of all the listening ears in the foyer.

"Yes, Mother is better now," she said when the doors were safely closed behind them. "She was distraught yesterday, however."

"So I understand," he said as he took a seat beside her and made a steeple of his hands. "Doctor Haynes was called, I believe? Tell me, Miss Eaton, as a man of God might I not bring some comfort to your mother, even though I am not a Methodist? She is alone in her faith here.

She must find it difficult. I would pray with her, comfort her, if I could."

He sounded sincere, honestly caring, but he was still a suspect in Sarah's eyes. And the thought of Mathilda's possible murderer praying with her mother was repulsive.

"It is kind of you, Mr. Blake, very kind, but I am afraid it will not serve. My mother is not seeing visitors, and I know she would refuse your help even if she were. She has this feeling that she must hold fast to her husband's faith; that anything less would be unworthy of his memory."

"I understand. He was fortunate in his wife," the curate said, looking a little sad. He was so impossibly handsome with his crop of dark curls, his fresh color, and his truly superb masculine form so beautifully attired, Sarah had to wonder why she had not fallen in love with him, instead of Miles. Then his dear face, those dark eyes, his long mobile mouth and firm jaw came to mind, and she smiled. Miles Griffin was only a well-enough looking man, but he was far dearer to her than the Adonis who sat beside her now.

"I understand Sir Harold believes a tramp was guilty of the foul deed?" Mr. Blake said, and she forced her mind back to him.

For a while they discussed the murder and its consequences. Mr. Blake was most concerned for other young women in the neighborhood, and confided he planned to warn them in church about strange men, and the folly of walking alone along country roads, especially at this time of year.

Sarah let him ramble on but she did not offer him wine, and as soon as it was decently possible, she excused herself, saying she had to see to her mother.

And as her guest bowed and made his polished farewells, she wondered once again if she had just been entertaining a murderer.

It was a most unpleasant thought.

Chapter 21

With her suspicion of him in her mind as well, Sarah was careful to avoid Daniel Horton for the rest of the day. She even sent down her excuses for dinner, which she said she intended to have with her mother in her room. She knew she could not stay away from him indefinitely, however, and the next morning she went down to breakfast with a feeling of dread.

The more she had considered Horton as a possible murderer, the more she began to think he might indeed be the one. Dennis Carten and Forrest Blake were pale substitutes; her butler because he so seldom left the Hall, and was a simple man at heart, and the curate because he was a man of God.

But Horton had the education, even, she suspected, the cunning, to commit murder. Why he had done so was still a mystery.

Daniel Horton was already seated in the breakfast room. As Sarah greeted him, she wondered at the level, considering look he gave her. Had she made him suspicious? she wondered as she took her seat, her heart beating so hard in her ears, she was sure the others must notice it.

"Just some oatmeal this morning, Carten," she told the butler, at his post by the sideboard. She had no idea how she was going to force the cereal down her tight throat.

"Your mother is better today, I hope?" Horton asked as he buttered a scone. "Surely she will leave her room soon, will she not? This lengthy mourning she indulges in is much more appropriate for a close family member. And, after all, no matter how fond she was of the girl, she was only a maid."

As Carten placed a steaming bowl before Sarah, he sent the solicitor a furious glance of scorn. Sarah was glad Horton did not notice.

"Yes, she is better, but I do not look for her to come down today," she said as she poured cream on her porridge. "I think it was the manner of Mathilda's death that has overset her so."

"Of course. Forgive me for sounding so callous. I fear the world of finance I deal with has ill-prepared me for women's little crochets."

Sarah ate a small spoonful of porridge. What was she to say to that remark, she wondered. And why was Daniel Horton so different this morning. He seemed almost abrasive. Could he have guessed she had begun to suspect him? Pray not!

Fortunately he changed the subject then, telling her of the agent's plan to turn more fields to mustard the following spring, and his consent.

Sarah let him talk, only nodding now and then. She managed to finish her porridge, but when he offered her the basket of scones, she shook her head.

"I do hope you are not sickening for something, Miss Eaton," he said. "Your excellent appetite appears to have deserted you this morning. Now, why should that be?"

"I am not feeling very well," Sarah said, delighted he had provided her with a further excuse to avoid his company. "Perhaps it was a mistake to come down," she added, putting her napkin beside her plate as she rose. "If you will excuse me, sir, I believe I'll go back to my room."

He rose and bowed, his clear blue eyes considering her carefully. "I shall hope you feel more the thing shortly," he told her as he went to hold the door for her. Sarah brushed by him, trying hard not to look as if she were hurrying.

Safely in her room, she began to pace up and down. Where was Miles? Why didn't he come back? she wondered. But it was too soon. He had only left yesterday at dawn. She could not look for him until tomorrow at the earliest, and her heart sank. She was as good as alone with Horton, for her mother was no help.

She took herself severely to task then. She was being ridiculous. She had no proof Mr. Horton was a murderer, no proof at all. All her suspicions were just that and nothing more. She must get a hold of herself.

She spent the day doing needlepoint and reading. When Fanny brought her tea, she asked her to tell Mr. Horton she would be unable to have dinner with him, for she was still feeling low.

And tomorrow, Miles might come back, she told herself as she drank her tea and ate a sandwich.

Much later, when she was thinking she might as well order dinner, someone knocked. For a moment she was startled, then she hurried to the door, afraid her mother needed her. To her surprise, a somber Mr. Horton stood there, candle in hand. As she stared at him, he raised a finger to his lips.

"Be very quiet, Miss Eaton," he whispered as he leaned close to her. "I have discovered something I think you should see. It has to do with the murders."

"What is it? Where did you find it?"

"In one of the attics, of all places. Mrs. Bonnet told me the roof has been leaking up on the north side, and I went up to the attics to assess the damage."

"Why are you whispering?" Sarah asked, whispering herself.

"Because I don't want any of the servants to know what I have discovered," he told her. "I am afraid your butler is the guilty man, but we must not alarm him till all is in place to arrest him. He is very dangerous. Will you come and see, Miss Eaton?"

Sarah nodded. How dreadful! And to think it had been Carten all along, and here she had been suspecting Daniel Horton. Well, at least he did not know that, she told herself as she followed him down the hall. At the end, behind a heavy door, were the stairs to the attics. They branched halfway up, one set going to the servants' quarters, the other to the box rooms.

Holding the candle high, Mr. Horton led the way up to the storage rooms. As he did so, he said in his normal tone of voice, "The evidence is in the last room, Miss Eaton."

Sarah was trying to keep her skirts away from the dusty old trunks, the stacked paintings, a jumble of boxes. She heard a noise suspiciously like one a mouse would make, and hoped they would not meet one. At last they reached the far room. To Sarah's surprise, it contained her grandfather's massive bed.

Mr. Horton did not hesitate. Going around the bed, he said, "Come here, Miss Eaton. See what is on the floor here."

"I can't see anything," Sarah said as she joined him.

"Look under the bed there," he insisted. As she bent to do so, she sensed him moving behind her, and she tried to turn. But she was too late, and the blow he struck sent her crashing to the dusty floor.

When Sarah regained consciousness later, she was confused for only a moment. Then her aching head, to say nothing of the gag in her mouth and the heavy cord binding her arms and legs to each of the four-posters, told her everything she needed to know. Horton had tricked her. Carten was not the murderer; he was and now she was his prisoner. Even though she knew it was useless, she struggled with her bonds. Horton looked up from where he was securing her ankle to the last bedpost and chuckled. Sarah was sure she had never heard anything more obscene. He had sounded genuinely amused.

"Awake, are we, Miss Eaton?" he asked courteously. "I was hoping you would come to yourself before I had to leave. Yes, I am off to London this very night, but I did want to tell you all about it, and how clever I have been. And there's plenty of time. The servants are all in the kitchens, and Mrs. Bonnet is entertaining Mr. Rogers to a few hands of cards. And since you have been pretending to be ill, they won't question it if you do not ring for your dinner. It was lucky for me when your maid decamped, but then, everything has gone surprisingly well.

"Of course," he added as he sat down on the end of the bed and made himself comfortable, "I have been put to a great deal of trouble one way or the other.

"Do you want to hear about it? Of course you do," he answered for her. "Not that there's a thing you could do to prevent me from telling you, or doing anything else that might strike my fancy," he added, leaning over to run his hand from her ankle to her calf.

Sarah concentrated on taking shallow little breaths. She did not try to move now; indeed, she was so terrified of what he might do to her, she felt as if she were paralyzed.

"Oh, you needn't think I am going to rape you, Miss Eaton," he said at his most debonair. "I've no inclination that way. And I certainly never raped that ugly maid. I only made it look as if I had, to reinforce the theory a passing tramp had killed her. But I get ahead of myself. Now, let me see . . ."

He paused for a moment before he went on, "I suppose it all started when your grandfather began to get suspicious of some discrepancies in his accounts. I had hidden my little thefts quite well, I thought, but he was an astute man, and unbeknownst to me, had sent for his papers when I was much involved with someone else. He had me down to Woodingham Hall to get my explanation for the missing money. It was only a few thousand pounds, but as I say, he was a canny old gent.

"Of course there was no way I could explain that discrepancy away, so I pretended horror, and told him we would both go into it the following day. That night, when he was snoring merrily, I stole into his room and smothered him with one of his pillows right on this very same bed. Fitting you are going to die here too, don't you think?

"The old man put up quite a fight before he died. He even knocked over a table near the bed. I set everything to rights, however.

"But when I was leaving the room, I thought I heard someone at the end of the hall. It was dark, and I was in a hurry to get back to my own room, so I didn't investigate.

"You do see where all this is going? Yes, I am afraid

when I heard the former housekeeper had been talking about knowing things about the Hall, I put two and two together. She had been the old gent's lover. I imagine she might even have been on her way to him when she caught a glimpse of someone in the hall. And, of course, when he was found dead the next morning, she was shrewd enough to suspect he had not met his Maker in the fullness of his years, so to speak. Still, she couldn't prove anything.

"Incidentally, I killed my Uncle Willis the same way. If you remember, he sent me an urgent message here, calling me back to London. He, too, had discovered I was stealing from the estate."

He sighed and shifted his back against the bedpost. "If only he had not meddled," he said regretfully. "I was really very fond of him, you know. It was such a shame."

Sarah closed her eyes for a moment. She could feel the vomit rising, and she swallowed hard. If she were to be sick, she would choke with the tight gag in her mouth. But to think she had been sleeping in the same bed where her grandfather had been murdered! No wonder she had been uneasy in his room.

"Mrs. Quigley was a problem, too," Horton went on. "Probably the most difficult, for she had every reason to distrust me. But I found out she drank, and then it was a small matter to sneak into the cottage and poison her bottle of daffy one afternoon when she had gone to the village shopping. Of course, I did have to go back later and arrange the supper of mushrooms on toast. A *most* unpleasant half hour, I do assure you. I was sick myself, afterward. But you see how it answered, don't you, Miss Eaton? No one thought it anything but an accident, no one except possibly the Marquis of Wexford. But there was no proof again. I am such a clever fellow, am I not?

"Oh, in case you are wondering why I returned to the Hall after I did away with my uncle, it was because Mrs. Bonnet sent for me. Yes, even though dear old Eudalia is no relation at all. She's a retired actress in need of money. I hired her to keep me aware of everything that was happening here, and when Wexford came to stay, she wrote to tell me."

He chuckled. "I imagine she'll be on her way as soon as she discovers me gone. To be fair to her, she had no idea what I was up to, and no suspicion murder was involved.

"Are you quite comfortable, Miss Eaton?" he asked. "Just nod. Not that it makes any difference if you aren't. You are going to die here, you know. Oh, yes, I would not tell you all this if I were going to let you live, no, indeed."

Miles, where are you? Sarah thought desperately. I need you!

"Now, the reason Mathilda Dents had to die is because she saw me coming out of Mrs. Quigley's cottage that afternoon. She went by the gate just as I was disappearing around the cottage to the backyard and the woods. She never said anything, so it was possible she didn't see me well enough to identify, but it was a loose end, you see. I do so dislike loose ends. It must be the accountant in me. I did try to get her sent away with no blood shed, by claiming I saw her trying to start a fire. Of course she knew I was lying, and she might have figured out why, so I couldn't take a chance.

"I am not, you understand, the kind of man who revels in doing away with his fellows. Murder was never in my plans. In fact, my dear Miss Eaton, I found it all most repugnant. But you do see how it became necessary through no fault of my own; how it all began to grow, get larger and larger just the way a snowball does when it is rolled down a hill? Most unfortunate.

"Well, now, where was I? Oh, yes. When I found out Mathilda had been freed by your mother, I decided I would make sure she had really left the area. The cottage was the first place I looked. Of course, she should have known that, but she was not a clever girl, to say nothing of being one of the ugliest people I have ever seen. Her death is no loss, except to your sainted mother. And I do sincerely regret the pain she is going to have to suffer when your body is found.

"I think that covers just about everything, doesn't it?" he

asked, for all the world as if they were engaged in an ordinary social conversation. "Well, perhaps not quite. I have no doubt you are burning to know why I took a shot at Wexford. Yes, that must be laid to my door as well.

"If you remember, I was assiduous at pointing out the advantages of marrying every male you met, even Wexford himself. You see, you were in mourning and no marriage was possible. Besides, I could tell you didn't care for any of them. Even after your betrothal, I did not expect it to last, you were both so cool. Still, I didn't want to take a chance. That, you know, has been the secret of my success, I believe. I leave nothing to chance.

"But I am sure you don't care to hear my bragging, do you, dear Miss Eaton?

"Yes, I fired at the marquis. Unfortunately he ducked. But I had no time for another shot. Instead I ran around the Hall, entering it by a little-used side door. Pausing only to hide the pistol under a handy cushion, I ran out pretending I had just then looked out and seen him there. When you were so concerned for him, I knew my original plan of asking you to marry me later had no hope of success.

"Besides, I was in the gardens that night hoping again for a clear shot when you ran out and joined him. My dear Miss Eaton, I swear I blushed at your wanton behavior. The way you kissed him, pressed up against him, even, I am sorry to say, wriggled most seductively . . . It was hard to believe in your innocence. Wexford was also an eager participant. So he had to die, because, of course, after your marriage not only would he remove me as steward of the estate, he would notice the missing funds immediately. Unlike poor naive you, who thought I was teaching you all about finance, Wexford is as astute as your grandfather was."

He rose then, and Sarah stared up at him with eyes wide with horror. "Yes, we are almost done. And if you are wondering why you are here now, it is simply because I suspected you were beginning to think I was the murderer. All this eating dinner in your mother's room, your feeling ill today—you were hardly subtle, were you? And the way you acted at breakfast this morning, so awkward and nervous. I fear you are not cut out for intrigue, Miss Eaton. Fortunately, I am.

"Now I am going to leave you and make good my escape. I told Mrs. Bonnet I've been called away on urgent business. My carriage will be at the door soon, and my baggage is packed."

He walked up to the head of the bed. Sarah could not look away from his pleasant, smiling face, his clear blue eyes. He did not look like a monster and that made it twice as horrible. Please, she prayed. Please don't let him hurt me.

"Oh, I'm not going to touch you, Miss Eaton," he said, almost as if he had read her mind. "I told you I've no inclination for forcing women. Or for murder. Fortunately there's no need for me to have to kill you. You'll be dead of thirst soon enough. No one ever comes to this part of the attics, and there's no way you can escape or call for help."

He stopped to check the ropes that held her, carefully, methodically, one after the other. At last he picked up the candle and went to the door.

"Do you want to hear my plans? I intend to abscond with as much money from the estate as I can when I reach London. Then I'm off abroad. I think I'll take ship to the Americas. Europe is so frightfully unsettled at the moment, don't you agree?

"But don't worry. There'll be plenty of money left to bury you. And the best part of this particular plan is that I needn't feel rushed. You won't die for a couple of days, and it will be even longer before a most peculiar smell causes anyone to investigate.

Sarah couldn't even shudder, she was so terrified. As she stared at him, he swept her a deep bow.

"Farewell, my dear. And many thanks, not only for your hospitality, but for your fortune as well."

He turned to go, then checked. "Oh, by the way," he

added, "You needn't fret about that roof. It isn't leaking at all."

He was chuckling as he went out and closed the door tight behind him. Relieved to be spared, at least for now, a still appalled, bound and gagged Sarah Eaton was left alone in the dark.

Chapter 22

The Marquis of Wexford arrived at Woodingham Hall at nine that evening. His face was stern as he strode up the steps and banged the knocker, while his groom drove his tired team to the stables.

"Where is your mistress?" he inquired brusquely of Carten while stripping off his leather driving gloves.

"In her room, sir," the butler told him. "She's been there all day. She said she wasn't feeling well."

Miles looked doubtfully up the stairs, then shook his head. "Come to the library, Carten," he ordered. "There's something you and I have to discuss before I see Miss Eaton."

The butler hid his surprise as he followed.

"There are things I must know," Miles said when the two were alone and the door was safely closed behind them. "Tell me, was Daniel Horton here the night Jonah Eaton died?"

Carten stared at him. "Yes, he was, sir. He'd come down from London that day to discuss some business, at least that's what we all thought. The old man, er, Mr. Eaton, was in some fine temper, I want to tell you. They were in here, and even with the doors closed, we could hear him roaring."

"And he was dead in the morning," Miles mused.

"Yes. We assumed the fit of temper had brought on a heart attack. The doctor thought so, too."

He paused, then he added, "See here, m'lord, if I could speak plain? There's something I have to say. I haven't

been completely aboveboard with you, because, well,
frankly I thought you killed Lena Quigley."

"I?" Miles asked, startled.

"Well, she said you'd come and threatened her, and she
was afraid of you. And I didn't know anyone else who
might have done it."

"You are so sure she was murdered?" Miles asked, ignoring the butler's assessment of his character.

"She had to have been," Carten said, both his face and
voice stony. "She never ate mushrooms. She couldn't. She
broke out in a terrible rash if she did. But whoever put them
there to make it look like she was having supper when she
died didn't know that.

"I'd give a lot to get my hands on the man who poisoned
her. A lot."

Putting out of his mind someone actually preparing a
meal while that contorted dead body lay on the floor in a
pool of vomit nearby, Miles asked, "How do you know so
much about Mrs. Quigley? Who was she to you?"

Carten stared at him. "Didn't you know, then? She was
my aunt. My ma's sister. She came to Woodingham after
her husband died several years ago. When the old housekeeper retired, she got the job here at the Hall. I—I was
sure Miss Eaton knew that."

"Did your aunt ever tell you what it was she knew about
the Hall?" Miles asked next

Carten shifted from one foot to the other. "No, m'lord,
she didn't. She hinted at something once or twice, but she
never came right out and said anything. And when I asked
her straight, she only said it was too dangerous for me to
know, and it was best to let sleeping dogs lie.

"Is what she knew what got her killed, then, m'lord?"

"I'm afraid so.

"Where is Mr. Horton?" Miles asked next.

"He's left the Hall, sir."

"What? When did he go?"

"Only a little while ago, m'lord. You must have passed
him on the road."

"Yes, I passed a few carriages, but I didn't pay any attention to them," Miles admitted. "I'm going after him. Mr. Horton has some explaining to do."

He almost ran to the door. There he paused for a minute to say, "Don't say anything of this to Miss Eaton or the other servants. Not until I return."

He was gone before Carten could even nod.

Only a few minutes later, the marquis, mounted on his favorite gelding, was galloping down the road to London in hot pursuit. He was trailed by a resolute Hal Wells, who had no intention of letting his master out of his sight. Miles didn't know what kind of team Horton was driving nor the pace he had set, but he thought with any kind of luck he would catch him up long before the outskirts of town were reached.

As he rode along, he thought about what the butler had told him and shook his head. All this would have been so much simpler if only someone had thought to ask Carten about his relationship with the dead woman. Instead they had all walked around each other keeping their thoughts to themselves, suspicious, wary. And if he had only considered Daniel Horton sooner, that unfortunate maid would not have had to die.

He was not looking forward to telling Sarah how Horton had been systematically looting the estate, more so recently since Jonah Eaton was dead. The other partner, Mr. Gavin, had not been hard to persuade to look into the estate files. And after they had found evidence of Horton's theft, he had confessed that although Willis Horton had been like a brother to him, he had never liked or trusted his nephew.

Still, stealing from the estate was one thing; murder was another. It was true both Jonah Eaton and the elder Horton had died while Daniel Horton had been staying in their homes. But there was no proof he had anything to do with those deaths. Both men had died in their sleep.

And there was no proof he had murdered Mrs. Quigley or the maid either; no reason to suspect he might have fired a pistol at Miles himself. Of course, the man would not want Sarah marrying anyone—perhaps he had even had hopes there, for certainly Sarah had made no secret of how much she liked him. But if she were to marry anyone with the slightest knowledge of finance, her husband would soon discover how the estate was being invaded.

He rode on, thinking hard. Perhaps he could bluff Horton, pretend he knew something, when in reality, he had nothing but a few straws and a lot of raw suspicion.

As he rode around a bend in the road, he saw a phaeton ahead of him, its pair traveling at only a steady trot. Miles drew abreast to look into the startled face of Daniel Horton.

"Pull up!" he commanded as Hal Wells rode to his side.

Horton raised his whip, and Miles waited no longer. Spurring his horse forward, and crowding the leader, he swung his leg over the saddle and jumped. He landed on the leader's broad back and grabbed a fistful of mane to steady himself.

As he pulled the team to a halt, he heard Horton cursing behind him, and then a shot rang out. Instinctively Miles ducked, although he sensed the pistol had not been aimed at him. It took him several minutes and all his strength to keep the team from bolting.

When they were quiet at last, and a grim Hal Wells had come to his side, he slid to the ground.

Looking over his shoulder, he saw that Daniel Horton was slumped over in the driver's seat. In the silver moonlight, the blood that covered his shirt was not red, but black.

"I had to shoot him, m'lord," Wells explained. "He had his pistol out. He was going to kill you."

Miles clapped him on the shoulder, gripping hard for a moment to convey his thanks, for he could not speak. Instead he climbed up beside the wounded man. To his surprise, Horton still lived, although his breathing was thready. When Miles saw the froth of pink foam escaping his lips, he knew he would be dead in a short while.

"So, you've . . . killed me . . . damn you," Horton got out. "Too bad . . . never find out now . . . where . . . Miss Eaton is . . ."

"What?" Miles asked, suddenly alert. "What do you mean? Where is Sarah?"

But he spoke only to empty air, for Daniel Horton was dead.

"Hal, I'll take your horse. Mine must be halfway to London by now," he said as he climbed down. "There's trouble at the Hall. I must get back. Take the rig to the nearest village and explain what happened to the justice."

"But what of your safety, sir?" Wells protested.

"I'm in no danger now Horton is dead, but I'm afraid Sarah is."

He mounted, wheeled the horse, and disappeared down the road that would take him back to Woodingham. And as he sped along, in his mind the words *be safe—be safe—be safe* beat in concert with the galloping hooves of the horse he rode.

Back at the Hall, it only took a minute to discover that Sarah was not in her room. Neither was she with her mother, for a maid was sent to find out, bringing some fresh towels as an excuse. Miles had decided he would not alarm Marion Eaton until he absolutely had to.

"When was the last time anyone saw Miss Eaton?" he asked Dennis Carten.

"Fanny, er, the upstairs maid, brought her tea around four this afternoon, m'lord," Carten told him. "There's something else, sir. Mrs. Bonnet's missing as well. Never said a word, she did, but she's gone off somewhere."

"I cannot concern myself with Mrs. Bonnett," Miles snapped, then he shook his head. "Sorry. Put my ill temper down to stress and worry, there's a good fellow.

"Was there someone in the front hall all the time after four?" he asked.

"No, m'lord. There wasn't any need, what with both Eaton ladies in their rooms, or so we thought, and Mr. Horton packing to leave. We were all belowstairs."

Having a bit of a holiday, Miles thought, but he didn't say so. He thought desperately. It was growing late, and he was tired. What the butler had just told him meant that Horton could have taken Sarah out without anyone knowing of it. But *where* had he taken her? He remembered how she had said once he always seemed to know what she was thinking. Where are you, Sarah? he begged silently. Tell me. That she might be beyond thinking, even breathing, he refused to consider. She was alive. She had to be.

"All right," he said. "Have men search all the outbuildings. Get the stable hands to help. Send someone to the cottage where Mathilda Dents died, and someone to Mrs. Quigley's cottage in the village as well. He couldn't have taken her far, not without a carriage. Hurry man, bustle about! We must find her tonight."

But they did not find Sarah that night, and at last Miles dismissed the tired searchers and told them to get some sleep so they could begin in earnest again at first light.

He forced himself to eat something and go to bed himself, a subdued Rogers waiting on him. Miles knew he would need his strength. It wouldn't do Sarah any good for him to spend the night pacing up and down, worrying. And the men could search more efficiently in the daylight. As a rational, intelligent man, he knew all this, but it was still hard to call a halt to the search.

After a hurried breakfast, he sent the men out again, riding beside them as they moved in a straight line across the fields surrounding the Hall. Some of the villagers had come to help as well, and he was grateful to them. Even the curate was there, although his bow to Miles was stiff. Miles knew he was still uneasy about the large bribe he had accepted to secure his endorsement for Mrs. Eaton's school, but he didn't care a whit. Most men had their price, and the pious parson was no exception.

Miles shivered a little in the early light. He hoped Sarah was warm enough wherever she was. It had been a chilly night, with more than a hint of the coming autumn in the air.

Later he rode to the two cottages that had already been searched, to inspect them himself. He set the men to walking the woods, and as every hour passed, he had to fight a growing despair.

Returning to the Hall, he was forced to tell Marion Eaton what had happened, for she had sensed something was not right when Sarah had not come to her that morning. For a moment, looking at her worn, fragile face, Miles had been afraid she would crumple under the shock of yet another tragedy. But to his surprise, she did not faint or cry out. Instead she told him not to worry about her.

"I shall be fine, m'lord," she told him in a firm voice. "In my heart I know Sarah is all right, and you will find her. Go now, keep looking."

Miles was delighted to do as he was bade, and as he closed her door, he saw Marion Eaton was already sitting down in her favorite chair by the window, her open Bible on her lap.

By noontime, when Sarah had still not been found, and all the nearby acreage had been searched, he slumped on a chair in the library, a glass of wine forgotten at his elbow. Although he hated to admit it, he was beginning to lose heart. She had been missing for a long time now, and all his earlier hopes of finding her safe were beginning to fade.

Where was she? Where could she be? He looked around the pleasant room with its walls of books, its globes and worn turkey carpet, the comfortable leather chairs and the handsome desk. The clock on the mantel ticked softly away, measuring out the minutes she was still lost to him.

It was then he realized that no one had even thought to search the Hall itself. And it was a large building, with a score of empty rooms. Jumping to his feet, he ran to the door, calling for Carten as he did so. The butler nodded when he gave the order, and sent the footmen running to tell the maids to help them search.

"Look in every room, every closet, Carten," Miles told him. "Don't neglect even the smallest space. I'm going to start in the cellars and work my way up. Quickly, man, quickly!"

When Horton had first left Sarah in the dark attic, she had tried desperately to free herself. Eventually, however, worn out and sore from her efforts, she had to admit it wasn't going to do any good. Neither could she get rid of the gag, although she rubbed her head this way and that against the mattress to try and slip it off. It was no use. Daniel Horton had made sure of that. She had cried a little then, before she forced herself to stop. Tears would not help, and they would clog her throat and her nose. It was hard enough to breathe now without deliberately adding to her discomfort.

Eventually, she fell into a troubled doze, waking often throughout that long night to stare at the darkness around her and pray as she had never prayed before. Sometimes, to help forget what was happening, she relived her life—her childhood here in Woodingham, her travels to India and her years there. And always, always, she thought of Miles and their love. She knew that love was the only thing that sustained her and kept her from total despair. Her wrists and ankles throbbed from where she had strained against the cord trying to free herself, but she welcomed that pain. It meant she was still alive.

Toward morning, a little pale light came in a small window set high in the wall at the peak of the roof, and by turning her head slightly, she could watch that light grow stronger. It told her it was now tomorrow, the day Miles would surely return. She just had to survive until then, because if anyone could find her, it would be Miles. She was certain of that.

But she had to admit she was growing thirsty, even though she scoffed at herself. On an ordinary evening, she did not drink anything after the tea tray had been brought in, and she never rose till eight. Fiercely she told herself she was not thirsty, she could not be, even as she wished Horton had not mentioned that was the way she was going to die.

Now she lay quietly and watched the little window as it grew brighter. She could do it, she told herself. She could survive just as long as it took for Miles to come to her. She only had to wait quietly, and not succumb to panic.

When the servants clattered down the stairs from their rooms in the other section of the attics, she could barely hear them. She knew then that even if she had been able to get rid of the gag, no one would have heard her calling. She

tried to imagine them busy at their morning routine—the
footmen setting the table in the breakfast room and arranging the serving dishes on the sideboard, the maids dusting
and sweeping the drawing rooms and the foyer, and the
cook bustling around the kitchen giving orders to the two
kitchen maids as she prepared breakfast. Surely then they
would begin to wonder when she did not come down,
wouldn't they? Surely then they would discover she was
not in her room and the bed had not been slept in, and start
looking for her, as her mother would as well. She wondered
if anyone would think to search the attics, and tried not to
despair when she couldn't imagine why they would.

Eventually, her muscles aching with cramp from the position she had been in for so many hours, she fell into a
troubled sleep again. When she woke, startled, she wondered why she was straining to hear in the dusty room, and
why her heart was beating so fast. It was then she heard a
faint little giggle.

"Sam Hatch, you're a bold one," she heard the upstairs
maid scold from quite a distance away. "This is no time for
you to be up to your tricks. We're supposed to be looking
for Miss Eaton."

""Well, but she's not in the box rooms, though, is she?"
the footman replied.

"Yes, I am," Sarah screamed in her head. She wriggled
desperately. Perhaps if she could make the bed creak, they
would hear it. But no matter how she struggled, the bed remained immovable. And the only sound she was able to
make around the gag was a throaty growl. Please come, she
thought. Please find me.

"But we're here," Sam Hatch went on. "Be a shame to
let such a chance go to waste, don't you think?"

Fanny squealed, then giggled again. "Oooo, you're
awful, you are," she scolded, although she didn't sound a
bit angry.

"Ah, come on, sweetheart, how about it, then? We've got
time. They all think we're searching, and I promise to be
quick."

"I'd rather you weren't," Fanny told him, and they both laughed.

It was quiet then, and the helpless prisoner in the last box room felt a wave of despair deeper than any she had felt before. They were not going to find her. They were going to make love and go away.

"Now, Sam, wait a minute," she heard a panting Fanny say a minute later. "It's too dusty here. Didn't you put old Mr. Jonah's bed up here somewhere? Let's find it. We might as well be comfortable, and I'd like to do it on his bed, wouldn't you?

"Now, Sam, you just *wait!*"

"Thank you thank you thank you," Sarah breathed.

"It's right along here," she heard Sam say much more clearly now. "Come on, hurry up. I want you bad, Fan."

Sarah held her breath until the door opened and the two stood on the threshold, their candles held high. Fanny, whose neat black housemaid's gown was open to the waist, exposing two round, pink-tipped breasts, screamed and fainted. Fortunately Sam was made of sterner stuff.

As he hastily buttoned his knee breeches, he said, "Why—why Miss Eaton, let me help you, ma'am." After putting his candle down on a box and making sure Fanny's had been extinguished by her fall, he hurried up to the side of the bed. He was still struggling to rid Sarah of the gag when Fanny began to moan.

"It's Miss Eaton all right, and not a ghost," he said. "And there's no time for any of your silliness, Fan. Run down and tell Dennis and the marquis we've found her. Hurry, there's a good girl."

The gag was loose now, and Sarah spit it out to take several huge gulps of air. "Thank you, Sam," she said in a voice that to her ears sounded both hoarse and rusty.

"Oh, I'm that sorry, ma'am," Fanny said as she pulled herself up by the bedpost. It was only then she noticed the state of her gown, and she whirled about to fasten it, the back of her neck red with embarrassment.

"Go and tell m'lord, now, Fan," the footman repeated. "You know how frantic he's been."

He was working on the knots of the cord that bound one of Sarah's wrists to the poster as Fanny nodded and disappeared. Sarah could hear him mumbling under his breath, and she said, "Don't bother being gentle, Sam. It's all right."

When Miles burst into the room, the footman had freed both of her wrists and she was sitting up and grimacing as she tried to massage away the aching cramp in her shoulders. Without speaking, he sat down beside her and took her in his arms. Smoothing her hair back with a hand that shook a little, he whispered, "Thank God you are all right, Sarah. I've been so worried."

She could only smile at him through her tears of pain and relief. He held her close until Hatch had freed her ankles. Then he lifted her in his arms to carry her down to her room.

"I think I can walk," she objected, then sighed and snuggled closer to him. "No, never mind," she added. "I'd rather be as near to you as I can get."

He kissed the top of her head. At the bottom of the flight, where all the servants were waiting for them, Dennis Carten began to applaud. At once, the others joined in, and Sarah smiled at them as her mother came to kiss her.

As Carten ordered everyone back to their work, Miles carried Sarah into her room. Marion Eaton, about to follow them, shook her head and smiled to herself as she went to her own room to give them some privacy. She could wait to hear what had happened. There was all the time in the world now for that.

When Miles asked what she would like, Sarah asked for a glass of water to ease her dry throat, and, reminded she had missed both dinner the evening before, and breakfast as well, something to eat. Miles looked around, and seeing Fanny still hovering in the doorway, he sent her to fetch the food.

He put Sarah down on the bed and poured her some water from a carafe on the table nearby. After she had drained the glass, he sat down beside her to pick up both her hands. The cords had burned her wrists raw, and he

kissed them, one after the other. "It is just as well Horton is
dead," he said in a conversational tone. "Because if he
weren't already, he would be soon for what he dared to do
to you."

"How did he die?" Sarah asked, wide-eyed. "Did you kill
him? And how did you know he was the murderer?"

Miles told her how he had returned last night, and what
he had learned in London. He also told her of his conversation with Carten, and his mad chase after Daniel Horton.
"But I didn't kill him. Hal Wells did," he concluded. "Horton was trying to shoot me at the time. You know, even
with all we know now, we still could not have proved murder, Sarah, not if he had not tried to escape after tying you
up in the attic. It's just as well Hal rid the world of that—
that—"

Sarah kissed him before he could say the word, and he
put his arms around her to hold her close.

"Tell me," he said after a moment. "Tell me how all this
came to pass."

Sarah spoke then of her growing suspicions Horton had
to be the murderer, and how after that she had tried to avoid
him.

"He told me I wasn't very good at intrigue; I guess he
was right," she confessed. "After he lured me up to the
attic, he hit me, and I lost consciousness. And when I regained it, I was tied to that bed."

She shuddered and the arm around her tightened. "You
know, the things he confessed were made even more
ghastly by the way he described them in such a sane, quiet
way. He even claimed he had never intended murder, he
had been forced to it by circumstance. But do you know
what the most dreadful thing of all was, Miles?"

"No, darling, tell me."

"It was being tied to my grandfather's bed, and not just
because Mr. Horton smothered him there, as he smothered
his uncle. No, it was because my grandfather never really
wanted me in the Hall, or in his room, or occupying his
bed. He only made me his heiress to spite my father. I think

that's why I never felt at ease here. I knew I was not wanted; that I wasn't *worthy* . . ."

"You? Not worthy?" he scoffed. "You're as worthy as the queen is! I don't want to hear you say such a thing again."

She smiled and shook her head before she remembered something else that had been puzzling her. "But Daniel Horton couldn't have set the fire in my dressing room. Who did, then?"

"I don't imagine we'll ever know. But I suspect it was Mrs. Quigley. If you recall, there was no further trouble after I spoke to her. And I think that is why Carten worked so hard to put it out, because he knew it had been started by his aunt."

"Miles, why was Horton stealing from the estate? Was he just greedy? Dishonest?"

He shook his head. "No, he was a gambler. Charles Gavin and I found evidence in his desk among his private papers of debts for thousands of pounds. I imagine he stole from others as well, to cover them."

"And to think he dared warn me about your weaknesses," she said indignantly.

"And speaking of those," he said softly, just before he kissed her.

When Fanny knocked and came in, they were lying wrapped in each other's arms in a deep embrace.

"Oh, Miss Eaton," she said in a shocked voice as she set the tray she was carrying down on a table. "I really don't think you should be doing that, no, indeed, ma'am."

Neither Sarah nor the marquis paid any attention at all.

"I mean, I know you're betrothed and everything, but what would anyone say if they could see you?" Fanny persisted. "On the bed with him like that and alone in your chamber, too, with the door closed? Why your mother . . ."

"Go away," Miles said, lifting his head a scant inch.

"Yes, that will be all, Fanny," Sarah told her.

"And be sure to shut that door again when you leave," Miles added.

Sarah gazed into his eyes, and neither spoke until they

heard the click of the latch as the reluctant maid finally did as she was bade.

"Now, where were we?" Miles asked, one finger trying to smooth away the red mark the gag had left on her soft cheek.

Sarah began to chuckle. "Oh, my dear, it is too funny," she said. "And for Fanny of all people to cry propriety—well! Do you know what she and Sam Hatch were about to do on Jonah Eaton's bed? They did not find me by a diligent search, you know. No, they had something else entirely in mind."

Miles raised one dark brow, and remembering what she had been about to blurt out, Sarah blushed.

"I wish I could ask you to demonstrate, my dear, for I am not perfectly sure I understand," he said easily as his hands tightened on her back. "Alas, it is not possible! But perhaps you could do so on our wedding night?"

As Sarah buried her face in his shirt, he chuckled and added, "And I have no intention of waiting until April when you are out of mourning for that happy event to occur.

"I honestly don't think I could," he added candidly just before he bent and kissed her again.